Cotton Dust

John Pether

Published: 2022 by breind

ISBN: 978-0-6452288-2-3 - Paperback Edition
ISBN: 978-0-6452288-3-0 - eBook Edition

for Sonia

Also By John Pether

Homo Derelictus: ISBN 978-0-6452288-0-9

Archaea, primitive organisms, attack Homo sapiens. The initial attack is cured but later multitudes of people rapidly regress to pre-hominids, labelled Homo Derelictus. The whole world must struggle to retain the remains of humanity. Children are in the forefront of the battle.

The Slow Apocalypse: ISBN 978-1780038094

A massive solar flare hits the Steppes of Mongolia, a mixing-bowl for devastating strains of the flu virus. Professor Jessica Patton struggles to control the outbreak but it is almost total. As one of the few survivors, Jessica leads a small band or people out of the catastrophe.

Deadly Botanicals: ISBN 978-1787197701

The horticultural market is overwhelmed with beautiful, cheap plants. The scent is strongly hallucinogenic, but genetically engineered to be toxic. Petra Wallace, a botanist and Julian Bailey, a scientist, detect an extraordinary plot created by the Kingdom of Plants to eliminate mankind. They have to unravel the plot by all the means at their disposal.

Available at all online bookstores

TARA'S COMBINED FAMILY TREE

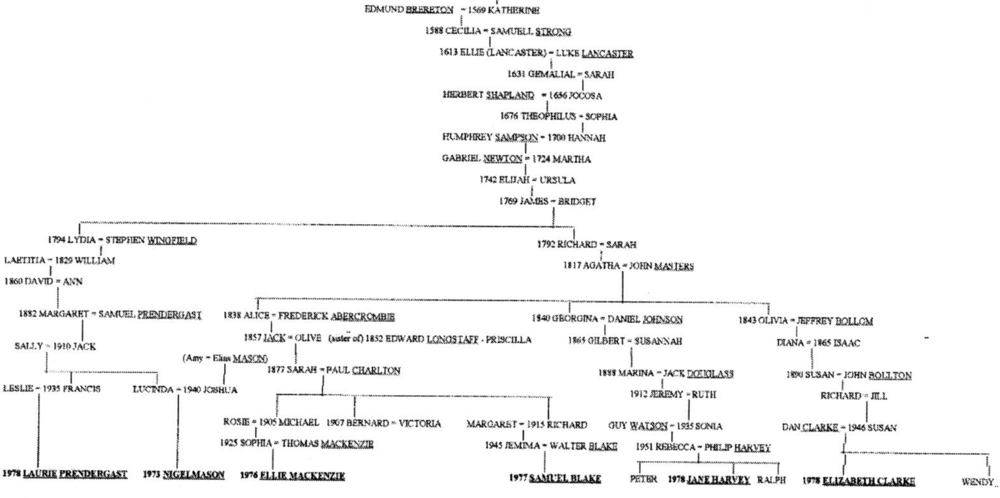

Affected cases emboldened
Surname changes underlined

Chapter One

"Why don't you try the bloody thing on instead of muttering about it? You can always change it if it doesn't fit."

"Perhaps I should, Angie. Expect me in five minutes."

Jane Harvey picked the parcel off the bed and began to open it. She let the tissue paper fall on the floor and held up her new dress. She stroked it, feeling the fine Sudanese cotton slip through her fingers like silk. She took off her shirt and jeans, threw them on the bed, put on clean tights and a new bra, and held the dress up in front of the mirror to remind herself of its pale soft green colour; what a relief, she still liked it! Tonight, was going to be hot, too hot to wear a slip at the university Midsummer Ball, so she threaded her way into the dress, adjusted the sleeves and smoothed the material over her thighs. She smiled at the result and stared in the mirror for some minutes tweaking the shoulder straps until she was satisfied.

Twenty years old, five foot five, fit as she could be, Jane was certainly attractive -perhaps even pretty - with an hour-glass figure and shapely legs. She was a moderately clever undergraduate with just a touch too much self-confidence. She winked at her reflection secure in the knowledge that her best attribute was her skin, a wonderful iridescent slightly olive-coloured skin inherited from her mother, Rebecca. She stroked her cheek; flawless skin that she loved to flaunt to the distress of her spotty friends.

A touch of lipstick and a final brush of the hair to complete the picture and, satisfied with the result, Jane left her tiny room and stood, ready for inspection, in front of her flat mates.

"What do you think guys?"

"Great, they'll be pretty envious," said Hilary, "let's have a drink."

"Don't, for Christ's sake, spill red wine over this one," warned Angela. "You made a right mess of that flamenco dress you nicked from your mother. At least it won't be so fire crazy as that one. You look good and deserve another G and T."

Jane helped herself to a second gin and tonic. "Hilary, are you sure we can all squeeze into Melusi's car?"

"It's all right there's only us, the other men are going separately."

Melusi appeared on time, and they set off for the ball to find most of their party in the hotel foyer. The women went to the Ladies where they joined the crowd making final adjustments to their clothing and applying not too subtle squirts of perfume to their necks and wrists. The consensus on Jane's dress was that they all loved it, the feel of the cotton, the flowing simple lines and the subtle colouring.

Wendy Clarke, a tall, almost beautiful nineteen-year-old with bright blue eyes and golden hair, was fascinated by the material. "You say it's made of cotton? It feels more like silk. What other colours are there? If there's a pale brown version it'd suit my sister Elizabeth. You remember her, the sporty one, spends most of her spare time in Africa?"

"Oh yes, how could I forget; she beat me riding the Bore up the river. As far as I know, the colour range does include brown, but Melusi seems to know more about them than I do so you'd better ask him. Being near finals has given him an obsession with reading about every obscure subject. Tell Liz to give me a ring, I expect there's only one shop in Bristol selling them."

The party gathered at the head of the stairs, and they headed to the ballroom where they found a table reserved in Melusi's name with bottles of wine and fizzy water. The dances warmed up and Jane's dress flowed and slipped around her legs, belling out as she turned. The dress appeared to have a dancing life of its own. After an hour's frantic exercise, she sat down with her heart pounding and drank a glass of water.

Melusi came and sat next to her. "Pretty dress, Jane; the colour's just right for your lovely skin, a good combination; let's dance."

Dancing with Melusi was in the top league; fast, smooth, and dramatic. He moved like a dream, muscles coasting with athletic precision, and he wasn't as hot and sweaty as the others. Outwardly, Melusi's face glowed with pleasure, but Jane sensed there was something wrong. There was just a hint of something in his eyes that she couldn't pin down. Melusi himself was puzzled, every time he touched Jane's dress, he felt the hairs on the back of his neck prickle, and a strange flash of fear went through him.

"What's the matter, Melusi? Are you going off my new dress? Not bright enough, too high cut?"

Melusi took a while to answer. Finally, he shook his head as if he had been far away. He replied. "Oh, I don't know. It's just… I have a very odd feeling which, I suppose, must have something to do with your dress…" his voice faded.

"Just what are you trying to say?"

"It's a wonderful dress, a beautiful dress, but every time I touch it, I feel there is something wrong. Sounds daft, I know. I can't explain… let's sit down," he abruptly sat her down before the end of the dance and left her.

"What's up with Melusi, Hil?" Jane asked her flatmate, "Is it the dress that's wrong?"

"Don't worry about him. He sometimes switches off into his own world, he's only a man. And it's a lovely dress. Let's go onto the terrace, fireworks are about to start."

The great glass doors opened directly onto the terrace and the night air was still, at last cooling. In the distance, the slope down to the river basin was lit by a line of wax flares and on the grass below the terrace the full moon cast an iridescent silver light, fit for romance, or seduction. The fireworks were scheduled for midnight, so the revellers crammed onto the terrace to watch the display, made more dramatic by being reflected in the water of the old docks. One of the fireworks failed to light properly. It sputtered and fell over sending a shower of sparks into the shrieking crowd.

"Ow!" Jane yelled. She looked down. "I'm sure a spark went right through the dress onto my arm." She looked hard at the painful area but there were no visible marks. "Oh well, I must have imagined it."

They moved inside and sat down for the entertainment. The usual comedian, only funny when you have had a lot to drink, was followed by a juggler with balls, plates and other objects flying around with a life of their own. For his final act the juggler went out onto the terrace and the lights were turned down.

"What's he doing now, Melusi?"

"Seems to be dunking lumps of wire into a bucket of what looks like paraffin."

The juggler lit the paraffin-soaked lumps from a flare and swung them round in blazing circles.

"Oh no!" Jane screamed yet again she felt that a spark from the burning wire wool had landed on her arm.

"I can't see any damage," said Melusi.

But Jane was not convinced, and she found the residual ache difficult to ignore.

In the early hours of the morning, towards the end of the ball, Jane was dancing hot and tired. She was uncomfortable and bad tempered. Why did she suddenly feel so desperately tired? And why were her arms so sore, especially in the place where she thought the spark from the burning wire wool had struck her? To cap it all, the hot sweaty patch in the middle of her back was on fire.

"Please don't hold me quite so close; I'm so hot and my arms hurt." Her partner's face clouded. "Don't be upset, Patrick, I love dancing close, but I've had it tonight."

Why the Hell did I say that?

"What's the matter with you? We've been dancing this close before and you haven't complained, how can your arms possibly hurt?"

"I'm sorry, they just do. I can't help it. Just don't touch me."

"Well, it's not my fault, and you're pissed," he said savagely.

"Oh, for Christ's sake shut up; don't be so bloody horrid."

They finished the dance in silence and parted in the middle of the floor. Jane went onto the terrace to cool off, but the chilly air failed to quench the fire from her arms.

Melusi followed and found her drooping over the railings at the edge of the terrace, sobbing. "Jane, cheer up. Come and have the last waltz with me. Hilary is sulking in the loo."

"Thank you Melusi, but please don't touch my arms, they're so painful."

Melusi held Jane as gently as he could, but even with lightest pressure the skin of her arms and back hurt. He was trying his hardest, but all his previous feelings flooded back. Melusi had a dreadful foreboding that some disaster was about to happen. Jane sensed his worry.

"You look so worried, Melusi. Have I said something wrong?"

"Of course not."

Jane felt a sense of longing for him, but she simply couldn't see past anything other than the fiery heat radiating all over her beautiful skin.

At the end of the last waltz Jane was crying with the pain and excused herself.

"Sorry, Melusi, must rush off. I'm dying for a pee and my skin's burning."

Hilary and Wendy had seen Jane crying and quickly followed her to the Ladies to find her leaning on a washbasin moaning softly.

"Please help me take off this bloody dress, there's something wrong with it."

They helped Jane to take off the top half of her dress and their looks of surprise quickly turned to sympathy at what they saw.

"Oh, God! Your arms; they're as raw as hell. They look just like burns. And your poor back. It's as if a giant red-hot iron hand had branded you. Those purple areas are oozing something horrible. Come on girls, see what we can plunder from the loo. There should be tissues and hand cream somewhere."

The women applied masses of soothing hand creams to Jane's arms and back and covered her with wads of tissues, anything they could lay their hands on. The pain eased a little.

"Oh, thank you, Wendy."

"We ought to call a doctor."

"No, please don't; just get me back to the flat." Jane was whimpering with the pain.

At last, they came out with Jane's arms wrapped in paper tissues and Hilary asked Melusi for his dinner jacket to cover her shoulders.

"Sure, anything else I can do; what's the matter with her? She did say her arms hurt earlier."

"Her arms and back are very sore with a horrible red rash. It looks almost as if she's been burnt."

"Hang on, I'll get the car quick as I can."

A few minutes later Melusi came running up the stairs to help the women down to the car. Hilary sat with Jane in the back and Angela in the passenger seat. The drive back to the flat was a nightmare; the slightest pressure on her skin made Jane cry out in pain. She was forced to sit bolt upright; if she slumped, the raw areas on her back rubbed on the car seat. They slowly climbed the stairs to the flat, Jane crying out with pain every time she brushed against the bannister. At last, they let themselves in and Jane stood while they helped her to undress.

"There, Melusi, full frontal," Jane tried to joke.

"The 'frontal' bit, happily for you dear girl, is the least affected," Melusi said gloomily. "But the tops of your arms and the small of your back are a nightmare. The pink flesh of your chest only made the picture more startling. This is no joke at all."

"What on earth can have caused this?" Angela asked the almost-doctor.

"It looks like a particularly violent allergic reaction to something. But I must confess I've never seen anything quite like it before. You poor thing, it looks bloody painful. Hilary, we need a lot of soothing cream as quick as you can."

"There's a big pot of something in the bathroom. Hang on, I'll bring some clean hankies as well."

They generously coated the raw areas with more cream and covered them with clean handkerchiefs.

"I'm sure you can find a couple of soluble aspirins in your medicine cupboard. Washed down with milk should damp down the reaction."

Jane swallowed the aspirin, drank the milk and they gently put her to bed. The three talked softly as they waited for her to go to sleep.

"What now, Melusi?" Wendy asked.

"If she's not better soon, we should ask her doctor to call. Give it twenty-four hours anyway but make an appointment for Monday morning. Just to be on the safe side we ought to take it in turns to sit with her for a few hours; I'll do the first stint and then buzz off." Melusi tiptoed into Jane's room, turned on a reading lamp and puzzled about Jane's skin.

Melusi Makuthwane was in his final year studying medicine at the university and therefore at that happy stage at which he knew, or thought he knew, everything there was to know about healing people. His parents had come from Zimbabwe and were now partners in a successful firm of solicitors in Cardiff. He had been born in Cardiff, worked hard at school, coping well with the almost inevitable prejudice. He had developed into a strong, handsome young man, well over six feet tall with broad muscular shoulders, arms, and legs, representing the university in the javelin and sprinting. Under a mop of black wavy hair Melusi's dark brown eyes were set in a firm face, unexpectedly paler than the average Zimbabwean; a contribution, he presumed, from a tiny percentage of Hamitic blood from the pre-Shona tribes that had swept into what was now Zimbabwe around 5000 BC. Family holidays in Zimbabwe were the highlights of his life and he was determined that he would return as a surgeon to what he took to be his own country.

Melusi waited until he was certain Jane had stopped tossing and turning and was breathing evenly. He rose from the chair, quietly exchanged the vigil with Hilary.

"I'll be back tomorrow afternoon."

He gave Hilary a peck on the cheek and left.

Chapter Two

Jane had a dreadful night; her mind was in the same turmoil as her skin; everything was on fire; and the dreams!

She was walking before dawn in a tropical forest. She looked down and saw she had dark skin and was wearing a cloth round her waist. It was not the near nakedness that worried her but the fear, which was all around her, gnawing into her. She knew she had no business to be there, her father had expressly forbidden her to approach the edge of the forest at night unless her brother was with her. Jane, or whoever she was in the dream, smelt a strange smell like wet chicken and she knew she was in deep, deep trouble. She started to run back the way she had come but tripped over a rope that appeared from nowhere. Now the smell was stronger, and she screamed as her arms were pinned to the ground by men talking in a strange language. She tried to struggle and screamed again as a hairy white man lashed her with a whip. Her arms were tied behind her back and a leather thong knotted round her neck. The white man pulled her to her feet, dragged her down to the river and forced her into the bottom of a canoe. Then she heard the urgent slosh of paddles taking her and perhaps others to the far bank. She was in despair; she knew she had been captured by slavers.

Jane awoke with a cry, drenched with sweat, still terrified by the dream. She lay quietly, dazed, until the door gently opened.

"How are the arms, are they bad? I heard you cry out." Hilary was holding a mug of tea. "Did you manage to get some sleep?"

"The arms are a bit better, but I had a rotten night. I had the nastiest dream I've ever had. I was terrified."

"I can offer you my one and only diagnosis: you are suffering from the combined effect of too much alcohol and not enough sex." This broke the tension in Jane's face and they both laughed.

"Not a snowball's chance in hell, last night anyway, I had a headache."

"Can't say I feel that good this morning. I guess too much of whatever I was drinking. Come on, let's have a look at you."

Jane bared her arms and they both looked at them gloomily.

"Shit! They don't look any better. We'll put some more cream on you."

They covered the cream with handkerchiefs and Jane gently put on her lightest clothing.

"I can carry your bag for you if that'll help. We both have lectures in the same building."

Jane's mind was wandering away from the subject of the lecture. A seriously boring study of the innards of an insignificant hermaphrodite animal. She dozed off in the heat. Immediately she dreamed that she was in the same humid, tropical forest as the night before and her dream-story continued where it had left off. The canoe had reached the far bank of the river and she and three other captives, two boys and another girl, were forced to walk for what seemed like miles as the sun rose. If they hesitated, they were lashed with whips until their crying became a whimper. She was utterly ashamed that she had been unable to contain her bowels and had soiled herself. All the four captives had soiled themselves as a dreadful hopelessness descended on them.

Jane awoke with a start as the others rose to leave the lecture theatre. One of her friends looked worried. "Are you all right, Jane? You look as if you've seen a ghost."

"I think I have," Jane replied as she left. She walked slowly back to the flat at midday worrying about the dreams. She opened the door and was glad to find she was alone. She ate some bread and cheese, took off all her clothes and lay down on the bed. She dared not sleep in case the dreams came back, so she read a novel in the warmth of the afternoon until her flatmates returned.

"How are things?" asked Hilary.

"My arms are still on fire, and I feel so depressed about them. They're awful." Jane burst into tears and collapsed. Hilary tried to stop her falling.

"No! Don't touch me, it hurts so much." Jane shrank away from her friend.

In the afternoon, Melusi appeared with a bottle of wine.

"Hair-of-the-dog, they say it should dull the pain. How about a gentle walk on the Downs?"

They walked over the sunburnt grass to the edge of the cliff from where they could see the gleaming white freshly painted suspension bridge. Jane told Melusi about her dreams; at first his response pleased her as she found he took them seriously.

"I do hope I'm not boring you, Melusi, but they are awful dreams. They seem to be a sort of resurrected story of the old days of slavery."

"Have you been reading any books about slavery in the last week or so?"

"No way!"

"Perhaps general books about Africa or the West Indies?"

"No I haven't, and I feel so tired. But thanks for taking an interest. You seem to know about dreams; what do you really think about mine?" She turned urgently to face him. "What do you think they mean? What's your interpretation?" Jane's voice was rising hysterically.

"I don't know just now. I'll have to mull it over, but I don't like the sound of them one little bit." He realised he had said it all wrong and tried to soften the impact. "Strangely, I don't even know why I should be worried. After all, they're only dreams and they could be the product of whatever you've become allergic to."

"I suppose it could be. Odd association, though. Let's go back to the flat."

That evening they made a Spanish omelette which they ate with Melusi's wine. The company and inconsequential chatter helped to take Jane's mind off her angry skin, but by the end of the evening the pain was as bad as ever.

Melusi returned the next day with a pot of steroid cream.

"We can try this. The chemist said it should work better than the usual simple creams."

They liberally smeared Jane's skin, bandaged her up and put her to bed with more aspirins.

Melusi called again on Sunday afternoon. "Show me a corner, please, Jane."

Jane very gently peeled off a tiny section of her bandages.

"This isn't working. You ought to see your doctor; there's just a chance there may be someone holding the fort in the surgery to make you an appointment on Monday."

"I suppose it's worth a try. I usually see Doctor Richardson."

Melusi handed his phone to Jane who brightened up a little when it was answered, and she was able to be seen first thing on Monday.

Monday morning came and if anything, the lesions were worse, so the three of them set off for the surgery in Melusi's car. The waiting room was crowded, and the other patients shuffled along the benches to give Jane room to sit down. She was thoroughly miserable and the slightest touch from the patient sitting next to her sparked agony in her skin. At last, she was ushered into the doctor's room.

"Good morning Jane, what's the problem?"

She told him the whole story and took off her blouse. He took a long look at the red raw areas on Jane's arms and back and listened to her story.

"The simplest conclusion I can come to, Jane, is that your clinical picture, while it is unusually severe, is probably an allergic reaction to something related to the material of your new dress. I noticed particularly that the inflamed area on your back is a mirror image of a hand pressing the dress against your skin. I will write you up for a stronger topical steroid which should damp down the reaction. I'm sure one of your flatmates can be persuaded to apply it two or three time a day."

Arthur Richardson was a typical Scottish wanderer. He had married twice; his first wife had died while they were both working in Brazil and the second after their car was hit by a lorry while they were on safari in Africa. Sadly, he had no children and perhaps because of this his itchy feet had led him to spend many years as a general physician in various parts of the world. Only in the last year had he come back to England to be a locum for an old friend who knew about his habit of talking to himself.

"It's because you live alone, old son; you need good company. People living on their own spend a lot of the time muttering to themselves; you know what I mean."

Perhaps I do, give it time. Let's talk about the present. How can it be that this beautiful woman with such flawless skin, has reacted so badly? I'm sure I have seen patients with similar rashes with a fast onset, but they are normally quite berserk, screaming. Jane is a somewhat docile, almost placid, young woman. But she reacts normally, and this strange acceptance of her lot is out of character. I need time to think and go through my old diaries. See if I can find similar cases. There's never time to think nowadays; Andrew's surgeries are so crowded, they're like a cattle market.

A motley crowd was waiting for him, and he had to put Jane's skin and its peculiar presentation to the back of his mind. Driving home that evening, he was still puzzling over Jane's rashes but could not come up with a satisfactory answer. It worried him; for some strange reason this young woman worried him more than any other patient he had seen in the last few years.

Monday evening, 17th July, back at the flat, Hilary smeared the topical steroid on Jane's arms and back.

"There, better to leave them uncovered. Let's see how you are after an hour. Doctor Richardson said it should work quickly if it's going to."

"Well, they are throbbing a lot less, and I do feel better. I'll be all right now; I'll go and lie down."

She lay on her bed to think about her predicament. At the surgery she had felt a strange, overwhelming tiredness; she had switched off, losing interest in her arms. It was as if she had been more interested to study the reactions of the doctor concerned with a particularly difficult patient. The awful wheals were someone else's problem, and her presence was merely to give the person comfort. She was acting the nurse, sympathetic but business-like, slightly aloof from everyday problems, this couldn't happen to her own skin, her lovely, beautiful, olive-tanned skin that everyone admired so much.

Suddenly she was wide awake. Her attention suddenly sharpened. She sat up; why had she been brought back to reality?

No! There was something weird about the way he had examined me. Why use a magnifying glass to see something so bloody obvious? And why did he ask me so many odd questions? Oh Lord, I hope I haven't got some dreadful disease; something so peculiar that even an experienced doctor is at a loss. Why me, what have I done to deserve such a punishment? I feel so tired. Where's that bottle of red wine Melusi brought. I'm sure there's a glass or two to knock me out.

There was a glassful in the bottom; she drank it together with a couple of aspirins and within a few minutes she was asleep.

The night started well, but around one o'clock, Jane started to dream again. The captives had reached what must have been a collection point. There were about forty of them all tied to a wooden fence. Her loin cloth was torn off and a bald fat white man roughly spread her legs and pushed his fingers up inside her. She screamed and he hit her face hard.

"You'll get a lot more than that where you're going," said the man. "Shame I can't pay to have you."

He licked his fingers and smiled. "Turn around." He pushed her violently. The man was now sweating profusely. He parted her buttocks and was about to enter her again when a giant African shouted at Jane's tormenter.

"Leave her for the boss, bring her over to the fire."

Another African pulled an iron rod from the fire and came towards her. Her head was pulled back. She screamed as she was branded below her left breast. Frantically, Jane had to wake up. With a shriek, she broke out of the dream drenched with sweat, trembling with fear as Hilary rushed into her room. "What's the matter, love? I heard you scream. Was it those ghastly dreams again?"

"It was, and they were even worse," Jane sobbed with the memory of the smell of her own burnt flesh in her nostrils, "I'll be all right soon. Don't go; please don't go." Hilary stayed until Jane had calmed down, just as dawn started to break.

The sun rose bright and clear, spears of light shone through the curtains. The exhausted Jane welcomed the new day as a blessed relief. She felt physically exhausted, ached all over and her arms hurt like blazes, but she got up and struggled to the bathroom. Hilary followed her.

"I'll help you wash your arms and back. I'll be very gentle. Perhaps a light polyester shirt would be the kindest thing to wear." As she helped undress her, Hilary's nose wrinkled. "Odd sort of smell; like decaying leaves."

"I must be disintegrating; I don't know what to do for the best. It's a lovely day so I'm going for a walk."

Jane put on shorts and sandals and at around six o'clock she walked up to the Downs. The sun sparkled on the dew to welcome a surprising number of people, taking advantage of the sweet cool air before the heat of the day. Dogs were being exercised, their legs and bowels made to move before they were locked away while their owners went to work. Jane walked over to see the suspension bridge and leaned for a while on the railings looking down into the gorge. Two children were trying to fly kites but there was too little wind to lift them into the air.

Jane took off her sandals and the cool remains of the dew on the grass felt wonderful on her bare feet; perhaps today would see the beginning of the end of her torment? She swished through the dew-damp burnt remains of the grass and started to hum to herself. An old man seated on a wooden bench reading his paper looked up to admire the pretty girl and a young man on a bicycle gave her a smile. Things were looking up at last and she turned to walk back to the flat. On her way, with the early sun in her eyes, Jane walked close to two boys playing with a Frisbee. They were hopeless, and the Frisbee sailed in her direction. Without thinking Jane raised her arm, caught the Frisbee, and threw it back. Immediately both her arms started to hurt with the same burning, tearing pain.

"Oh, no!" she cried out in disappointment and collapsed onto the grass crying with pain.

The boys ran over to her. "What's the matter, Miss?" The boys sounded genuinely worried.

"I'm so sorry, it's my arms, I shouldn't have reached up, it was my fault not yours. I used to be good at throwing a Frisbee."

"Can we do anything to help, Miss?"

"No thank you lads, it's very kind of you," she tried to smile, "I must go back to my flat, it's only at the top of Whiteladies Road."

"We'll come with you, Miss, just in case." The three walked back to Jane's flat. She staggered as she walked, and the boys put their arms out to help her, but she shrank away just in time.

"Please don't touch my arms, they hurt so much. It's just me."

"Sorry, Miss." The boys were puzzled by their newly found friend who seemed to be in such pain.

At the door of the flat she turned to them. "Thank you, boys, your very kind and I really am most grateful."

"That's all right, Miss, anything for a pretty face."

Jane laughed and felt better about the pain. The boys laughed with her as they ran off to play. Hilary was making tea and there was a delicious smell of toast. They had breakfast in silence which Angela eventually broke. "Well, Jane, how are the arms? Come on, let's have a look."

"I had a lovely walk on the Downs. It was so peaceful; there were people walking dogs and children playing. A couple of boys were playing with a Frisbee, and they weren't very good at it. It sailed towards me, and I stupidly reached up to catch it, and…" Jane choked the tears back, "then that terrible pain started again in my arms. The boys were very sweet; they came with me all the way back here."

"Come on, let nurses do the treatment."

They both carefully smeared a thick layer of the steroid cream to Jane's arms and after a few minutes the pain gradually lessened.

"Jesus, that's better. Perhaps soon I'll begin to feel human again."

"What's on for you this morning; can you stay here and rest?"

"No, I'm afraid I can't, there's a long, boring practical animal psychology experiment that I'm supposed to design; it's all to be done in that festering laboratory that ought to have been torn down ages ago."

She had known about the practical for some time and had not been looking forward to it; the point of the experiment seemed puerile. To cap it all, the pain in her arms made the idea of trying to concentrate on such an idiot subject almost unbearable. The practical was to be held in an old laboratory built many years before the advent of air-conditioning.

"That awful building is so hot it's bound to make my skin worse. It was a bloody stupid idea to put a glass roof over the laboratory; it's just like a greenhouse, totally unsuited to animal work, or even for humans. I'm supposed to design an experiment to investigate the direction-finding memory of our common house mouse. They're sweet little animals, fun to play with until they try to run up my sleeve. They must be bored silly, cooped up in their cages for most of the day. But, I suppose, overall, they are quite clever, just with memories like sieves.

"How any of this can be applied to humans is beyond me. Doubtless, it's someone's idea, but I think it's daft. The only thing I'll get out of it is a tick on my work sheet, so it has to be done some time."

Jane dressed in her coolest blouse and light skirt. She didn't want anyone to see her ghastly arms, so she chose a blouse with long sleeves and a high back, despite her comments on the inquisitiveness of her mice. She walked the mile to the School of Zoology and wearily climbed the stairs to the laboratory. The practical started well; Jane devised a learning experiment using a maze that could be altered quickly to give alternative routes. Time passed but as the afternoon progressed, she noticed that her mice were making silly mistakes. She was sure they were trying their best but there were several routes the mice did not seem to be able to learn. The heat was rising, and Jane's mind began to wander. She looked up, her attention distracted by the glorious day visible through the glass roof, cotton wool clouds meandered lazily across the pale blue sky.

"Just the day for photography," she muttered, as she casually picked up one of the mice in too much of a hurry. The mouse objected and bit her finger.

"Ouch! Bloody hell serves me right, you poor little thing, I'm so sorry. Oh God, I must wake up."

Jane gently returned the mouse to its metal cage and gave it fresh food and water to make up for the insult, then she found the first aid box and bandaged her finger.

"I must concentrate," she said softly.

After half an hour, Jane's finger started to throb and, as if in sympathy, so did the patches on her arms; by the end of the morning her arms were as sore as they had been at the end of the ball. She started to cry with the pain, excused herself, walked miserably home to the flat, let herself in and tore off the blouse. Her arms were again a livid red and the worst areas were oozing slightly. There were also a few ominously raised lumps on her elbows and wrists. Jane bathed her arms in cold water, smeared on more steroid cream and lay on her bed. Later, she got up, took two aspirins washed down with a large gin, shed the rest of her clothes and, in the cool of her nakedness, lay down. As sleep descended the dreams returned with a vengeance; they continued with yet another chapter in the gruesome story.

She was in a long line of naked captives following a narrow trail across the savannah. Her wrists were tied behind her back and her neck was trapped by a heavy forked stick tied to the shoulder of the captive in front. Two of the captives had cut their feet earlier in the day and when they fell yet again, they were shot in cold blood by a white man. He showed no emotion and immediately ignored the bodies to shout at the miserable line of captives. Jane woke up screaming and again

Hilary came quickly into the room and started to put her arms round Jane's shoulders.

"Please don't touch me. I've had those awful dreams again," she sobbed, "they're so real and so frightening and I don't understand them, if they have any meaning at all. Oh Hilary, I feel so ill. I'm sure Melusi thinks I've got something terrible; he seems to know it from the dreams. Please believe me, tell me I'm not going bloody mad."

Hilary looked at Jane's arms and they were as bad as ever. Even the bitten finger was a peculiar colour. Her ankles also had a red tinge and were covered in scratch marks so they obviously itched.

Hilary was becoming tired of Jane's illness. "I've rung the doctor and he said he would come over at once." Ten minutes later he appeared and was horrified at the state of Jane's skin.

"Oh dear! I don't like the look of this. I know an excellent dermatologist at the hospital. And if I may, I'll ring him from here and have you admitted as soon as possible."

"Am I really that bad?" Jane was at the end of her sanity. "Do I really have to go to hospital?"

"That's my advice. The trouble is, I'm not the best person to give you a full answer to that question and I'm referring you to Doctor Bhekitembo Makuthwane. He will probably do a battery of tests that I can't do in general practice. Don't worry, you'll be in the best possible hands; he's a very good dermatologist."

"He must be Melusi's famous uncle," said Angela. "We all know Melusi, he's just about to qualify as a doctor."

"I'll be very surprised if he fails to do so," said Arthur with a laugh, "He's a bright lad."

Arthur Richardson was relieved that Jane accepted his suggestion, but he had a strange feeling that there was something more sinister going on. Whatever agent was the cause of her terrible skin, other organs were also under attack. He identified a trace of blood in Jane's urine and there was something odd to be seen at the back of one of her eyes. Early on Tuesday 18th July, Melusi took Jane to the hospital where she was formally admitted as an inpatient. Bhekitembo's ward rounds were in the afternoon. He had heard of the women through their friendship with Melusi, so he was able to greet Jane with some familiarity.

Jane told Bhekitembo her story. At first, he felt intrigued and then, in some strange fashion, felt out of his depth, mystified by the speed with which the lesions had deteriorated. At first glance, Bhekitembo tended to agree with Arthur Richardson's diagnosis: the rash was a severe allergic reaction to a yet unknown agent related to the material of the new dress. However, there was something about Jane's skin that made his clinical hackles rise, it was too indurated and most of its normal elasticity had gone, as if there was a hardening agent just underneath the skin surface. Jane's attitude to her illness was also strange; at times she appeared to be disinterested; at other times she would become hysterical. Overall, she seemed to be more ill than was justified by the state of her skin. As he ran his fingers over the affected areas, Bhekitembo felt suspiciously solid areas suggesting deeper tissues were also affected.

Jane was obviously relatively fit, her systems functioned normally, and she enjoyed a work-out at the gym every week. During her trip round the world before going to university she had been no more ill than any of the other travellers, and Jane related no sexual experiences while abroad. Her bowels had naturally complained at the strange foods and germs poured into them at various stages of her wanderings, but they eventually recovered. She returned from her travels over nine months ago, so her present illness was most unlikely to have been due to one of the nasty tropical viruses. Remotely, Jane could still have a few parasites lurking somewhere in her body, but these normally disappeared with time and again were not usually associated with such an acute rash. Importantly, Jane gave no history of allergy and no skin complaints. Bhekitembo noted the unusual beauty of the unaffected parts of her skin, particularly startling was the contrast between the soft flawless skin of the breasts and the angry patches below them. He was pondering on the list of possible causes when he noticed that Jane was becoming uncomfortable at his concentrated gaze. He shook his head as if to dismiss a strange thought, smiled and she relaxed.

"What a mess, we must pull all the stops out to get to the bottom of this one." Bhekitembo acted the benign father-figure and his calmness infected Jane with a glimmer of hope. He went over the history again and it was quite clear that initially, the rash had been sharply limited to the area of maximum contact with the material of Jane's dress. It had started on her arms and back and was now affecting her abdomen; but the complete absence of rash in the bra and panties areas struck Bhekitembo very forcibly. He wondered grimly where it would spread to next and which of her internal organs were the most at risk.

The colour of the rash was becoming dark purple, and he was worried that the skin underneath the lesions was hardening, as if the small blood vessels were giving up and leaking fluid. He turned over in his mind an enormous list of conditions, most of them genetically determined, obscure connective tissue diseases; but he knew that they all developed much too slowly. They simply did not fit Jane's clinical picture. He dismissed an allergy to food, it was most unlikely to be an over-reaction to something that Jane had eaten at the ball as a great many people had eaten the same dishes as Jane and, as far as he knew, Jane was the only person affected by the peculiarly vicious rash. Bhekitembo straightened up and stretched his back.

"Well, for now, I am forced to the conclusion that your skin rash is due to an allergy to something connected to the material of your new cotton dress. Either the actual material of the dress or some process that has been applied to it may be responsible. I don't believe there will be a simple explanation and I shall have to do my homework with the modern processing of cotton. You are not exactly a textbook case, not even in the small print. That would be so boring!"

Bhekitembo chatted on general matters until he was happy that Jane was calming down. As he busied himself organising a series of blood tests and a skin biopsy Jane's confidence began to return and she tried to relax. She ate the hospital food that evening with surprising relish, snuggled down into the bedclothes and fell asleep. That night the dreams were not quite as bad as they had been, but she still awoke after a few hours in a fearful sweat and needed to be calmed down by the nursing staff. Bhekitembo sat late into the evening surrounded by empty cups of coffee, talking to himself. "I have a sneaking suspicion Jane won't be the only one."

Chapter Three

Elizabeth Clarke was in her first year reading African History at the university. A striking woman, twenty-two years old, tall, slim with long black hair and very dark eyes. She was obsessed with keeping fit and could out-run, out-jump and, at tennis, outplay most of the others in her year. Elizabeth's father had for many years run a farm in Zimbabwe. With the hopeful relaxing of tension, he had sold out to his African foreman, but the family often returned to visit old friends. They loved Africa. Elizabeth particularly enjoyed the enthusiasm of the local children, and she spent a great deal of her time planning what she was going to teach them during their next trip. She missed the huge open spaces, the freedom to ride for miles at dawn on the plateau; that was real freedom. It was not surprising that her skin was golden olive.

Elizabeth's sister, Wendy was more interested in the vanity of clothes.

"At least, dear sister, you ought to try on something new. Jane has a new dress and tells me it's environmentally friendly. Not sure what that means, but it sounds good to me. Come on, there's only one shop selling them, at the top of Whiteladies Road. I'll take you there this afternoon."

"I have to say, Wendy, the fabric feels more like silk. Something… not sure what to say… not sure. Stupid, I know, but there is a sort-of background effect."

Elizabeth shook her head as if to get rid of a thought.

"As if someone who had something to do with the dress is watching me."

She turned, but the only other person in sight was Wendy who was examining a jump suit at the other end of the shop. Elizabeth shrugged her shoulders, picked up a pale green dress and took it to the changing cubicle. She took off her jeans and sweatshirt and slipped the dress over her head. She brushed her hair back and saw herself mirrored against the cubicle curtain, which was a dark patterned material with intertwined giant trees and flowers, simulating a tropical forest. She shivered although there was no draught and shook her head to dismiss a particularly silly thought – that the dress seemed appropriate to the subject matter printed on the cubicle curtain. She emerged from the cubicle still puzzled by her emotional tangle.

"It's only a dress," she said to her sister, "but it's almost as if there was a compulsion to have one. You must admit it's unusual for me to have any interest in clothes."

Wendy was puzzled by her sister's attitude. Instant decisions were more in Elizabeth's line. So why was she taking such dickens of a long time to make up her mind?

"Which colour do you like?" Elizabeth asked.

"The brown one suits you best." Wendy was struggling to hide the impatience in her voice.

"Don't be cross with me, darling sister. You know I don't buy many clothes. I suppose it's about time I took it more seriously. All right, I'll try on the brown one." The fit was perfect, the colour was just right and carried away by Wendy's enthusiasm, Elizabeth bought it.

"I'm sure you'll be over the moon when you wear it."

"I hope so, but will the moon be pleased with me?"

Wendy would always remember the strangely doubtful overtone in Elizabeth's voice and the far-away look in her eyes.

The major tennis tournament between the colleges was at the end of June. Elizabeth's team won and the coach organised a celebration to be held in a marquee on the Bristol Downs, just over the road from the college.

"Come on Liz; let's splash out and have a real party for once. You can wear the new dress, ideal for a hot night." The party grew, of course, until twenty people were due to cram into Elizabeth's tiny room in college. Towards six o'clock, Wendy came over and they dolled themselves up ready for the kill. They laid out glasses, dips, crisps, and nuts on every available surface. Two of the men had promised to bring the drink but the sisters prepared themselves with the remains of a bottle of gin and some flat tonic. The party eventually overflowed onto the stairs and only when all the bottles were empty did they stagger across the road to the Downs and the marquee. It was packed and very hot, but they managed to find a table near the band, the food, and the bar.

Elizabeth felt good, she knew she looked good, and she knew that the other women were admiring her dress. Her boyfriend, at least she thought he was her boyfriend, Patrick Neill, said he loved her with a complete lack of conviction, but she didn't mind; he was fun. She danced with all the men in her party. The evening was going well. At midnight the buffet was in full swing, the bar packed, the noise dreadful and the heat intense.

Elizabeth suddenly felt dizzy, she was uncomfortable, too hot, and the dress clinging to her, almost burning. She needed fresh air and quiet but stumbled out to find her sister in a steaming embrace with Patrick Neill.

"Sorry Wendy, didn't mean to interrupt."

"Don't worry, Liz, he's all yours, including his spiky moustache. Hey, what's the matter with you? Come on, little sister, you look like death warmed up."

"I'm sorry to be such a wet blanket. I just feel like shit. I'm too hot, my arms itch and it feels as if there's something crawling all over my back and tummy."

"Patrick didn't get that far with you? Give him another go!" As soon as Wendy had spoken, she wished that she hadn't. There was something dreadfully wrong with her sister.

Elizabeth collapsed to the ground and burst into tears. "For Christ's sake shut up!" Her voice rose to a shriek.

This was so unlike her that Wendy and Patrick marched her over the grass, across the road and up the stairs to her room. Patrick tried to put his arms round Elizabeth to give her a cuddle, but she whimpered and cringed.

"I'm sorry, Patrick, but everything hurts, and I feel bloody."

As soon as they entered Elizabeth's room, she tore off all her clothes and crouched down by the side of the bed covering her weeping face with her hands. Patrick was embarrassed and started to leave the room, but he stopped at the door when they saw the angry red areas on Elizabeth's arms and back. The skin of her breasts and her tummy looked normal, making the inflamed areas look worse. Elizabeth looked as if she had been attacked or burnt, the wheals looked so bad.

"Oh, Wendy, what's wrong with me?"

"Oh my God! I hope and pray this isn't the same thing that Jane's got."

"What do you mean?"

Wendy told her the story of Jane's skin lesions and how Jane was now in hospital under the care of Melusi's uncle.

"I don't like the sound of that at all," Elizabeth covered her nakedness with a sheet that Patrick had pulled off the bed. "At least I feel cooler now and not so burnt. I can understand being allergic to something but why do I feel so bloody ill? Now all I want to do is lie down and die. I'm sure I'll be all right in the morning if I go to bed now. Please, just let me lie down and sleep."

"Bed it is," said Patrick, "but you had better have a slug of this with a couple of aspirins, if you've got any." He produced a hip flask and Elizabeth took a great swig with two pills that she hoped were aspirins.

"I'll ring the doctor first thing tomorrow," said Wendy.

Wendy's description of her sister's rash was so clear that for the second time in a week Arthur Richardson had the strange premonition that he was going to be asked to deal with an unusually weird problem. He arrived within the hour and examined Elizabeth in minute detail. The lesions were identical with Jane's, and he gave her a steroid with an antifungal cream, hoping that it would have a better result than the steroid cream alone had with Jane. Arthur Richardson said he would ring the dermatologist that afternoon and arrange for Elizabeth to be seen as soon as possible.

"The creams have helped a bit and I do feel better, but what now? At least I feel like getting dressed." Elizabeth slipped into a light silk dress and stood up. "That's better! What now, little sister?"

"Let's go and see Jane in hospital, I'm sure we can persuade Patrick to drive us."

"That's the last thing I want to do, but if you say it's a good idea... I suppose I won't be the only one with horrible rashes."

An hour later they took the lift to the ward and sat by Jane's bed, feeling thoroughly miserable listening to Jane's story.

When she mentioned the dreams, Elizabeth cried out that she too had terrible dreams the night before.

"Horrible dreams; so horrible, I tried to forget about them. They… I want to go home… leave this place."

She turned and came face to face with Bhekitembo and Melusi.

"Sorry to prevent your retreat. This is my official ward round and I have already had a call from Arthur Richardson about you, so don't worry, I'm very pleased you happen to be here. I presume you came to see Jane. The reason doesn't really matter, anyway you're here so it gives us plenty of time to talk. Now, we will all sit down, and you will tell us the whole story."

Bhekitembo's warm, smooth voice and his reassuring words helped Elizabeth to relax as he continued to question her in minute detail. He looked at Elizabeth's skin and compared her lesions with the latest lesions on Jane's skin; they looked identical. He took a blood sample, ordered a skin biopsy and a range of further tests.

"I am inclined to agree with Arthur. There must be something, perhaps in the dye, however 'natural' it is, or in the chemical processing of those dresses or even in the material itself, that has caused this to happen. The only snag is apparently many thousands of these new dresses have been sold and so far, you two appear to be the only ones with this reaction. Despite that, I think there is a range of possibilities to be investigated. I'll ring round my colleagues in the southwest to see if they can identify any more cases."

Bhekitembo was outwardly confident but clearly worried. He had one very sick woman and another who was going the same way and he still had absolutely no idea of the diagnosis. During the afternoon he telephoned colleagues and heard that ominously two more females and, strangely, two males had recently been seen by dermatologists at hospitals in the Plymouth area.

Bhekitembo reached for the phone and dialled his nephew.

"Melusi, I have a job for you. Find out if those patients were wearing garments made of the new cotton."

Melusi phoned within an hour. "The two women had indeed been wearing dresses and the men, shirts made of the new cotton before their skin erupted."

"Interesting – well done!"

Chapter Four

"Let's start again," Bhekitembo muttered. "There must be something odd connected with the newness of this blessed cotton material. But that's ridiculous; more than three-quarters of the world's population wear clothes made of cotton or mixtures that contain cotton. Well, our now six people must have reacted to some peculiar or unusual substance used at some stage in its manufacture. On the other hand, a change in the production process might have affected the cotton in some malign way and the six affected people possessed an unusual reactive substance in their make-up, possibly a rare genetic mutation. I need Kit Pearson's help. I bet she's at work to get away from her ghastly grandchildren."

Bhekitembo drove to the university department run by his formidable friend and was relieved to see her car parked in its usual spot. Kit was a cheerful, plump fifty-year-old lady who knew everything there was to know about fibres and materials. Unfortunately, Kit's encyclopaedic knowledge of fibres failed to help her look after herself. Attempts to lighten her hair could often be traced to an array of empty bottles of peroxide resulting in the disastrous straw-coloured mop that partially covered her head.

Bhekitembo found Kit in her office at the laboratory fanning her face in the heat.

"Can you help me, Kit? I have a very strange problem."

"I hope not a personal problem!" said Kit gently; she knew Bhekitembo only too well. "Most of the time you mean your patients' skin problems, and they're usually pretty revolting. Go on, tell me."

"I have two patients in my acute ward, and I gather there are four more in the region. They all have horrendous rashes that seem to be related to hot sweaty contact with what I gather, is the fashionable new cotton material. I know that thousands of dresses and shirts made with this material have been sold, but I have the nagging suspicion that the six patients I've told you about are reacting to it. Tell me about cotton and what is different about this new material."

"Well now," said Kit as she leaned back in her chair. "How long have you got, Bec?"

"I can give you two hours."

She laughed. "You can always come back for another session tomorrow. The story of cotton goes back for longer than historical records. Half a million years ago primitive cottons probably grew wild in East Africa and then spread throughout Asia. We know that about 5000 years ago people in the northwest of the Indian sub-continent cultivated cotton plants. The industry was adopted by the Persians and Alexander the Great brought it to Europe in about 300 BC. In the 700s Muslims adopted more advanced manufacturing methods and brought them to Western Europe. Later, we have a few beautiful examples from Italy and Spain who started to weave cotton garments in the 1400s. In the 1600s the English took to weaving in cotton in a big way. Mostly the raw material was sourced from the Levant, later imported from America in the 1700s. It was the English textile manufacturers who designed the machines that made it possible to spin thread and weave cloth in large quantities, so much so that a thriving export business developed.

You should have learnt all that at school, it was part and parcel of the Industrial Revolution. You must have heard of Arkwright and his spinning-jenny. You still listening, Bec?" Bhekitembo nodded. Kit bent back in her chair and continued.

"Most of the cotton grown nowadays is produced in China and America, with America being the biggest exporter. Incidentally, you may be interested to know that the early explorers in America discovered that the native Indians knew how to make beautiful articles of cotton clothing. Other areas producing cotton are India, Pakistan, some Central and South American countries, especially Brazil, and a belt of countries across Central Africa. Some is grown in Spain and Greece and a little in Australia.

"In the southern United States, cotton became so important that people called it 'King Cotton' and slave traders sold huge numbers of African slaves to provide cheap labour to cotton farmers. Slavery also was the mainstay of the cotton industry in Brazil."

"How about the actual cotton plant?" asked Bhekitembo.

"Modern plants are, of course, selected variants of the primeval ones. Cotton plants are classified within the mallow family. Only a few species of cotton, part of the genus *Gossypium,* are cultivated. American upland cotton, *Gossypium hirsutum*, has creamy-white flowers and white fibres between 22-32 millimetres long. Egyptian and so-called sea-island cotton are varieties of *G. barbadense.* Egyptian cotton has lemon-coloured flowers and long, light tan fibres. Sea-island cotton, mainly grown in the West Indies, has brilliant yellow flowers and white silky 44-millimetre fibres and it is the most valuable cotton."

"And cotton cloth itself?"

"Cotton cloth is made from the fibres that are the main constituent of the boll. The boll is the seed pod and forms as the flower withers. It grows to about three to four centimetres in diameter, rather like a green golf ball with a pointed tip. As it matures it cracks in four or five straight lines from the tip and splits open showing what are called locks or groups of eight to ten seeds each with the cotton fibres attached. Finally, the boll turns brown, opens out, dries and the cotton fluffs out. At first cotton was harvested largely by hand with the help of the odd mule. At the height of the slave trade in 1850 it was estimated that nearly two million slaves were put to work in the cotton industry in America. It was extremely hard work with very long hours. It has to be said conditions were only marginally better than those in the sugar industry at the time."

"Yes, Kit, I have read about the horrors of the slave trade. Slavery has been going on for thousands of years, but it's reckoned that up to thirty million Africans were forcibly taken from their country by Europeans. Many of them died on the way; they were probably the lucky ones. Almost all European nations at the time were involved in one way or another."

"I know. It was terrible and, strangely, it was probably abolished purely for economic reasons. Indentured labour is, in the end, cheaper and more productive. Today cotton is produced in a much more scientific fashion with little labour and a great deal of machinery.

"The production of the final material is an interesting process," Kit was happy to return to her speciality subject. "Six to ten months after planting, defoliants are sprayed on the plants and ten days later giant machines strip off the mature bolls and take the harvest to the processing factories. The first stage of processing is by a machine called a cotton gin which separates the fibres from seeds, rubbish, and the remaining leaves. The raw cotton is compressed into bales which are graded and sold to the textile mills. At the mill the bales are opened, and various pieces of machinery attack the cotton eventually turning out a rolled sheet of relatively clean lint which then goes to a carding machine which separates the fibres, rejecting the short ones. It's now the turn of what, you may remember, is curiously called the spinning-jenny whose product is the yarn that is warped onto a gigantic spool known as a beam. Yarn from this beam is then fed through a vat which contains a mixture of starch, gum, and resins. This strengthens the yarn which is dried and rewound ready for weaving, knitting or other processes. Once woven, the sizing is removed from the cloth in hot water. It may also be boiled in alkali which removes the natural colours and waxes. Wrinkle-resistant and so-called easy-care cloth is treated with chemicals that link the fibre molecules and makes them malleable."

"Fascinating," said Bhekitembo. "That gives me a range of chemicals to investigate for a start."

Kit thought for a while. "Your problem is that the new cottons have fewer treatments than previously. That's the whole idea behind the sales push. Perhaps we should revert to the Middle Ages when cotton used to be dipped in urine and left in the sun to bleach before being coloured with a range of vegetable dyes. It was a particularly inefficient way of doing things, but at least it was cheap and didn't require the tons of chemicals used nowadays.

"I'm afraid the new cotton is a development of a very old idea," Kit continued, "Various wild species of *Gossypium* are naturally coloured but their fibres are very short and therefore can't be machine spun. But by selection techniques and a degree of crossbreeding, even the tweaking of the odd gene, a range of naturally coloured cotton plants have recently been developed that have a much longer fibre length so they can now be spun by machines. The colours are lovely, greens, browns and pale pinks. Today these colours are fashionable, perhaps tomorrow they won't be."

"That doesn't help my theory very much," said Bhekitembo gloomily.

"Ah! But I have a further depressing story for you. At the same time as the fashion for natural colours, there is a significant move towards a reduction in the use of pesticides."

"Oh dear, my theory is coming apart at the seams," Bhekitembo sounded depressed, "Whatever else have you got in surprise for me?"

"Sorry about this but there is yet another activity of the environmentalists that we must consider. Weeds and insects are great destroyers of the cotton crop. Have you heard of the bollworm, sometimes called the boll weevil?"

"No, I have not, it sounds disgusting. Can the little beast affect humans?"

"Not as far as we know. But bollworms are very difficult to control; they attack the plants, crawl inside the bolls, and eat the seeds and cotton fibres. To combat them and the weeds, farmers use huge amounts of agrochemicals. In fact, cotton farmers use around twenty-five per cent of the world's production of pesticides and up to ten percent of all the herbicide produced. In some countries the crop is sprayed thirty to forty times a season. Round the Aral Sea most of the local water supplies used for drinking are heavily contaminated with agrochemicals, and these chemicals also run off into the Black Sea and kill the local fish stocks. They usually kill everything. They even distort the hormonal balance of the fish and humans so you are left with vast areas that, as I told you, are full of cancers in humans and abnormal fauna; areas that can't support anything except primeval slimes. They are extremely dangerous compounds; you may have heard of the PCBs that mimic human hormones and distort the generative structures of the next generation."

Bhekitembo, feeling desperate, leant forward.

"There must be something in that list of toxic chemicals that could have affected my patients."

"Not even sure I can help you there. Farmers can now use chemically altered pheromones which resemble the airborne sex hormones of the bollworms. This changes their mating behaviour and so there are no baby bollworms to continue the destructive process. They can also spray the crops with sterile bollworms or even varieties of lacewings or tiny parasitic wasps that naturally kill bollworms. But it must be said that these methods are expensive and to be economic they must be used selectively. Egypt has controlled the bollworm problem by using pheromones in over half of its crop area.

"The latest gimmick is to listen to the bollworm eating! Scientists working on this idea selected bolls in a portable soundproof box surrounded by very sensitive sound detectors. Apparently, a munching bollworm sounds like a horse munching hay. If you know where the infestations are you can use your expensive methods more efficiently.

"And I have to remind you about the weed problem," she continued remorselessly. "It has been rediscovered that chicken manure and hoeing is just as effective and costs just about the same as the use of toxic agrochemicals; that's including labour. You see, the more we discuss the new cotton the less plausible appears your hypothesis. Sorry about all this. On the other hand, I find your story worrying, perhaps the very purity of the cotton may relate to the problem. Is it possible that the very absence of all these nasty chemicals has left some active agent in the cotton and this might have something to do with the rashes? Just a thought, Bec?"

"Good point, Kit; I'll have to mull over everything you've said."

Chapter Five

Bhekitembo left Kit's office feeling thoroughly deflated. All his ideas seemed to be falling on stony ground. However, he did know a lot more about cotton. He drove back to the hospital and telephoned his old friend, Dan Karnel, at the Institute of Dermatology in London. "Dan, I am puzzled about a batch of very odd skin rashes."

"Tell me all, I could do with a good story to liven up the day."

Bhekitembo described the two women under his care and mentioned the four other cases in the Southwest, emphasising the association with the new cotton material. "Do you have any views on that idea?"

"I don't know whether it will cheer you up or depress you, but I've just had a very similar query from colleagues in Liverpool and Harwich. Come to think of it, they're all seaports, worth remembering as a possible clue, like the proverbial needle in a haystack."

"I don't think we ought to dismiss anything, however farfetched." Bhekitembo remembered his long lecture about the cotton industry. "We must keep in touch and hope for a few more clues."

Bhekitembo thought for a while and then phoned Dan for a second time. "Sorry to pester you again but do you think the consultants in Liverpool and Harwich would mind if Melusi, my nephew who is a medical student, looked into their cases to see if we can discover a common link?"

"I'll give them a ring right now. I guess they or Melusi could also look for an equal number of matching controls who live in the same areas. Unfortunately, this all takes far too much time, and we don't appear to have that luxury, bearing in mind the speedy development of your cases."

Bhekitembo put the phone down carefully, deep in thought. Even with Dan's cases, the total number was still a tiny fraction of all those who must have worn dresses made with the new cotton. The manufacturers assured him that many thousands of dresses and other garments had been sold. There had to be a link between the cases for them to all have reacted so violently.

Early on Sunday, Bhekitembo found Jane and Elizabeth very down in the dumps. The rashes seemed to have stabilised, but the two were dreaming horrific dreams and when asked about the substance of them, they both became wild-eyed with fear.

Later in the day he had a call from an old friend, Doctor James Fisher. "I hear on the grapevine, that you're collecting some peculiarly nasty skin rashes. Is that correct?"

"That's quite true, do you have another one?"

"I gather you think there may be some association of these rashes with the new so-called 'environmental-friendly' cotton clothing," said James, not directly answering Bhekitembo's question, "well, I have a twenty-one-year-old patient by the name of Samuel Blake who bought a pale pink shirt made of this new material. His arms and trunk are badly affected and curiously there is a sharp cut-off at the level of his underpants."

"I would be delighted to see him as soon as possible. I have a free slot tomorrow afternoon."

"Many thanks; I'll ask him to bring along his shirt."

"Good idea, thank you James."

Bhekitembo phoned his nephew, "Melusi, come to my clinic tomorrow afternoon, I think I have another case, a man this time from James Fisher's practice."

"Thanks uncle. Incidentally, we must remember to ask him if he's had any weird dreams."

"What intrigues you about the dreams? Do you think they have a related significance?"

"I have been talking a lot with Jane and Elizabeth," said Melusi, "both they and the four cases from the Plymouth area have had the most frightening dreams. Could it mean that there is evidence of irritation of the central nervous system? Incidentally, we have both recorded that all the cases have had crashing headaches. Might that indicate some degree of brain irritation? Perhaps there is a hallucinogen involved?"

"Good point, we'll ask him, unless he volunteers the information."

Samuel Blake, a frightened little man, appeared in Bhekitembo's clinic clutching a plastic carrier bag. Mary Challenor, the Jamaican Staff Nurse smiled at Samuel.

"Do come in Mr Blake. Would you please undress in the changing room and put on the gown hanging behind the door? I'll show you which is Dr Bhekitembo's office when you are ready."

Samuel entered the doctor's room still clutching the carrier bag, which he put down on the table. He looked thin and ill and seemed to breathe with some difficulty.

"Thank you for coming, Samuel. I was telephoned about you by Doctor Fisher. Tell me about the rash."

"I am very grateful to be seen so quickly. Doctor Fisher says you think it may have something to do with my shirt, so I've brought it with me. My mate and I saw this new type of shirt in the shops a few weeks ago. He bought the brown version, and I bought a pink one. It was nice and cool and comfortable to begin with sitting in a chair in the garden but by the end of the afternoon I suddenly became very hot, and my chest and arms began to itch. Then my back started."

"Do you remember what date that was?"

"It started sometime in the middle of June."

"That's over three weeks before Jane!" Melusi burst out, unsettling Samuel.

"I had not missed that fact," said Bhekitembo severely.

"Sorry to interrupt," said Melusi.

"I'm glad there are other people with the same thing," said Samuel. "Not that I would wish it on anyone. This Jane, has she also had frightening dreams, and does she feel so ill she could give it all up?"

Bhekitembo looked at Melusi who this time said nothing. "Tell me about the dreams, Samuel; have you had headaches as well?"

"My head hurts most of the time; my skin is on fire, I can't breathe, and I don't seem to be able to pee properly." Samuel's voice was rising. "And if you can't do anything for me, I am going to jack it in." He obviously didn't want to talk about the dreams now, so Bhekitembo proceeded to a very thorough history and examination. He discovered that Samuel was twenty-one years old and an only child. His father, Walter Blake, had been a ship's captain and had died at sea. His mother, Jemima, had worked in a laundry and had died at the early age of thirty-five of a bad chest. Samuel had been born in Bristol and when his parents died, he went to live with a distant cousin, Ellie Mackenzie, who lived in Africa.

Samuel was now crying. "Recently; I was told Ellie had died of some peculiar disease in Africa. She was only twenty-five, my Ellie. I loved her as if she'd been my sister. We had some wonderful times together." They had to wait as Samuel broke down with his returning memories. "She was in South Africa and the illness that killed her started with a rash. Do you think the same thing is going to happen to me, doctor? They said everything just clogged up and Ellie didn't stand a chance."

"When did she die?"

Samuel pulled out a much-used handkerchief. "She died at the end of June this year. They said that she had funny things in her organs, so it was better that she was cremated."

Mary fetched him a mug of tea. "Do you take sugar, Samuel?"

"Oh, yes please, two." Samuel was brightening up with the sympathy.

"Drink this and you'll feel better."

After a while Samuel was able to continue. "Ellie died in a hospital in Zimbabwe. I've got the name of it in this letter." He extracted a dirty piece of paper from his pocket. "They sent this to me soon after her death and I haven't wanted to part with it ever since; it's all I've got."

Bhekitembo looked at the letter and noticed that it also had the names of the physician, Doctor Gabriel James, who had looked after Ellie and the pathologist, Doctor Valentine Johnson, who would have done the post-mortem. He wrote the names down in his diary together with the telephone number of the hospital.

"What a lovely old-fashioned name: Ellie."

"Yes, they named her after an Ellie Lancaster who, it's said, we're all descended from. She lived in the early 1600s and was apparently a real beauty. Anyway, it didn't do my Ellie any good, being beautiful. She's dead now."

Samuel's eyes filled with tears for the third time. He pulled out his grubby handkerchief again from his trouser pocket and blew his nose. They waited patiently for him to recover.

"She used to be a wonderful swimmer, my Ellie. She went to Southern Africa to do scuba diving and surfing. You see our family has always had something to do with the sea, going back many generations; quite a few were sea captains or pirates, I wouldn't be surprised." The last statement seemed to cheer Samuel slightly as he rambled on. "Perhaps that accounts for the dreams. Do you know what keelhauling is? I can't imagine anything worse, but they did that to me, in the dream. You were tied up and dragged under the boat right under the keel, across the barnacles. You were very lucky even to survive to come up the other side. If you didn't survive, sometimes even if you did, they just chucked you over the side to feed the sharks, like the others from below."

"Who were the others, Samuel?" Melusi said, suddenly wide awake.

Samuel was quiet for a while until he finally erupted. "I don't understand; when I tell anyone about the dreams, I come to a block. As if I mustn't tell any more."

It seemed better to leave any further questioning about the dreams for the time being.

Samuel's skin rashes were in a more advanced state of decay than Jane's or Elizabeth's. The areas were now spreading but it could clearly be seen that the original rash had ended sharply at the top of his underpants. On examination, Samuel's chest sounded noisy. In the next room, Bhekitembo and Melusi stood in front of the X-ray viewer.

"See here, Melusi, those odd-mottled areas that appear to be spreading over both lungs. They bear some distant resemblance to cases of Farmer's Lung Disease. I remember we used to have a lot of those after a damp summer."

"I thought I could see some odd little white spots on Samuel's retinas using my new ophthalmoscope. I don't think it was the dirty lens. Do you think, uncle, Samuel is slightly jaundiced? And I found a trace of blood in his urine, so his kidneys are not in the best condition. And he is a trifle anaemic."

"There's a lot going wrong with the poor fellow."

When the examination was finished, Samuel was shown into the changing cubicle to get dressed again.

"I wonder what his father died of. Remember he said his father had died at sea," Bhekitembo mused, a curious look in his eyes.

Ignoring his Uncle, Melusi was anxious to get on. "Let's have a look at the shirt. Mary, would you open the bag, please? Maybe pop on some gloves, just to be on the safe side." Mary rolled on latex medical gloves and went over to the table, picked up the bag and pulled out the shirt. It looked very smart, a most attractive pinkish colour. Mary held up the shirt by the shoulders facing the three men.

Melusi stepped forward for a closer look, then gently took the shirt from Mary with bare hands. He felt no fire or pain.

"Put it back in the bag, please, Melusi." Melusi did so carefully. "Thank you. We will examine the shirt again later; keep it in a safe place for the moment, locked away."

Samuel was admitted to hospital on Monday 24th July. He cheered up a little when he was tucked up in bed, especially when he was visited by Jane and Elizabeth. "Very susceptible to the female form, you know." He spoke to the ward sister in an oddly old-fashioned way. Melusi's visits did not produce quite the same effect and Samuel, although he liked the young man, felt a fear he could not explain. Samuel was confused, in pain, and plainly out of his depth.

Melusi's questioning was very thorough. He felt something was driving him; he had to get to the bottom of these cases. He already had answers to a great number of questions but was not sure what other questions to ask and his questions were beginning to unsettle Samuel.

"You asked about relatives, doctor. I have a very old great uncle, Bernard Charlton. He must be very rich, and he lives in a large house in Clevedon. He's a lovely old man, very generous to me, and he spends most of his days studying our family tree. He showed me one old document that linked my dead cousin Ellie back to her namesake in the 1600's."

"This is very exciting. Do you think I could visit your great uncle?"

"I'm sure you could, he would be pleased for any interest in the family tree. I warn you; he talks for Christmas!"

That evening Melusi telephoned Great Uncle Bernard.

"Come over, dear boy; Samuel will give you directions. I look forward to wining and dining you."

Chapter Six

Bhekitembo managed to get through to the General Hospital in Harare on Wednesday 26th July.

"Can I have a word with Doctor Valentine Johnson, your pathologist, please?"

The switchboard operator located Valentine who came to the phone in a state of some agitation.

"So glad you phoned, Bhekitembo. I have to say, the entire hospital staff were deeply upset at Ellie's death; by her youth, by our inability to reach a diagnosis and the uselessness of all the treatments we tried." Valentine needed time for his voice to calm down.

"I remember the wonderful times we all had with Ellie. Several the staff joined the same scuba diving school down on the coast at Beira in Mozambique. It's a good organisation. There are a few wrecks just off the coast that are easy to reach. Ellie was an expert diver and since she had all the right PADI certificates the school had taken her on to supervise the beginners. I was a beginner and rather frightened at the whole idea, but I've always wanted to explore the bottom of the sea. Ellie was very patient, especially with me. On Monday 29th May, I think it was, I managed my first dive down to fifteen metres; it took me quite a long while to get down as I had some difficulty getting my ear pressures right. Then when I got down to the sea floor I got carried away with excitement and started to paddle off into the gloom. Ellie came batting after me and I had a wag of her finger in front of my goggles to re-join the group. She very gently tore a strip off me when we came up. I was better behaved after that."

Valentine took a deep breath. "I'm certain she wouldn't have done anything silly in the sea. When we were trying to establish a cause for the awful rashes we even thought of some toxin from an unusual fish as the cause of her disease, but the scientists at the local marine biology school didn't know of any local poisonous fish, nor could they throw any light on the problem. There is still, I suppose, a remote possibility that the cause was something chemical, perhaps leaking from one of the wrecks. Goodness knows what chemicals some of those ships were carrying."

"Tell me everything you possibly can about Ellie's illness. Tell me about her signs and symptoms, the development of the disease, the treatments that you tried and so on. Leave nothing out, however irrelevant it may appear to you. You see there is a possibility that whatever she had may now be affecting her cousin and two other women under my care in this country. I gather there are four more cases in the Plymouth area and some in the north of the country.

"OK, I'll tell you everything I know of Ellie's last few weeks." Valentine was working up speed again. "The night the rashes were first seen was when Ellie was staying with some friends in the hostel used by the divers. Our dive had been the day before, in fact. The dive was fun, and we came up without any need to decompress as we were only down to fifteen metres. The guys in the boat leant down and took our cylinders, masks and flippers and having washed our faces in the sea we spent the next ten minutes splashing about in the lee of the small island that sheltered us from the swell that can sometimes be quite severe in the Mozambique Channel. We climbed the steps to the boat, and I did notice that Ellie took rather a long time to climb up, as if she was tired. This was odd because she always had a tremendous amount of energy, far more than any of her pupils. We were driven back to the shore at speed, and we were laughing and singing as the boat ran up alongside the floating platform owned by the school. But Ellie was a bit down; not her usual self at all. We left our kit on the boat and took off the wet suits and rinsed them, then we showered in whatever we had on beneath the wet suits. That evening back at the hostel she complained that her chest, neck and back itched so much that they hurt. She said she felt hot and desperately tired, which I suppose could have been down to her working hard the day before. She went to her room and a friend of hers, Alice, went with her. As soon as Ellie took off her shirt, she saw that there was a dark reddish rash on her chest and back. Alice came out of Ellie's room and called through the door of my room. She was very upset and since I was a doctor, she asked me to come and look at Ellie.

"Ellie burst into tears and said she felt tired and ill, and the bloody rash was the last straw. How right she was! The rash had an odd distribution in that it sometimes missed the natural folds of the skin. For instance, beneath her breasts there was a crescent moon shaped area that was unaffected. Likewise, there was no rash under her armpits and only a little at the inside of the elbow. There was a line of rash round her neck as if she had worn a collar that was too tight. On her back the rash was mainly in the middle, much worse on the areas that had taken the pressure of the tank support. It only reached to her waist with an abrupt cut off at the level of the top of her pants and her legs and feet weren't affected."

"Was the whole of the breast affected?"

"Sorry, perhaps I didn't explain it very well. The main area of each breast was as affected as any other area of the chest wall. It was the curious crescentic new moon areas under each breast which looked the most startling."

"Did Ellie wear a bikini when she went scuba diving?"

"I'm not sure, but I can ask one of the others at the diving school. Are you suggesting that if she had been wearing a bikini it may have protected the skin from the agent that caused the rash?"

"Precisely. The next question is related. What was the garment that Ellie was wearing on her top half? Perhaps a seemingly strange question, but we have a very strong suspicion that the rashes are caused by contact with a newly developed cotton material. This material has only been on the market for a relatively short time and many thousands of dresses, shirts and so on have been sold, but it seems to be a common factor in our cases. I find it difficult to believe that it is the only factor, but maybe it is a trigger that sets off a train of events that so far we don't appear to have been able to stop."

"Ellie was wearing a shirt of some sort, but I wouldn't know what sort of material it was made of. I have Alice's phone number, so I'll ring her this evening and ask her if she remembers. Then I'll ring you as soon as I know."

"Thank you, I would be most grateful, sooner the better."

"To continue with the sad story, Ellie's rash deteriorated, and she was admitted under Doctor Gabriel James' care at the General Hospital in a pretty bad state on Friday 2nd of June. In any case associated with a rash we look for evidence of our current range of nasty viruses or other infections that are common around here. We even started up the electron microscope but failed to identify anything. As well as doing our own tests we sent some of her serum, eventually with further samples, to

Porton Down, the research place near Salisbury, UK. They are supposed to be your experts in rare diseases, and they sometimes come up with a diagnosis when we have failed. So far both we and they haven't come up with anything. Feel free to ask for those samples if you have any bright ideas what to do with them; they should be frozen down somewhere. I can give you the actual numbers of the samples from our files in a minute.

"Poor Ellie's rash gradually spread, and the worst areas became purple. The centres gradually darkened and looked almost black. The picture looked as if it could remotely have been anthrax, so we did the whole range of tests all over again but failed to come up with anything. She developed a bad cough, but there were no identifiable germs in her spit. On the X-ray of her chest there were strange, mottled areas rather like those you see in advanced allergic chest disease from almost any cause. I remember a bad case of Farmer's Lung disease when I was on a respiratory course at the Brompton Hospital in England. His chest X-ray looked like Ellie's. We used to call the areas fluffy cotton wool balls in the old days.

"Towards the end, Ellie's systems simply ceased to function one after another. Her bone marrow was infiltrated with some, probably fibrous, material that we haven't yet identified. All the cell lines in her peripheral blood failed one after another and transfused blood just vanished. Her kidneys packed up and she went into renal failure. Finally, her heart rhythms changed in an unusual fashion, and she died in ventricular fibrillation that we failed to reverse on Tuesday 27th of June."

Valentine sighed deeply. "Just before her death the inflamed areas that had been quite black became covered with a curious white fluffy deposit on them as if something was coming out of the skin. The skin was slightly sticky, and it could have been cotton dust from the bedclothes."

Bhekitembo felt as if he had been hit in the pit of his stomach and the hairs on the back of his neck stood on end. "Go on." He struggled to regain control.

"From start to finish Ellie took a month to die. It was awful, she needed huge doses of opiates in the last week as otherwise she would have been in torment. We tried every treatment we could think of. Local steroid creams seemed to have some effect in the early stages, but the usual mild skin creams were quite useless. We tried intravenous steroids and again these worked for a few days, but you could see that even though the inflammation was less, nothing had any effect on the progression of her lesions to the black stage where one had to presume that the skin was dead. We tried the usual supportive treatment for the failure of her systems, but it only gave her temporary benefit.

"Frequently, and especially in her last days, she would cry out in terror in her sleep. When we woke her up, she said she had just had the most terrifying dreams. Even in her sleep Ellie said strange things like, '*We didn't do it; you can't blame us, it's too long ago.*' When we had time to ask her what the problem was and who she was she talking to, she never replied. She just looked very sad. It was as if she was in another world."

"Did she ever describe the dreams to you or anyone else?"

"Something about forests, great heat, guns, screams, the noise of chains and a great terror in everyone around her. Sorry not to be more specific, but the dreams weren't our prime concern at the time." Valentine thought for a while and continued slowly. "Before she died, she was really terrified of something. She was crying out, '*Please don't, please don't!*' She had such a far-away look in her eyes. I have never seen such a haunted look on a face before."

"Well, Valentine, I'm sorry to have to tell you but all our cases have had dreadful dreams. There are so many loose ends. To be more practical, what were the post-mortem findings?"

"I found a whole range of odd things. Firstly, I must tell you that we had a major power failure during a tremendous storm and the pathology fridge packed up. Now this would normally have only been a smelly disaster, but, strangely, after two days, Ellie's body looked the same as the day she died. There were no apparent signs of decay. Even in the heat there seemed to be no change; her face was still beautiful; it was as if she had died a few minutes before. I particularly noted this as you can understand I was personally not looking forward to doing the post-mortem."

"I can understand that."

Valentine was silent for a minute and then continued when he had control of his voice. "Her organs looked superficially normal. We took pieces of all the major organs and sectioned them all. Under the microscope it looked as if every organ had been infiltrated with fibrous material that resembled some weird version of one of the rare congenital diseases that affect the connective tissues of the body. But Ellie was the wrong age, wrong sex, and wrong race for any of those conditions. I am hoping to get this material analysed, so far with no success. Would you like me to send you some sections?"

"Yes please. I'm sorry; I seem to have distressed you. It must have been terrible for everyone. You've given me a great deal to go on and I am very grateful for all your help."

"It's kind of you to say so. We were all very upset indeed, and I hope never to see another case like it."

"Many thanks again for your help, Valentine. I look forward to receiving the slides. We must keep in touch, and I will let you know if we find any useful information from any of our cases. Goodbye."

Bhekitembo sat for a few minutes in silence. Could Ellie's rash have also been an allergic phenomenon with a hereditary basis? If Jane, Elizabeth, Samuel and Ellie, the cases in the Plymouth area and the two other cases in the north of the country could all be found to have a common ancestor, it would reinforce the hypothesis. The story of the namesake, the unfortunate Ellie Mackenzie in the early sixteen hundreds, was too good, or too awful, to be true.

Bhekitembo dialled a number. "Ah, Melusi, you should know the latest in such things. Where can I find a clever molecular biologist who can look for an aberrant section of Jane and Elizabeth's genetic material that is common to all cases and cause them to react in such a horrendous fashion? Another project, can you find a biochemist to identify a toxic substance in or on the new cotton?"

"Uncle, I am afraid we don't have the time. It is theoretically possible to identify parts of the DNA that would over-react to a unique substance. If there was a strange but identifiable section of the DNA that could be demonstrated in all the cases with the rashes and none of a similar number of control people who had not been ill after wearing the new cotton, this would reinforce your idea. But – and it is a monumental 'BUT' – how long would that take? Probably months! Out of the question.

"Our best bet, uncle, is to study the hereditary origins of the cases. We need to study their family trees. There are lots of books and some computer programs to give us some clues to find that sort of information. It still takes a very long time, though. We could try parish records of births, marriages and deaths and the stored wills at the Public Record Office? They're all available to the public."

"My dear nephew; then it is just the job for you! I want you to trace, as quickly as possible, the family trees of Jane, Elizabeth, and Samuel back to the 1500s or even earlier if possible. We already know that Ellie is related to Samuel, so that's a start. When you've done that, do the same for all the other cases."

"Certainly, uncle, I can start tomorrow with the help of Samuel's great-uncle Bernard. Samuel has told me a lot about his ancient relative and says he is a bright old spark; he must be at least 90 but sounds as fit as a fiddle on the phone. I'm dining with him tomorrow at his house in Clevedon."

Chapter Seven

Melusi arrived at exactly seven o'clock at the gates of Great Uncle Bernard's house, a magnificent Edwardian mansion with a wide view of the Bristol Channel high up above the commuter town of Clevedon. Melusi identified himself to the intercom, the gates opened as if by magic and he drove up the steep winding drive and parked in front of the house. An elderly man wearing an apron opened the door.

"Do come in Mr Makuthwane, we are expecting you."

Melusi was ushered into an ornate hall with spectacularly high painted columns that ascended further as iron fingers to support a magnificent glass dome under the sky.

"May I get you a drink, Sir, while you are waiting for Bernard?" asked the old man.

"Thank you, a gin and tonic please."

Melusi was ushered into a large comfortable room whose floor to ceiling windows glowed with the evening sun. In the distance, the sea shone like rippling gold.

The old man reappeared. "Please make yourself at home. There are some nuts and crisps in the bowls on the table. Bernard is looking forward to meeting you."

"Thank you," Melusi sat down in a well-worn comfortable leather armchair facing the dying sun. He looked around him at the walls of the room covered with maps and old framed pictures of virtually every continent. Africa seemed to hold pride of place, especially the central and eastern states. Many of the maps had little flags with what appeared to be file numbers on them. Melusi presumed these related to information held in half a dozen cabinets in the far corner of the room. The furniture had an ageing elegance, showing extreme signs of wear, and the room oozed the Edwardian era while still confessing to intense use. This puzzled Melusi, knowing the great age of the owner. Samuel had said his great uncle was about ninety years old and Melusi was hard put to imagine how someone of such an age could still beaver away at a family tree. But for the last two weeks Melusi had been presented with so many strange happenings that he supposed anything was possible. The old man came in with Melusi's gin and tonic, followed by another man whom he presumed was Great Uncle Bernard.

Tall, possibly a trace over six foot, slim and nattily dressed, great-uncle Bernard looked not a day over sixty. A mop of wild silver hair sat on top of a narrow strong tanned face covered in smile lines. The eyes were a startling dark brown and radiated an intensity of feeling normally only seen in much younger men. But Melusi was to discover great-uncle Bernard was no ordinary man.

Bernard's hands were as dark as his face, burnt by many years of working in the sun. The skin was thinning, the veins standing out like a medieval map. Melusi's host walked across the room with a spring in his step and thrust out a hand. Melusi was not expecting the crushing handshake. What was the magic preservative used by this man? And yet, there was a hint of sadness about great-uncle Bernard's general demeanour; could this reflect grief for the death of Ellie Mackenzie?

"Melusi, how nice of you to come and see me, dear boy." His host had a powerful voice. "I am generally known to the world as great-uncle Bernard, but I answer just to Bernard. I see Hobson has been looking after you. Thank you, Hobson, I'll have a whisky and water."

Hobson ambled off.

"It is so nice to have a clever young visitor; this is a celebration. Sit down by the window, that chair has the best view of the estuary. I'm sorry not to greet you in person, Melusi, but I was held up for a minute trying to organise a flight out to Zimbabwe. Sadly, a young relative has died there in rather unusual circumstances."

"Yes, I am very sorry to hear of Ellie's death. It's very sad, she was so young."

"Of course, how silly of me, you must have heard of her death from Samuel. How is he, by the way?" The question, put in such a casual fashion, belied the obvious concern felt by Bernard for his young relative.

Melusi carefully phrased his answer. "I think he'll be all right. Currently he's in rather a bad way, his rash has not yet responded to treatment, but we have several more routes to follow." He wished they had, but economy with the truth seemed to be appropriate; there was little point at this stage in saying that they were desperate to find anything that could be relied upon to stop the progress of the disease in any of the three patients.

"Now tell me about yourself and your family. Where you come from, what you are doing and why you are kindly taking such an interest in an old man?"

"My mother and father originally came from Zimbabwe. They came over separately to study law. They met at law school, fell in love, married, and settled down here as it seemed to be a relatively civilised country without an excessive amount of colour prejudice. I was born here, went to school in Cardiff and managed to get into the medical school at Bristol. I hope to qualify next year, then train as a surgeon so that I will be of some use when I return to my country. We go back most years to Zimbabwe, and I can't wait to live there."

"What a lovely ambition. I could tell you a few stories about surgery towards the end of the nineteenth century in what is now called Zimbabwe, later perhaps. Now, to what do I owe the pleasure of your visit?"

"I came to see if you can throw some light on Ellie's death. Samuel's illness is also a puzzle, and the illness of the two women who are currently in the same hospital. I have to confess that I have no idea why I think you can help, I simply have a feeling that you hold at least one of the keys."

"I do hope you're right. How about the other half?" Bernard had already drained his glass.

"I'd better not drink too much. I'm driving. And I need a clear head to glean the maximum amount of information from you."

Bernard laughed. "Fair enough, let's go and eat. Hobson! The young man must be hungry." Hobson was obviously used to being summoned in such a fashion and came in immediately.

"Dinner is served, Bernard."

Bernard stood up and led the way to the dining room. He held one of the massive double doors open for Melusi to reveal that the walls of the dining room were also covered with maps, most of which had notes attached to them. In the centre of the room was a magnificent refectory table, some twenty feet in length, with a complete set of fourteen chairs. Bernard sat at one end and Melusi sat next to him.

"I hope you're not a vegetarian. Mrs Hobson has cooked us venison that arrived yesterday from my estate in Scotland. Had

I known you were coming I could have pretended it was specially brought for you! Will you have some wine? It's from Chile and should be rich enough to match the venison."

"I love venison, it sounds delicious and Chilean wine sounds fun."

The venison was followed by mango ice cream and, finally, cheese. Over the cheese they talked at length about Ellie's death. Bernard was obviously determined to discover the cause of her illness and come hell or high water; nothing was going to stop him. Was this an obsession or was there some other factor in the equation?

"I know a great deal about Zimbabwe, but I have never heard of anyone dying in such a peculiar way. I had a word with the doctor who had looked after her and he seems to have been completely confounded. I intend to go and see if I can discover anything further about her death."

Bernard rubbed his hands together to hide his sadness, and Melusi felt the time was not ripe to tell Bernard about his uncle's phone call to the pathologist. They sat for a while in silent thought.

"What you will not know, Melusi, is that there has always been something unusual about our family. I may interest you with the mammoth story later. We have had close connections with Zimbabwe, previously Rhodesia as you know, for many generations. My great-uncle, the Reverend Edward Longstaff, known as Ted, went out as a missionary in the 1880s. I suspect you know the history of your country much better than I do, but I'll give you my version, so please correct me if I am wrong. In the 1880s the region we now call Zimbabwe was known as Mashonaland and Matabeleland. Around 1890 the area was controlled by the British South Africa Company. Officially the name Rhodesia was not in general use until about 1905.

"Ted was a very tall man; he was six foot seven, the same height as some of the tribes. Perhaps that's why he was sent out there by the Missionary Society. I have never been convinced that was true, but it made a good story at the time. I fear Ted was rather an outspoken man, always getting himself into deep water. Towards the end of his career, he was constantly getting into trouble with the bishop. Ted wasn't convinced that the bishop was sympathetic to Africans. Ted thought he looked down on them. I remember him saying that once he overheard the bishop complaining about 'these damned Africans'. Ted apparently burst into the bishop's room and tore the bishop off a strip. I suspect it'll all be in Ted's diaries. In fact, as you doubtless know, there were civilizations in Africa that were at times far in advance of those in Europe. It was the guns that upset the balance.

"Ted hadn't been there very long when he got a bee in his bonnet about the availability of health care, as we now call it. So, he purchased a copy of Gray's Anatomy and a set of knives, scissors, and other implements that surgeons use and did quite major operations, apparently with very good results. I have his original notes somewhere in the top of the house. I don't know what the witch doctors thought of Ted, but he must have been a dramatic man. His first wife, Priscilla, sadly died of some tropical disease and he eventually married his Scottish housekeeper, a wonderfully tolerant woman. He finally retired to this country, and they lived in this house for a while with various other members of the family. He died in 1920 and his second wife died soon afterwards. There was a son and a daughter by his first marriage, but I've lost touch with them, I'm afraid. I doubt they are still alive; one was particularly accident-prone. He had his shoulder bitten off by a crocodile!" Bernard obviously found this funny, but he laughed in a kindly way. Clearly Bernard liked to talk about his great-uncle Ted, but this evening he was running out of steam. He rose from his chair, walked to a corner cupboard, took out a decanter of port, filled two glasses, placed one in front of Melusi and sat down himself with the other.

"Now I have been rambling on and you came with a specific request. How can I help you?"

"Well, it's only a slight change of subject. Samuel said that you had been working on the family tree and were able to trace it back to the 1600s or even earlier. He thought this tree included the dates of birth and death of the original Ellie Lancaster, the beautiful namesake. Would you have any information going further back than that?"

Bernard thought for a full minute. "That's a tall order. Those filing cabinets are stuffed full of information, as you call it." He gestured dismissively towards the end of the room. "You are looking at the result of sixty years of research and you will need many hours to take in even a fraction of it. Oh yes, I have, indeed, got an enormous amount of data on the family tree which you may study, but I am afraid you will have to study it in this house as the documents are personally very valuable. To help you I have a photocopier, scanner, and printer in my study that you may use, and I can offer you any secretarial help you may need. My personal secretary will help you in that direction, but I have an unnerving feeling that time is running out for us."

Bernard spoke fast and Melusi was overwhelmed; this was far more than he had hoped for. Why did a 90-year-old need a personal secretary and a collection of modern state of the art office equipment? Surely this was rather over the top, almost verging on an obsession. Melusi dismissed some fleeting salacious thought about the status of the 'personal secretary', although he was not certain how to interpret the twinkle in Bernard's eye when he had mentioned her.

Seeing Melusi's puzzlement, Bernard laughed, "I can see you think that I'm much too old to need all that kit. I can assure you that they are all necessary for the mammoth book I am writing; more of that another time." As an afterthought he added, "I have to admit the secretary is very cheery."

"But why, with respect, at your age, are you putting so much energy into discovering all this information about your forbears?"

Bernard refilled their glasses. "You may have thought you were changing the subject. One subject frequently links to others, you know. There has been a family legend going back through a great many generations that there is a curse hanging over members of our blood line. The curse is reputed to have originated well over two thousand years ago. I heard about it when I was very young, and it so intrigued me that I have been studying the subject ever since. I suppose it all started as a hobby, but it quickly became my life's work and sadly, I suspect, the beastly thing has now come home to roost. You see, until now, no one in their right mind would have said that the family was cursed, just the opposite. To an outside observer we have had more than our fair share of good fortune. That is fortune in terms of worldly goods, you understand. I fear some of these worldly goods have come from that very part of the world that we are discussing. You may think that my shares in the mines of central Africa are tainted, but I can assure you that most of the profit goes back to the various countries."

Bernard waved his hands around the room as if to emphasise the richness of his surroundings, but it was obvious that there was a guilty feeling about it all and he was trying to justify the opulence to his visitor. Melusi was unsure how to take this. He knew of the European companies that contributed little to the countries that were host to their mining interests, but he forbore to make any comment. Another time, maybe.

Bernard was firing up again. "One thing I can tell you is we have always had a lot to do with the sea. There are several semi-famous mariners in the family tree. I am afraid their histories are a trifle suspect. As a result of this we reaped the unholy benefit of participating in the slave trade and, going back even further, in the 1400s and 1500s, we were pirates on the sea and militant robber barons on land. Someone called me a robber baron the other day, so I hit him to add the militant bit!" Bernard laughed at the memory.

Although he did not like the sound of some of the things done by Bernard's forebears Melusi could not help liking the old man.

Was Bernard a rogue or a disinterested historian?

"Let us get back to the family tree. You may think it seems like cheating to lead straight to the first Ellie, but when you're given a clue, you should follow it up. Great-uncle Ted said that his sister-in-law Olive's side of the family was descended from a great beauty in the early part of the seventeenth century and so when little Ellie was born the name was there to be used." Bernard shook his head as the tears came to his eyes. "Oh, dear, I am sorry, I can't get over it and I'm sorry if I sound flippant. It is as if the curse is beginning to take effect after all this time; but why did it have to kill the loveliest of us all?"

"I am afraid there's a standard answer to that question. I would humbly suggest that to kill the one that was the most beautiful or the most loved would be guaranteed to have maximum emotional effect. If it killed a member of the family who was mean and nasty, you might be tempted to say it was a good thing. Ellie's death was the worst thing that could have happened to your family and therefore even more devastating. Or does that sound too philosophical?" Had he really said those words? They seemed to come to Melusi's lips as if they were spoken by somebody else through him. He felt he was simply the mouthpiece for a voice from many hundreds of years ago; it unnerved him. How many more members of Bernard's relatives were going to die? Remembering the purpose of his visit, Melusi still had to find out if his patients were connected to the same blood line.

"Is there a remote possibility that my patients are connected in the same blood line?"

Bernard was thankful for the change of subject. "I suppose it's possible. As you have probably gathered by now, all these maps on the walls and the thousands of references in those filing cabinets in the drawing room are a life's work to get to the bottom of the curse. For the last twenty years it has increasingly worried me that despite all my work I still don't have enough answers, and what answers I do have seem to lead on to yet more questions. Perhaps I'm too late." He stood up. "Let's go through to the other room and I'll show you some of the family history over coffee and brandy."

"I had better forego the brandy, remember I'm driving, I don't want to get any more points. I've already been done for speeding twice."

"In that case you must stay the night," Bernard said in the tone of voice that was not prepared to accept a refusal. "You might be lucky enough to meet my secretary tomorrow. Will you accept a brandy now?" Bernard's eyes were full of fun.

"Twist my arm, thank you, both for the brandy and for hopefully introducing me to the lovely lady!"

Bernard pulled the bell rope and Hobson came with a tray of glasses and a bottle of brandy. He poured two generous glasses and Bernard sampled one.

"That is excellent, Hobson."

"Yes Bernard."

"Melusi Makuthwane will be staying the night. Lend him a pair of my pyjamas and a toothbrush; I'm sure there's a new one somewhere. He can sleep in Tara's room, it's nice and airy and he can wake to the morning sun."

Hobson's face lit up with pleasure. "How splendid, I will get Mrs Hobson to make up the bed at once. I do hope you like tea in the morning, sir, and a hearty breakfast."

"You're very kind. I would love to stay the night, and I do like breakfast and particularly early morning tea."

"That's settled then."

Chapter Eight

"Let me show you something really dramatic." Bernard opened the top drawer of one of the filing cabinets and took out a roll of stiff vellum. He unrolled it very carefully and placed it flat on a table by the window.

"There, Melusi, can you put those four Baccarat glass weights on the corners while I hold them down. Isn't it beautiful?"

The sun was just touching the horizon and the golden light on the old writing brought it alive. The document was a genealogical tree of extreme age, written in black ink in letters so small they were difficult to read. The dates were quite distinct and started in the 1500s with decipherable dates up to the mid-1800s. Melusi studied the writing.

"This is absolutely wonderful and incredibly detailed. How old is it? Silly of me, of course, since 1850 is the last readable date, it can't be older than a hundred and fifty years."

"It is three hundred years old at the very least," Bernard said quietly, very serious. "The clever scientists using carbon dating and other methods can tell the age of the parchment and the inks. I'm sure you have noticed that there are no names connected with the dates after 1700. But I can put names to all the dates up to and, of course, beyond 1850."

Melusi was startled. "That is just eerie. You are suggesting that someone drew up this document three hundred years ago and was able to predict the births, marriages and deaths that would occur at a series of accurate dates until the eighteen fifties?"

Bernard switched on a powerful lamp. "Quite so! That's the first surprising thing about the vellum. But look harder, if you look very closely you will see indentations on the parchment that seem to indicate dates up to the present time."

In the slanting light of the table lamp there were indeed impressions of dates on the parchment, as if the ink had run out of the marking pen all those years ago.

"All those dates, young man, are exactly right. They are the lifetime events of persons that could not possibly have been known to the creator of the document."

Melusi was silent, his mind whirling.

"But who could have made this document and where did it come from? It's weird."

Bernard was enjoying the effect the conversation was having on Melusi. "It came into the possession of great-uncle Ted when he was in Africa. Ted said very little about where it came from or under what circumstances. All I know is that he had gone on a long journey and when he returned two months later, he had this roll of vellum. The bishop was reported at the time to have said that Ted had been very frightened, but I am rather wary about that comment. As we know, Ted didn't hit it off with the bishop. I have to hope the full answer will be in Ted's papers in the loft; there are eight boxes of papers and for ages I promised myself that I would go through them, but you know how it is."

Bernard took a sip of his brandy.

"Well now, I've told you something about the curse. You will understand when I say that I have a terrible suspicion that the answer to Ellie's death lies somewhere in one of those boxes. Perhaps there might have been a remote chance if I had pulled out all the stops, I could have saved her but until now there's been no urgency to examine the confounded boxes. I can't do it on my own now and Hobson isn't strong enough, so I need help." The implied request was left hanging in the air and Melusi was unsure how to reply.

"You're not being very fair to yourself. There must be a limit to the amount of work that even you can get through. Look at you, you are ninety years old, and you are still working harder than most medical students." Bernard's deep dark eyes looked as old as the vellum they were both studying.

After a while Bernard unwound, and his taut cheek muscles relaxed. He gave a grim laugh. "Perhaps you're right. You're very kind. Incidentally I knew a crowd of medical students in my younger days, and I can say that I didn't drink as much as they did even during the Depression. I wouldn't dare to comment on the present consumption."

"Never mind that, can we return to our patients. My uncle Bhekitembo is the dermatologist looking after the three of them and he has suggested that there may be some hereditary basis for the severity of the rashes. He gave me the job of tracing the lineage of all the cases. This vellum will help us enormously. I'm afraid we don't have any sort of a diagnosis to account for Ellie's death. My uncle telephoned the pathologist in Zimbabwe, Valentine Johnson, who had the sad task of performing her post-mortem. Uncle had a long discussion with Valentine, but he is as foxed as everyone else. He has promised to send sections of various bits and pieces to the UK, and we might stand a chance of at least identifying the cause of her death."

"Well young man, you and your uncle have got further than I have so that's hopeful. Shall we see if we can glean anything further from the vellum?"

The two men bent over the ancient document and studied it for some time in silence. The earliest dates were rather smudged, but the surname of a forebear of Ellie, someone who had been born in 1528 and died in 1570, seemed to begin with the three letters 'Haw' and had the initial 'J'. He, or she, as the sexes were unusually written in what looked like a random fashion had consorted with a person whose surname began with a 'T'. This 'T' was covered in gold leaf and there were specks of gold leaf further along the continuation of the name.

"Can we presume, Bernard, that T was a female, and judging by the gold leaf, was a very important person? So according to this chart they had one child who was a great-grandparent of the original Ellie?"

"A reasonable presumption, Melusi. I have another document for you."

Bernard produced a modern roll of thick paper from the same drawer, unfolded it on the next table and placed four more weights on the corners. "I have collected the names from 1700 without much difficulty and constructed my own chart on a second roll."

"So, the original Ellie was born in 1613. I wonder who this J Haw was, born in 1528, and the gold encrusted T?"

"Have a guess, Melusi, remember there is a very strong tradition of my family going to sea. Perhaps I shouldn't say 'my' family as there is a mixture of families in these charts. We are all such mixtures that, on a mathematical basis, Ellie would only have had six per cent of J Haw and the same amount from the golden T."

Melusi exploded.

"Good God! John Hawkins, possibly the first Englishman to take part in the slave trade. I remember questioning my parents as to the usefulness of studying the history of a country far away from our homeland. At last, it's beginning to show dividends."

"Hole in one, Melusi! Yes, he did several slaves runs and was as unpleasant as most of the others, unlike Drake who only did one voyage to snatch slaves and sell them. He found the whole process so awful that he refused to have anything more to do with it on his subsequent voyages."

Melusi wasn't satisfied. "The dates fit, but who on earth was T? At least we can assume that T was female. Surely the gilding must have indicated that she was of royal blood; just a suggestion."

"It is, indeed, more than likely. I think we must presume that J Haw had bought or captured her amongst a batch of slaves. He obviously wanted her for himself and looked after or, more likely, raped and imprisoned her until she had delivered."

"Bernard, that would explain Ellie's beauty; just a touch of African blood would be likely to give her skin its wonderful colour."

Bernard choked back his emotions and fetched another bottle of brandy. "Let's do a little lateral thinking; there are so many lines of investigation to follow and so little time. Tell me, why are you so interested, Melusi?"

Melusi sat back in his chair. "Those two are personal friends of mine. I've known them the whole time I've been a student. The rashes appeared quite suddenly and seem to be progressing inexorably. My uncle Bhekitembo has performed a battery of tests but there have been no useful results so far. And, unfortunately, standard treatments have had only minimal effect on the rashes. He has discovered there are four further cases in the southwest, all in the Plymouth area, and two other cases in other seaports. These cases don't sound as severe as the ones in Bristol and are still under the care of their general practitioners."

Bernard interrupted. "John Hawkins lived for most of his life in Plymouth, for what it's worth. Carry on, Melusi."

"Then Samuel was referred by an old general practitioner friend of uncle, and it was Samuel who told us about Ellie's death in Africa and about your interest in the family tree, so that's why I'm here. Uncle has always had a huge number of ideas about his patients. But in these cases, he is suggesting that they are suffering from a unique hereditarily-determined reaction to something in the newly-developed cotton material used to make the currently fashionable range of dresses."

Bernard brightened up. "This is fascinating. I wonder how many other cases there will be and if they have all been wearing your new cotton? I have booked to fly to Zimbabwe next week and I'm sure I could find out if Ellie had been wearing any of this material you talk about. I am not an expert in the subject, but it does seem rather odd that an allergic over-reaction, however exaggerated, should then take such a short time to kill a previously fit adult. I believe there is something much more sinister at work, and I don't think that's a product of anyone's imagination."

They talked for a while longer, but they could come up with no better theory of the cause of rashes. Eventually, well past midnight, Bernard stood up.

"We should have a get-together with all the people involved with the cases. In the meanwhile, the time is speeding towards one o'clock in the morning and I think we should go to bed. Hobson will still be up, and he will show you Tara's room. I'm sure he can provide you with all the necessary bits and pieces for your night's stay. I will see you at breakfast on the veranda at about eight in the morning."

Bernard held the door open for Melusi as Hobson came out of the door opposite.

"Good night, dear boy, and thank you for coming. It has been the most stimulating evening and it has given me great hope."

"Thank you for inviting me. I've enjoyed this evening enormously; let's hope it will be productive. Good night, Bernard."

Melusi followed Hobson along the upstairs corridor to Tara's room. He had forgotten to ask who Tara was, but there were some beautiful dresses in the open wardrobe. He sniffed the perfume on the dressing table and his head spun with the intoxicating smell. There was a picture of a laughing attractive girl on a tractor and another of a handsome couple in their fifties sitting on a bench in front of a rose-covered thatched cottage. Yawning, Melusi undressed, washed, cleaned his teeth with the new toothbrush, put on Bernard's or Hobson's pyjamas, climbed into bed and within seconds was asleep.

Melusi dreamed of the high seas, the cries of men thrown overboard to the sharks, the cruel laughter and the shame of others onboard. He dreamed of a royal princess who, as she was forced to give herself to the captain of the ship, cursed him and his offspring for ever. She used a curse known only to the royal family, a curse as old as the spoken wisdom of the tribe, a curse so terrible that it had never been used before and would never be used again. She would die and many others would follow, but in the fullness of time there would be revenge. It would take a long time but have a devastating effect.

Melusi awoke with his thoughts in turmoil. On the one hand, he could well understand that there would be a desire to be avenged for the dreadful excesses of the slave trade, on the other hand he was professionally involved in trying to help three people whom he liked and for whom he felt medically responsible. *Somehow*, he mused, *I must weigh my professional responsibility to my patients against a primeval urge to exact retribution for the activities of the slavers. But this is crazy; the suggestion that it could remotely be justified to attack people who had been born between eighteen and twenty generations after the activities of the slavers strikes me as grotesque. Few, if any, of those in the family tree alive today will have any concept of what it must have been like all those hundreds of years ago.*

Melusi lay quietly mulling over the problem for some time and was now convinced that the right path to follow was to heal and to forgive. But to heal, he had to find a cure, and at last he felt he had one or two clues to steer them all onto the right track.

Chapter Nine

Melusi awoke just before 5 o'clock on Friday 28th July. The sun flooded in through the window, warm and friendly. At last, he felt he was going to succeed in his search for the cause of the rashes. With tremendous optimism he felt today was the day to find something exciting; with luck he might even find the cure for the suffering patients. He had no idea why he was feeling so optimistic, simply that after the exhilarating discussion with Bernard last night, today could not possibly be all doom and gloom. What was the meaning of the curse that for many years had made such a deep impression on Bernard? Was it to be taken seriously? Could the curse have anything to do with revenge for the monstrous four hundred years of the slave trade? But if this was the case, what was the point of leaving the culmination of the curse for so long? There were a lot of questions and very few answers. After an hour's thought sitting by the window, Melusi decided to go for a walk. The ever-thoughtful Mrs Hobson had left clean socks, underwear, and a short-sleeved shirt for him on the chair. He gratefully put them on. Descending the stairs, he opened the front door to the early morning sun and went out into the garden where he saw a woman in a bright red bikini watering the plants down by the gate.

"Hello there."

She smiled. "Bernard said he was going to have a visitor last night. You must be Melusi. Knowing how much he talks I guessed you'd be staying the night. I'm Tara Vaux, and you probably slept in my bed. I'm Bernard's personal secretary. I'm not quite sure what the difference is between a personal secretary and any old secretary. And before you get any ideas, our relationship is, unfortunately, wholly innocent. While we are on about innocence, did you sleep in my bed?" She looked mischievous.

"I am happy to say I did, but sadly all on my own."

Melusi flushed with pleasure at the thought of not being on his own last night and he tried to imagine what fun it would have been to have had this woman beside him. But then he thought that even he might have been too tired.

"I hope you didn't have to sleep out, Tara."

"Don't worry, I had to go and see a dear old aunt in Cornwall in a hurry. Anyway, Bernard wanted your company for himself. Auntie seemed to be all right so I left as soon as I could and drove back, early enough to help old Jack. Jack's the gardener and he's getting on a bit. He's eighty and rising, so I thought I'd help him with the watering."

"You must have driven like the wind," Melusi was taking quite a shine to Tara, who talked so freely to a stranger.

"Getting difficult now with all the speed cameras."

"Let me help."

"That'd be nice I'm getting a bit hot."

Tara found another reel of hose, connected it up and Melusi watered the back of bed by the garden wall as he watched every movement of Tara's superbly fit body. She was a fount of knowledge about Bernard's plants; knowing the binomials for most of them.

"The majority were brought from Africa by Bernard's great-uncle Ted. I expect you've already heard about Ted."

"I heard about most of Ted's life last night, he seems to have been quite an adventurous character, with all his operating."

"Oh yes, he certainly was, he even did a few hysterectomies for massive fibroids. His anaesthetics were a mixture of alcohol, witchcraft and hypnotism, but they worked."

They were silent for a while. Melusi's heart resumed its normal pace as he studied her. Tara's dark-brown hair, with its natural wave, enhanced a pretty face with high cheek bones and large dark eyes. Her honey-coloured skin glowed with health in the early morning sun. Melusi guessed her age at about twenty-two, five foot six inches tall with a gorgeous firm figure. As she yanked the hose from place to place her breasts hardly moved in the bikini top. She was perfection to him. The muscles in her arms and legs looked strong and fit and she moved with a grace that was made even more attractive by her bright red bikini.

They watered for a while in silence until she looked up and smiled at him. "Now you've had a good look, I'll tell you about me; then I want to know all about you."

Melusi was very happy with this idea, he wanted to see her mouth move; it made her face light up like a goddess.

"My grandfather was an Indian all-in wrestler in one of those wandering circuses. The circus landed up in this country and then went bust. Grandfather ran through what little money he had and finally shacked up as a toy-boy for a rich middle-aged heiress in Devon. It sounds an unlikely combination, but they lived very happily together, and much to her surprise my grandmother became pregnant and my mother was the happy result. She had a spoilt childhood and married a Somerset farmer, and I was one of four children, all girls. We're all still very close friends; two of them are happily married and they both have children. I'm supposed to be the clever one, getting to university. I love sport; I'm a black belt at Judo and swam for the university, and got a good degree in history. Bernard advertised for a genealogist, so I applied and surprisingly got the job. I love working for Bernard. Has he told you anything about me?"

"He offered me your services."

"Did he now?" Tara laughed. "And I bet he said it in just the same way."

As Tara laughed her whole body seemed to be laughing, a lovely fluid flowing laugh. Her generous mouth was so inviting Melusi had to restrain himself from kissing it.

An upstairs window opened, and Bernard's head appeared. "Your laughter starts the day well, Tara. Oh good, you've met. I'll be down for breakfast in five minutes. What a wonderful day, meet you both on the veranda then."

"He's probably been awake for hours," Tara whispered. "He works so hard. Has done ever since his wife Victoria died twenty years ago, according to Hobson. It's almost as if he's driving himself to finish all the projects he started before he joins her. But the harder he works, the more he seems to survive. Bernard's a lovely man and we'll miss him when he does go. Oh well, you'll have to tell me about yourself another time."

As Melusi helped Tara put away the hoses she suddenly shouted. "Last one up to the house is a sissy!" She ran off to the veranda at the back of the house where breakfast was laid on the table in the morning sun. Despite her speed, Melusi caught up with her as she reached the corner and grabbed her round the waist. She turned to him with a look so flushed and expectant that he kissed her open mouth. She pressed herself to him for a second, said nothing, but gave him a wonderful smile. They linked hands and walked the rest of the way.

Bernard was already at the table. "Isn't she lovely?"

"I keep on telling you that you shouldn't be such a naughty old man; fancy offering my services without asking me first." There was deep affection in Tara's voice.

Melusi was floating on air.

"I think Tara is the loveliest woman I have ever seen."

"Oh dear, this is too serious." Tara blushed under her tan which made her look even more attractive.

The sun was now high in the sky and the veranda was the perfect setting for a leisurely breakfast. They sat for some time basking in its warmth, chatting about nothing important.

Suddenly Bernard stood up.

"Tara, work to do. Can you confirm the bookings that I tried to make last night to fly to Zimbabwe? I am not sure if the airline understood exactly what I wanted. I also want a hire car and a good, tough driver, capable of driving anywhere. A four-wheel-drive, air-conditioned Toyota would be ideal. The cost doesn't matter."

"Certainly, Bernard." Tara turned to Melusi. "This must be important; Bernard isn't usually so specific."

Bernard was about to give other marching orders when Melusi interrupted him. "Before you go to Zimbabwe I would very much like you to meet my uncle and Arthur Richardson, the general practitioner who referred Jane and Elizabeth to hospital. Arthur has also spent a good part of his life in Zimbabwe. There's also one other person that I hope you will meet one day. He is Jane's mother's boyfriend who lives with her in the South of Spain. He's a retired Professor of History at the School of African and Oriental Studies."

"You mean Simon Lancing. Good heavens, I've known him for years. He's in this country now; he telephoned me two days ago. I presume he's come over with her mother to see Jane.

How about all meeting here for a meal on Sunday evening? Hobson!"

"Yes, Bernard?" Hobson always seemed to be waiting in the wings.

"Can Mrs Hobson cope with six people on Sunday for dinner at seven o'clock sharp? I suspect they would also like to stay the night. I hope you can be with us, Tara?"

"Of course, I would love to. Is that OK with Mrs Hobson?"

"I am quite sure Mrs Hobson will be very happy; quite a social event," remarked Hobson.

"And I wouldn't miss it for the world," said Tara looking at Melusi.

Bernard missed nothing and smiled happily to himself, remembering how exciting life had been when he was young. How many years ago was it that he first set eyes on Victoria; would he ever set eyes on her again and feel his heart turn over?

"Right, that's fixed," said Bernard. "Tara, can we contact Simon? I think I know where he and Rebecca are staying." He turned to Melusi, "Would you invite your uncle and Arthur Richardson? Say it is a matter of some urgency and is intimately connected with all their patients."

Melusi thought it was extraordinary that a man rising ninety years of age could so easily take control. He must remember to ask Bernard if he himself had been a ship's captain. From the little that he had gleaned about Bernard's life there appeared to be a very big gap in his host's story. The dinner party sounded as if it should be interesting and there was, of course, the bonus that Tara would be there. They finished breakfast and Melusi went to thank Mrs Hobson for looking after him.

"It was a pleasure," said the beaming lady. "It's so nice to have young people staying in the house. We don't have very many nowadays with Mr Bernard working all the hours that God gives him."

Melusi came through to the hall where he found Tara, who had changed into more practical clothing.

"Can I do anything to help you in preparation for the dinner party?" she asked. "I've done all the calls to Zimbabwe."

"I am sure you can, if you can stand travelling in my car," Melusi said, his heart pounding.

"I'll go and ask Bernard if he needs me today."

Melusi thought that his own need for Tara's company was greater than Bernard's, but at least Bernard had the excuse that he was employing her; Melusi's need was more physical.

Tara came out of the study slightly flushed. "It's fine. Bernard doesn't need me until after lunch tomorrow. Let's go and find these doctors and their patients."

Melusi drove carefully down the drive and as before, the gates opened by some mysterious command and quietly shut after them.

"Where shall we go, Tara? How about the country club at Long Beeches? My uncle's a member and they don't mind if I use his guest card on the odd day. We can play tennis, swim, have lunch and generally while away the day."

"Why don't we get the work done first, then we can relax and enjoy ourselves?" Tara sounded so sensible.

Melusi felt a little deflated by this practical approach but did see the sense of it.

"I suspect at this time of day my uncle will be at the hospital doing a ward round. Would you mind waiting, or perhaps come up to the ward and see Jane and Elizabeth? They need moral support and I'm sure they would love a visit from you. It'll be a great change from endless silly conversations with Samuel."

"I don't know about moral support. But I would be fascinated to see the rashes. Yes, of course I'd love to come with you, and I promise I'll do my best to cheer them up."

Chapter Ten

Bhekitembo was in deep conversation with Jane and Elizabeth when Melusi and Tara appeared.

"Uncle, can I introduce you to Tara, Samuel's great-uncle Bernard's personal secretary."

"Pleased to meet you, Tara. In turn can I introduce, Jane and Elizabeth."

He turned to his nephew. "I have been trying to do some of your work for you Melusi. I found a beginners' guide to genealogy which may help, but I fear it's going to be very slow work."

Tara interrupted Bhekitembo's ponderous flow.

"I'm sure I can help. My thesis was on the study of genealogical trees and I do have several valuable contacts. I suspect Bernard's research has turned into an obsession, but it keeps him going. Melusi has had first-hand experience of Bernard's work."

"I certainly have, we stayed chatting until the early hours. I can tell you a lot more at a more appropriate time."

"Well, I've got something to tell you, Melusi," said Bhekitembo, looking remarkably smug. "To start the ball rolling, I have discovered that Jane and Elizabeth have a common ancestor called Agatha who was born in 1817. Thorough history taking, old son; an excellent aspect of the trade to study for the final examinations." He looked hard at Melusi who had to think fast.

"Fantastic, so they have a common mother seven generations ago."

"I am sure you're right," said his uncle, not having worked out the number of generations, however, his pompous manner was only slightly dented. "We may have to go further than that to bring in the Plymouth cases. Then there are the cases in the north, perhaps they'll have to wait for a while. Can you go down to Plymouth today, Melusi? I have the addresses of the patients and the phone numbers of their general practitioners. I am sure Tara's expertise would help. Would you mind going as well to keep an eye on my nephew, Tara?"

His uncle's eyes twinkled just enough to reassure Melusi that the planned afternoon at the country club was to be sacrificed in a good cause.

"Of course, we will. Give me the addresses and we'll call as soon as possible."

Melusi was about to leave when he suddenly remembered why they had gone to find his uncle.

"Oh uncle; an invitation from great-uncle Bernard; he invites you and Arthur Richardson to come for dinner on Sunday evening at seven o'clock and stay the night. He's also asking Professor Simon Lancing."

"That's mummy's boyfriend!" Jane blurted out before Melusi could explain who Simon was. "He was here yesterday. You'll like him; he's great fun and knows a tremendous amount about African history."

"Thank you, Jane. Yes Melusi, I would love to come and dine at Bernard's and I'm sure I can persuade Arthur to come as well. It should be a stimulating evening."

"It's a lovely day and I am to drive a lovely woman all the way to Plymouth. Just a minute!" Melusi said as a thought occurred to him. "Why did Jane mention Africa? I don't believe any of us said anything about Africa in her presence. I thought I was being so careful to keep off the subject."

Tara shrugged. "Rather a strange coincidence. Perhaps it's just chance, after all Simon is a well-known authority on Africa and he was a professor of history; maybe Jane was just emphasising how knowledgeable Simon is."

"You could be right. But I'm not convinced; all very odd. Come on. Let's talk about each other. Ladies first, naturally. And we'd better get a move on."

Tara's voice carried the gentle tone of familiar and pleasant memories, "I had a blissful childhood in Somerset. We had a prize herd of cows, some corn, and acres of apple orchards, ideal for making cider. I loved riding on the Quantock Hills in the early morning.'

Melusi glanced across and saw her wistfully looking out the side window at the passing landscape. He waited for her to continue.

"In the autumn the families from neighbouring farms used to join us to make cider. It was a tradition as old as the hills. We used to crush the apples in an ancient stone trough crusher, then scoop the resultant mush onto cloths interspersed with straw."

"To press for the cider?" Melusi asked.

"Yes. It all went under a massive block of wood. When we released the block, it squeezed out all the juice. Loads of it. Nothing was wasted; the dry remains of the unused bits of the apple were spread on the fields to lighten the soil or as cattle feed; the cows loved it."

"And the cider?" Melusi asked and glanced again at the smiling face of the woman, lost in her childhood memories.

"It was collected and left to ferment in old sherry casks." She gave a sudden laugh.

"What?"

"Oh, just remembering the smell when it all went wrong one year. Some nasty bug infected it, the acid took over and we had to throw the whole lot away. It stank, but it was a bit sad. All that hard work; it didn't even make lousy vinegar."

"And do they still do it that way?"

"No. Not now. Even sadder I think. They take the apples to the professionals and get it done properly. The fermented apple juice or rough cider, known as scrumpy, is stronger than beer and it goes straight to the legs."

"Lucky scrumpy." Melusi put his hand on Tara's bare thigh.

Tara allowed it to rest there and said softly, "Scrumpy and driving don't mix, Melusi. You're driving now. How about your life?" She smiled at him and gently, but firmly, put his hand back on the steering wheel.

"My parents were born in Zimbabwe, they did well at school, and both had won international scholarships so they could come to the UK to study law. It was almost unheard of for a Black African woman to study law. She thought it a great laugh when she beat most of the men in the final exams. Their love blossomed at the end of their courses they married and they're now successful solicitors in Cardiff."

"How romantic," said Tara.

"Even the whites come to us nowadays."

"You shouldn't speak like that; it sounds bitter. You had a happy childhood by the sound of it, and your parents are successful, so you should be thankful for the good things."

"I guess you're right. But there is still too much prejudice where colour is concerned."

"I can tell you one place where there seems to be no prejudice: Mauritius. It's the most wonderful feeling to feel free to talk to anyone, whatever their colour, and have a normal cheerful reply. I had a super holiday there a couple of years ago. You should try it."

Melusi prayed that one day, if the gods cast the dice in the right way, they both would be on holiday together. He was already falling in love with Tara, and he hoped she was with him. They drove on for a while in silence.

"Why did you take up medicine?"

"I suppose it's ridiculous really. Because I had an overwhelming fear of spiders. I tried to get over it by studying biology and one thing led to another."

Tara laughed. "I don't believe it."

"It's true. When I was a child, I couldn't bear them. Some people can pick them up and put them somewhere safe, but I used to run a mile. Not a very useful attribute for someone who wants to live in the tropics. The biology lessons were fun and interesting and at that time most of the pupils doing biology went on to study medicine, so I followed the clan. I managed to get into medical school at Bristol and won loads of prizes. I hope to qualify at the end of this year. I am afraid the devil is still in there and I still don't like spiders.

"But I do like medicine. It's like an up-market detective story with the bonus that people might derive some good from my efforts; at least I hope they do. I like dealing with patients. They're usually frightened and even though they often whinge a bit too much, there's usually a good reason behind their whingeing. Some patients are even grateful for your treatments and say so, that bit is really satisfying. The miserable sods that you sweat blood over and spend a fortune getting them better, who then complain about everything, are the downside. I guess that's what we're paid for, so we have to lump it."

They came down the slip road from the dual carriageway and with Tara guiding them from the map he drove into the city of Plymouth, down through the narrow streets towards the inner harbour and parked the car by the fish market. Melusi's uncle had lent him a 'Doctor Visiting' sign, so Melusi placed it behind the windscreen to fend off traffic wardens.

"We shouldn't really use this, but time is valuable, and we are actually visiting patients."

Chapter Eleven

"Twelve, The Barbican, Tara; this must be it. Looks like a block of very up-market flats – great location!"

The door was opened by an immaculately dressed woman of about fifty showing distinct signs of strain.

"Mrs Lesley Prendergast?" asked Melusi. The lady nodded. "We've come from Bristol…"

"Come in, you have no idea how welcome you are." Mrs Prendergast's deep voice had been modified by rivers of gin. "You must be the clever research people who are going to find the cure for my daughter's awful rash. I am afraid it isn't getting any better with the creams that the doctor has given us. Come in. Would you like a drink?"

Mrs Prendergast gestured towards the drink's cupboard. She was obviously used to alcohol at any time of day but as her guests failed to respond she showed them into a large comfortable room that overlooked the harbour. A picture window with a magnificent view filled one whole side of the room. There was a slight breeze, and they could clearly see the busy weekenders trying to keep their sails filled with what wind there was. Gulls screamed overhead, occasionally snatching at the sandwiches of unsuspecting tourists and promptly depositing the partially digested contents of their guts on the cars parked by the quay. Fishermen sat on the low stone wall smoking pipes, mending their nets, and putting the world to rights.

"We'd love a coffee, if that's possible."

"Of course, of course, wrong time of day. It's a super view, isn't it, if only we could just sit and enjoy it?" Mrs Prendergast disappeared into the tiny kitchen recess. "Laurie! The scientists have come to ask you some questions."

Laurie Prendergast, a tall, sad-looking girl with pale skin, appeared in her dressing gown. She certainly looked very unwell. Melusi and Tara sat down with Laurie and drank a very welcome cup of coffee.

Melusi opened the questions, "I understand, Laurie, that you recently wore a dress made of a new type of cotton that had been treated in a different fashion, a recently developed natural, so-called environmentally friendly cotton. Can you tell us more about it and how the rash started?"

"I wanted to look really good at a friend's twenty-first party and I happened to see this in a shop that was going on about wonderful new materials."

"When exactly was the party?"

"About two weeks ago. I specially bought a lovely pale green dress of that new type of cotton that feels like silk."

Tara thought that with Laurie's pale skin it was the last colour she should have worn. She would have looked like a half-peeled cucumber.

Laurie was crying now. "Towards the end of the party, my shoulders and arms itched so I came home and when I undressed, I saw these red raw patches all over the itchy areas."

"Did you have any itching on your tummy or back?"

"No, I didn't."

Tara stepped in. "What were you wearing underneath?"

"A bra, pants and a long frilly slip to give the dress a better line. At least I hoped it did."

"That must explain why there were no lesions in other places. Laurie, most of your skin was protected. Can we have a look at the rashes?"

With Tara's help, Laurie struggled out of her dressing gown. Her abdomen was startlingly pale when compared with the angry skin above the line of her slip. Some of the areas on her arms were oozing slightly and there were a few stains on the inside of the dressing gown.

"The strange thing is, I tried on the dress for a few hours before the party and one reason for putting on the slip was because the dress felt odd, and it didn't hang correctly. I thought at the time it was because it was this so-called new material and may have been sprayed with something to keep it looking fresh in the shop. But when I had the slip-on underneath the dress, it did look better, and I felt better in it. I'm glad I wore that slip as otherwise, from what you're saying, I would have been covered in these horrible things. Come to think of it, if I had worn a shirt with long sleeves underneath the dress, nothing would have happened at all."

Laurie started to cry again, and Tara moved over to comfort her, careful not to touch her shoulders.

"I'm all right now, thank you. No one has dared to touch me recently. Even the doctor kept me at arm's length as if I was some sort of outcast."

"Don't worry, nobody is going to catch it from you, it's not infectious." She looked at Melusi and he nodded in agreement. They both hoped that, at least, was true.

"Thank goodness for that, anyway."

Melusi helped Laurie into her dressing gown. "One reason for our visit was to obtain some rather unusual information from you. Tara is an expert on genealogical trees, working out who you are descended from. It is rather a tall order but is there any hope Laurie, or perhaps Mrs Prendergast, that you would be able to help us trace your family back to the 1500s?"

"I can." The deep male voice came from the doorway.

"Francis!" Mrs Prendergast nearly jumped out of her skin as a scruffy weather-beaten man entered the room. "What are you doing home at this hour? Sorry darling, it is lovely to see you." She greeted her husband with a kiss, tidied his grubby shirt collar and turned to the others.

"Doctor Melusi Makuthwane and Doctor Tara Vaux, can I introduce you to my husband, Francis."

"Very pleased to meet you," said Tara.

"Did I hear you correctly just now?" Melusi asked, "Can you really identify your family line back to the 1500s?"

"Certainly, I can, it's a hobby of mine. I must show off sometimes and since I only work just over the road at the yacht club it's easy enough to pop into the local library which has an incredible amount of data to do with sea-going families. Lesley telephoned me to say you were coming so I came over to see if I could help. Family tree, eh? So, do you suspect that there may be some sort of hereditary basis for this peculiar rash?"

"It is possible that there may be, but we haven't enough data yet to firm us up on the subject. So, we are visiting all the sufferers and asking them the same questions."

"Well, for a start, Nigel Mason, who should also be on your list of patients, is Laurie's cousin. He is my sister's boy. She died in childbirth and the father has married again so the connection may not have been obvious. He also has some of these nasty inflamed areas but they're not half as bad as Laurie's."

Melusi and Tara looked at their list and there was the name, Nigel Mason. He was the next person to be visited and he lived just two hundred yards away.

"Do you know if Nigel has been wearing any clothing made of the new material, Laurie?"

"Oh, he certainly has. He was at the same party, and he was wearing a pale green shirt that matched my dress. I was a bit cross with him at the time. I thought he'd done it deliberately, but I'm sorry now."

Francis stood up. "Let me show you the family tree. You will have to excuse me while I clear a way through the forest." He disappeared through a door on the far side of the room to the picture window. They could see him moving mounds of paper from the floor trying to make room for them all.

Mrs Prendergast whispered, "I daren't go in there. The last time I did I fell over a pile of papers and scattered them everywhere. Francis was awfully cross. His filing system appears to be mainly on the floor. Now, before I forget, Francis told me to find some paper for you, I have some in this drawer together with a clipboard to write on."

Tara, with Laurie's help, started to write notes on the clipboard detailing the recent family relationships by name, date of birth, marriage, and death. A few minutes later Francis appeared.

"Come on in to the holy of holies. It's a bit crammed in here, makes it rather on the warm side."

They crammed into the hot little room and watched as Francis very carefully removed a cloth that covered most of one wall. Like a magician he revealed the most perfect genealogical tree stretching back to the 1400s.

"This is an absolute gold mine; fantastic!" Melusi felt on a high. "This is the sort of information it takes years to produce; there are mighty few gaps. How long did it take you, Francis?"

"Oh years; a lifetime, it feels like. It seems to be par for the course if you spend a lot of time at sea, there were so many hours to while away just on the lookout for something on the horizon that I found it the ideal way to occupy myself. I'm happy with the result, although there are a few loose ends. It is actually very difficult to identify people before 1500 because the spelling of names is done in such a random fashion. I'm afraid phonetic spelling was the norm so you can have ten written variants of one surname or first name."

"Did you have any problem about verification during the civil war?" asked Tara.

"You sound like an expert. Yes, I did have some problems, particularly with local parish records. The parishes were often taken over by the non-religious 'intruders' who couldn't be bothered, or who probably didn't think there was much point in keeping the register properly. You will be pleased that I did not have to resort to certificates for the touching for the king's evil, scrofula, tuberculosis of the skin, or settlement certificates." He turned to the others. "In case you haven't heard of those, settlement certificates are documents for the removal of the poor." Genealogy was plainly Francis' favourite subject, and he was excited with the chase. "The most useful documents to help fill in the gaps were wills when they were registered with the Diocese. Then there were the apprenticeship books in the eighteenth century. I even found a few ship's musters from the late 1600s. It has been the most absorbing hobby and I'm very pleased that it has at last been some use instead of just a wall decoration."

The heat in the room was rising and Melusi was acutely aware of the warmth of Tara's thigh against his. His attention was wandering, and he was daydreaming about being somewhere cooler and more horizontal with Tara, when quite suddenly his attention was caught by an entry on Francis' chart dated 1528, associated with the letters J H.

"John Hawkins, I don't believe it. It must be, this is wonderful, too good to be true."

Francis looked puzzled. "How do you know that? All there is on the chart is J H; you must have seen it before."

"I haven't seen this chart before, but I have seen a similar chart and rather assumed that your J H stood for John Hawkins."

"Oh yes, I was very excited by this connection with an old sea captain. If it was John Hawkins he was as much of a rogue as all the other sea captains at that time, but he was famous and it's always fun to be related to someone famous."

Melusi interrupted. "Famous for his activity in the slave trade. Great!"

Tara had been enjoying the academic discussion with Francis and was put out by Melusi's interruption: she thought that constantly harping back to the slave trade was at best, unhelpful, and, at worst, bloody-minded.

But Francis did not seem to have been upset by the interruption. "Yes, I take your point. But Stalin and Genghis Khan were famous, evil people at times, but still famous, or perhaps more accurately infamous."

"I guess you're right," Melusi had to concede, realising that he could have made his point with a great deal more tact. He tried another question, "Can you tell me the identity of J H's consort, she is indicated only by a capital T?"

"I am sorry I can't, and I don't know, without having access to the Hawkins papers, how it would be possible to identify her."

Melusi decided to leave the question in the air. "You've done the most wonderful job. Congratulations! Would it be asking too much to have this wall photographed?"

Francis waved his hands in the air like a magician and went over to the desk, "I thought this might happen one day, so I had a professional photographer make me several copies. You can have a print, a negative and a thirty-five-millimetre slide for a projector. All rather old-fashioned but they can be transferred to PowerPoint."

He handed Melusi a roll of paper and a small envelope.

"Fantastic, you have no idea how valuable this is to our investigation."

"I know Bernard still has a projector so the slide will come in useful," said Tara.

"Well, now I've done my good deed for the day. You both have come all this way to help our daughter and the least we can offer you is a bite to eat. I am afraid I have to go back to work."

Tara was hungry but Melusi thought otherwise. "Thank you, but no. I think we should move on to see the other patients and we have to get back to Bristol tonight. Thank you again for these. Nigel is next on the list." He tapped the roll. "You have filled in many of the pieces in the jigsaw puzzle."

Turning to Laurie, Melusi said, "I am sure we'll find a cure for your skin, just give us time."

"I do hope you can. Thank you very much for coming." She showed them to the door. Francis and Lesley Prendergast were sorry to see their visitors depart.

Melusi and Tara found Nigel Mason in one of the new flats that had been constructed in an old warehouse on the north side of the inner dock. Nigel's unshaven tired face poked out of the door of the flat.

"Come in, I gathered you were coming. My doctor telephoned me yesterday evening to say that someone may come, but he didn't give me a time. Anyway, I managed to squeeze in an early morning shift." Nigel stood to one side to let Melusi and Tara into a neat little sitting room. They now had a clearer view and saw a tall, twenty-five-year-old man of massive build. His dark, fierce look was accentuated by a dense mass of black hair and dark brown eyes.

Melusi introduced himself and Tara.

"I know who you are," said Nigel rudely. "Laurie phoned me to say you were on your way. OK, you want to see the rashes. I'm sick of 'em. You doctors seem to be useless. Here, have a look at my arms." He took off his shirt and showed them a range of tattoos that made Tara blush. The red areas were in just the positions described by Laurie.

Melusi studied Nigel's arms.

"Hm. They're not as bad as Laurie's, and with a little imagination, one or two of the areas might be healing from the centre. What do you think, Tara?"

"You could be right, Melusi. Nigel, tell me more about the cotton shirt you wore at the party. How many times had you worn it before the rashes appeared?"

"Only that one time. The rash must have taken about a couple of hours to come on. My friend also bought a similar shirt from the same shop, but his was a different colour and he hasn't had a rash; nothing wrong with him." He looked at Melusi. "And there's nothing else wrong with me, if you're thinking of asking me any more questions."

Melusi got the vibe that his questions were falling on stony ground, and he said he needed to use the loo. When he returned, the atmosphere was a lot calmer, and Tara and Nigel were joking about something.

"Why don't we go for a bite to eat in the pub next door?" suggested Melusi. "Is the beer drinkable?"

"The beer's brewed in the back of the pub; we reckon it's the best in Plymouth."

They ordered sandwiches and a round of drinks and Nigel opened up at last. "I'm sorry Melusi. I always feel defensive about my forebears. Uncle Francis is very well meaning but he can turn a blind eye when he doesn't want to know something. You see, my grandfather was African, hence my darkish skin, dark eyes, and black hair. He was probably the nicest person in the whole family, my grandfather, but was frequently snubbed because of his colour. I loved him dearly; I used to sit on his knee while he told me wonderful stories of Africa. He trained as an engineer and had come over on a ship to Plymouth. Unfortunately, the owner was bankrupted just as the ship docked, so grandfather was dumped in a strange port with no money, very few possessions and nowhere to go. He was walking down from the Hoe when he saw a lady, my future grandmother, struggling to get down from an apple tree. The ladder had fallen sideways, and she was trapped, so grandfather righted the ladder and helped her down, more likely fell into his arms! He picked the rest of the apples and when she discovered he was out of work she took him on as a sort of general handyman. He was good at everything." Nigel, now on his second pint laughed at his own joke. "Don't ask me too closely on that subject. They were married within a year and were blissfully happy until he died only a few years ago at some advanced age. He worked hard and they became well off. They eventually had four children, one of whom was my father, Joshua."

Melusi was enjoying Nigel's history. "Sounds like Adam's apple with a difference, what a lovely story."

Nigel was now in full flow. "Father was also a clever engineer. He had all his exams and eventually bought a chandler's shop on the Barbican quay. Lucinda, my mother, walked in one day to buy something; she came back the day after and the day after that, until father asked her out. They were married in a few months, and I was born a year later. Sadly, mother died in childbirth, not so common nowadays, but it still happens. So I was brought up first by a housekeeper, then by my father's second wife. My stepmother is very kind, but she's always been a bit distant. She had two children by my father who don't like me. The feeling's mutual." Nigel shook his head at the effort of telling this long story.

"I hope you can understand why I was a bit off this morning. You see, I'm proud of my African blood and then to be talking with you both somehow threw me. I'm sorry, no offence meant."

Melusi smiled. "And none taken, have another drink?" When Melusi returned from the bar with another tray of drinks, they started to talk again about the rashes.

"Why are my red areas so much less than Laurie's? Do you think it is because of my mixed blood?"

Melusi shot forward in his seat, his adrenaline pumping. "Nigel, I think you're brilliant; if that really is a clue you deserve a medal." Nigel was a good-looking young man when he laughed; he was at last becoming optimistic.

At that moment Nigel's flat mate joined them, obviously pleased at the emotional change in his friend. "You two have done a fantastic job cheering up Nigel. Let's hope you can come again."

Sadly, they had to leave the two tipsy friends to track down the final two patients. As they searched for the houses on one estate after another Melusi remarked, "I think the Royal T, whoever she was, was captured and raped by John Hawkins and she is the source of the rashes."

"What leads you to that conclusion?"

"I dreamt about it."

"Go on, let me into the secret of these dreams."

"Jane and Elizabeth's dreams are the most startling. As if they had been abducted and sold into the slave trade. Even Bernard confessed that he had had similar dreams. He wasn't abducted, of course but they related to the same time in history."

"Well, I think we had better get on and find the other patients."

They found the third and fourth patients and quickly discovered that the same new cotton had been worn by both, but they could not be made to understand that Tara and Melusi had a very good reason to wish to know about their forebears. They tried for more than hour to ask about deceased relatives but found the going too time-consuming and eventually gave up in the face of a strangely belligerent attitude. They decided to call it a day and consolidate what information they had. At the last house there was a message from Bhekitembo to say that he had something very important to tell them and would they please meet him after lunch tomorrow. "Take the morning off, my dears. You have made splendid progress and we need to have a meeting to discuss strategy. Not over the phone and not today. See you tomorrow refreshed, bright-eyed and bushy-tailed."

Chapter Twelve

"Well now," said Tara, "that means we're not expected back by bullet train. I wonder what your uncle meant by bright-eyed and bushy-tailed?" She smiled. "I know, let's go and see Auntie in Cornwall; she lives just over the border."

Melusi's face dropped a mile. "If you insist, Tara." He slumped in the driving seat of the car.

"Silly man!" She held his face and kissed him hard on the lips. "We can go for a swim first in a secluded cove that is just below Auntie's house, and we can stay the night with Auntie. She is very broad-minded and sleeps like a log!"

"That sounds better. I'm all for secret coves, away from strangers."

They drove over the Tamar Bridge and a few miles further along the A38 Tara directed Melusi to turn up a narrow road on the left towards Trewithin.

"Now, go slowly, just after the Old Post Office there's a tiny track and Auntie's little farmhouse is at the end, only a few hundred yards from the edge of the cliff." Melusi parked the car by the open front door and Tara leaned over and pressed the horn. A little gnarled, white-haired old lady wearing ancient sweater and baggy trousers appeared. Her face lit when she saw Tara, revealing a cheery map of smile lines.

"Tara, my love, but you have only just been to see me; who is this handsome young man? You must introduce me."

"Auntie, meet Melusi Makuthwane, Melusi meet Lady Sibyla Penrose, known to everyone as Auntie."

"How nice to meet you, Lady Penrose."

"Auntie, you dear young man. You must take Tara's cues!"

"Auntie, may we please borrow some towels, your sun brolly from the garden and four cans of beer. Tara says she would like to take me for a swim in her secret cove."

Auntie gave them both a beaming smile and waved her hands with pleasure. "You lucky man, help yourself to anything you need, but do mind the jellyfish, there seem to be a lot around this year. They're not those horrid Portuguese Man-of-War ones but they can still give you a nasty sting. I'll have a meal ready for you this evening."

"Come along now, exercise time." Tara gathered up their belongings and they walked to the edge of the cliff. "The path is behind this line of bushes. It's more of a slither down rather than a path. Mind the brambles, they can cut through skin like a knife. We can use the towels to protect our arms."

Golden sand greeted them after their descent, undisturbed and still warm in the afternoon sun.

"What do you think of this place, Melusi?"

"It's absolute heaven! Picture postcard material. No wonder you like coming to see Auntie."

"Actually, she's not all that well. But for an eighty-five-year-old she's not that bad either."

Tara placed the cans of beer carefully in a hollow in the sand under the shade of the umbrella. "Last one in is a sissy."

"When you said that last, I won."

"You kissed me."

"Was that my reward?"

Tara quickly slipped off her shoes, undid her blouse and skirt followed by bra and knickers. Her beautiful body was trembling for Melusi to chase her. He followed her cue, just as Auntie had told. They ran over the hot sand and plunged into the warm incoming tide. Tara swam with powerful strokes, easily outdistancing Melusi who, despite his strength, had never been a good swimmer. After five minutes of splashing about they came up the beach and lay on the towels in the shade of the umbrella.

"Who was the sissy?" Melusi feasted his eyes on her firm breasts and the sleek lines of her body.

"I would like to be." They pressed together and he ran his hands over her back and the soft skin just beneath the buttocks. He kissed her breasts, feeling the nipples harden under his tongue. He put his hand between the warmth of her legs.

She held his hard manhood. They made love quietly, exploring as they went until they exploded and were at ease with the world. After a while they drank two of the beers and went for another swim, but the sight of Auntie's jellyfish made Tara rush to the protective arms of her lover.

"Too cold in the water," laughed Melusi.

They made love again on the beach. They talked quietly in the evening sun until hunger drove them to dress and climb the cliff back to Auntie's cottage and the promised meal.

"Dinner is almost ready," said the old lady as they came into the little kitchen, with its low ceiling and polished flagstones. "I hope you had a lovely time on the beach?" Her eyes twinkled.

"Yes, thank you, Auntie," said Tara sleepily. "The sea was lovely and warm, and you were right about the jellyfish."

"I hope you like pork and crackling?" Auntie asked Melusi.

He laughed. "Love it! I just wish I could make really good crackling."

"The pork has to be quite dry, then just a little sea salt and plonk into a very hot oven."

They were tired, calm, and happy and they ate quietly while Auntie chattered away about her cooking and triumphs at the flower festival.

"Auntie has the best collection of mallows in Cornwall. She has visitors from all over the county."

"Tara, dear, you know they only come because they want to see a frail old lady who is the last of a line of robber barons. Now, why don't you two go for a walk and see the twilight? I will clear up and go up to bed soon. Your room is on the left at the top of the stairs. Breakfast is at seven, as I must be collecting eggs to take to the village shop by eight. Good night, my dears; sleep well."

She kissed them both and dismissed them for their evening exercise.

"Let's walk to the headland and see the sunset."

"I love your Auntie."

They walked in single file to the great rock that crowned the headland and watched as the sun slowly drowned in the sea. The Eddystone light began to wink at them as the sky darkened; two flashes and then a pause, two flashes and a pause. There was a big cruise boat on the horizon, lights shining like a Christmas tree, sailing into Plymouth Sound. The only noise came from a lone fisherman making his way back home to Looe; they could hear the powerful diesel engine with the familiar 'phut phut' sound. They waited until he was out of sight and Tara shivered.

"That was one of Bill's boats. He's been fishing here for years, and his father before him. I overheard him say he had never learnt to swim. That's typical of fishermen. They used to say if you were washed overboard in a gale without a life jacket there's no point in prolonging the agony. Strange sort of fatalism but understandable, I suppose." They were silent for a while. "I love this place," Tara murmured.

"I love you."

"Too soon, young man; love in the afternoon." Melusi found it difficult to interpret Tara's enigmatic statement.

They kissed and walked back to the house. Breakfast was laid out on the table with a torch and a note from Auntie asking them to bolt the door, turn out the lights and, with her blessing, sleep well. The note also hinted that they could either share a bath or there was just enough water for two showers. This was added as an afterthought and an exclamation mark.

"What a wonderful, practical old lady, your auntie."

They took it in turns to go to the tiny bathroom and have a shower. On the bedside table was a small glass decanter with coloured liquid. Melusi sniffed the stopper.

"Auntie is more than practical; this is whisky, and just enough water. Well, I never!" They entered the big bed, put their arms round each other, kissed and went to sleep; it had been a long wonderfully tiring day.

Auntie knocked on their door at a quarter to seven. "Wake up children, breakfast in quarter of an hour. I've left some of your clothes outside the door, Tara, and there is a pair of George's socks and some rather old-fashioned underpants for Melusi if he would like them."

"Bless you, Auntie, yes please, he would," Tara put a finger on Melusi's mouth before he could reply. "She would be really upset if you said no," she whispered. "The pants will certainly be warm enough knowing Uncle George's choice of clothing. George was Auntie's husband, he died about ten years ago. She misses him terribly; so do I."

They dressed and came down to the delicious smell of bacon and eggs with proper fried bread and wild mushrooms. At eight o'clock Auntie announced that she had gathered the eggs so Tara and Melusi decided to be on the road at the same time. After hugs and kisses, they drove off, leaving Auntie sadly waving by the door. Melusi's heart sang all the way to the Tamar Bridge where he felt he had to say something.

"That was the best overnight stay I have ever had."

"The service was first class as well," Tara laughed, as she gently removed his hand from her knee and placed it on the driving wheel while she found the money for the toll.

"I had forgotten we need money going this way. Something tells me I must have been thinking of other things."

"How am I supposed to interpret that?" She let forth a bubbling happy laugh of a woman, perhaps in love? Melusi had not heard such a laugh since his mother had greeted his father with the news that they had both been accepted to join the solicitors' practice in Cardiff all those years ago. His parents were still very much in love and his heart turned over with the thought that this beautiful woman sitting next to him might be in love with him. Perhaps his profession of love was a trifle 'too soon', but he had to strike while the iron was hot; he had to have her.

Chapter Thirteen

Back in Bristol at 11 o'clock on Saturday 29th July, they found Bhekitembo in his office in a great state of excitement.

"I've just received those sections from Valentine. You remember, the pathologist in Harare who had to do Ellie's post-mortem? They arrived this morning and I got Bob Hewlett, our histopathologist, to have a look at them. He thinks the fibres are vegetable origin, all the tissues are stuffed full of them. One thing is certain, they are certainly not fungi. Bob has taken them to a research pathologist at the Ministry of Agriculture. When I asked him to hazard a guess at the plant, he plumped straight away for cotton. I have done biopsies of the lesions from Jane, Elizabeth and Samuel and asked the histology department to give the highest priority to the preparation of those sections as well. With luck Bob may be able to give us a provisional answer this afternoon or this evening. Also, Bob suggested electron microscopy of some of the material to see if there are any more clues at a magnification of forty thousand. Anyway, I am sure I'll have some news for the dinner party. Don't worry, I haven't forgotten about it."

Melusi turned to his uncle, eager to tell him of their success story in Plymouth. "Thank you for leaving the message at the last house. Are we anywhere nearer a diagnosis? I'm afraid the last two patients were pretty useless at giving information, but we were definitely in luck to get the complete family tree of the first two of the patients."

"How on earth did you manage all that in such a short time?"

"We'll keep that for after dinner at Bernard's house tomorrow evening, as it's a very long and complicated story. We even have visual aids."

"Ah, you remind me, the dinner party. What time are we expected? Arthur and I will be coming by taxi as we both have full clinics the next morning."

"Seven o'clock sharp; don't be late. And by the way, don't dress up; this is a working evening, not even a tie."

"I shall most certainly wear a tie." As they were leaving Bhekitembo thought of something else. "If I can persuade Bob to take them, I might be able to bring along copies of the electron micrographs. I have to keep up with Melusi sometimes." He smiled at Tara.

"So, do I," said Tara with a knowing laugh that Melusi's uncle was not certain how to interpret.

Melusi and Tara went to the Three Feathers pub near the hospital to have a drink and a bite to eat. "What now, Tara? Any ideas to occupy us for a few hours?"

"I know what I would like to do. But I suppose we ought to go and help Bernard prepare for the dinner."

"We certainly should. You're right – just when I want to spend weeks, months, and years with you. They say patience is a virtue, but I don't seem to have much of it."

"Down boy! Seriously, Bernard will be doing his nut and driving the Hobsons up the wall with his fussing. We ought to go straight to the house and help him. If we ring, he'll only say that he can cope perfectly well."

"When I woke this morning and felt you in my arms, I just looked at you and thought that life was unbelievably wonderful."

"Please Melusi, don't be in too much of a hurry. It was wonderful and it will be wonderful, but remember softly, softly, catchee; and so on. Come on, let's go."

They arrived at Bernard's gates early in the afternoon. As before, the gates opened at the sound of Melusi's voice and shut silently behind them. Bernard was, as Tara predicted, fussing the Hobsons, but he was pleased to see them.

"Bless you, my dears; you've come to help. Very grateful, I'm sure. I hope your time has been well occupied?" Was it a trick of the light or did Bernard's eyes always twinkle like that? He continued, "Thank you for asking your uncle and Arthur Richardson. I've had a call from your uncle's secretary to say they're coming by taxi but won't be able to stay the night as they must work early on Monday. Not got the stamina you know, these young people."

Melusi interrupted, "Uncle is sixty-five and I am sure Arthur is at least seventy..."

"Oh dear, poor old things," Bernard gave a condescending laugh, "Simon will be here and staying the night; he's always late, but never mind. I hope this evening we can have a restful meal and relax before the dinner tomorrow. I hope you can stay the night, Melusi?"

"I'd love to."

Melusi and Tara helped Mrs Hobson make up beds and open another bathroom; the big house seemed to have spares of everything. It was quite an eye-opener helping her in the kitchen to prepare for the big meal for Sunday. Mrs Hobson was full of the joys of spring at the social activity and simply wouldn't stop talking.

"Just like the old times, people used to come for weeks on end. I could hear the murmur of their long discussions, they used to go on until the early hours of the morning, talking, talking. The next day I used to find all the wastepaper baskets full of screwed-up paper covered with odd writing. I remember even one Sunday Mr Hobson was asked if he knew where to buy reams of paper so they could continue their writing.

"It's all because of this so-called Curse on the family," she continued chatting. "I think it's a load of rubbish, but Mister Bernard takes it all very seriously. There was a time when Mister Bernard's wife, Victoria, was alive when he thought he had got rid of the curse, but then she died, and he had a fit of the glooms for a year. Anyway, he seems to have recovered and he's all go again. It's all due to you two."

"I can understand being in the company of Tara would cheer up anyone, but how can it possibly have anything to do with me? If it has, I am very pleased, of course."

"I don't know," Mrs Hobson was quite determined. "But it's true."

Bernard came into the kitchen, "Is there any machinery we need for tomorrow evening?"

Melusi shot up. "Oh, my goodness, yes there is. We need a large board, about five feet square. Come to think of it, two boards, and an old-fashioned slide projector."

"Where can we borrow boards from, Tara?"

"Actually, the village hall has some very good display boards. Melusi and I can collect them tomorrow morning."

"Excellent, and Melusi can also help to move some more comfortable chairs into the sitting room before lunch. I think you should both take the afternoon off."

At four o'clock Mrs Hobson brought in a pot of tea, four mugs and a plate of home-made biscuits. "Time for the workers' tea break. Stop organising us, Bernard, and relax."

Bernard did not appear to know the meaning of the word. "Is there anything else I should know, perhaps the reasons for the board and the projector?"

It seemed to be the right time for Melusi and Tara to tell him about the amazingly detailed family tree that had been compiled by Francis Prendergast in Plymouth, and how there was a J H in the early 1500s, and how Francis had confirmed that the J H could well have been the initials of John Hawkins.

"Did you ask who his issue was and was there any indication of the identity of the Royal T?"

"No, I'm afraid that still remains somewhat a mystery."

"Never mind! We are getting very close. I have been at it for over seventy years and I'm not going to be beaten at this late stage. We'll find the answers."

Melusi was curious about Bernard's use of the word 'we'. Guessing his thoughts, Bernard said softly, "Yes, I mean 'we', Tara, Melusi and Bernard, there's a prediction for you," he ended lightly. "Is there anything else we have left out? Oh yes, Melusi would you mind helping Hobson with the drinks? We're all right for the driving problem as your uncle and Arthur Richardson will be returning by taxi and Simon is staying the night. Don't get them all plastered as we have a lot of serious discussion and thinking to do. Perhaps we are up to schedule after all. Why don't you two go for a walk until seven, come back for a quiet supper and we can plan tomorrow's dinner over a few glasses? Hobson can provide you, Melusi, with spare clothing so you don't have to go back to your flat tonight. They will be on the bed in the room next to Tara's. She may not want you in her bed tonight." He was laughing as he left the room.

"That naughty old man knows everything, and I don't care. I do want you in my bed. It is plenty big enough for two." She had a fleeting worry that perhaps she was acting a trifle too brazen, and it might frighten Melusi. But the loving look on his face reassured her that she could say no wrong.

"Bernard has reminded me that I am still wearing Great Uncle George's underpants which are giving me the hottest crotch for miles."

"Oh good; I look forward to that."

They walked hand in hand through the gates, down the road and into the gardens by the Bristol Channel. The tide was slowly coming in, disturbing the oystercatchers which rose in little speckled black and white clouds, singing their twittering song before they settled again to plunge their beaks into the softening muddy sand at the new water's edge. Curlews were busy probing the mud near the pier with their curved beaks, and little dunlins busied round their feet picking up minute specks from the surface. Most of the background noise came from the scruffy moulting gulls making dirty white floating islands on the almost still water.

There were few people about; it was hot, and the tourists had retreated to their campsites, bed and breakfast houses, or moved on to explore different parts of the country in their frenetic search for something new. Fishermen at the end of the pier waited patiently for the Big One, the one that had escaped from all the other fishermen and was just about to snatch at the end of their line. There's always hope.

"There's such a lot to think about, Tara. I must remember that I have to persuade the examiners that I am fit to be a doctor. At the same time, we must help Bernard solve his Curse and its strange connection with Jane and Elizabeth and all the others suffering from these weird rashes. It's tricky to work out what should be next on the agenda."

"We have to go with Bernard to Africa."

"I was thinking along the same lines. Funny that! Must be telepathy between us."

Back at the house there was more work to be done for the tomorrow's dinner; later, they relaxed for the evening meal. Mrs Hobson had cooked a bass her nephew had caught earlier in the day. It tasted delicious washed down with a 1990 bottle of Mersault.

Bernard started to give his instructions.

"As our guests arrive, Melusi, will you do the introductions, using the simplest name for each? For instance, I will be known as Bernard. Is that all right?" Melusi nodded. "And then we should have drinks in the drawing room and repair in due course to the dining room. We have only one female so the seating must include Tara in the middle of one side of the table. Do you think we should have a seating plan, Tara?"

"I don't think that's necessary. I will be ushered in first and I can sit down in the middle of one side and the others can then sit at random. They all talk so much you'll be hard put to keep them from interrupting each other."

"You're right as usual. After the meal we'll come back into the drawing room and have coffee and brandy, or soft drinks. Then I would like to introduce the evening with my little talk which is essentially to explain why I have been so obsessed with the Curse and how it has led me to the study of the complications of my family tree. I will include some of the work that Ted did on behalf of the family. Then, perhaps Arthur Richardson should talk about his patients, followed by your uncle and then yourself, Melusi, and finally Tara. Simon is so unpredictable that I have no idea when to slot him in but I'm quite sure that he'll have his say. I don't want to prejudge what either of you are going to say, so no more on that subject."

They went through other minor points that could arise and eventually decided that they had done as much as they could towards the organisation of the dinner party, so at ten o'clock they went to bed.

The next day dawned bright and clear; they worked most of the morning in the house, tidied up the garden and by lunch time there was no more to do so Melusi and Tara went for a walk. Melusi could not take his eyes off her.

Tara smiled a shy smile. "You keep on looking at me and I love it. You're worth looking at yourself you know; I love the sheen on your skin and the smile lines that join your mouth to your ears." She touched his face. "I love the way you walk and the way you hold me. We'll go to Africa and solve Bernard's family problem and cure your patients. Later, I hope, we'll go back to Africa again."

Suddenly she laughed and ran off. Melusi chased her back to the gate where they kissed and walked together up to the house. They changed for dinner to join Bernard in the hall waiting for the guests.

"Remember, Melusi, you do the introductions; make them informal."

Bhekitembo and Arthur Richardson arrived first in the taxi which they paid off and walked up to the front door, where they were greeted by Bernard.

Melusi did the introductions. "Let me start with our host, great-uncle Bernard, to be known as Bernard, my uncle Doctor Bhekitembo Makuthwane, dermatologist, to be known as Uncle. Doctor Arthur Richardson, general practitioner, to be known as Arthur. Tara Vaux, you have met Uncle. Meet Arthur, the doctor who first saw Jane and Elizabeth. My name is Melusi Makuthwane, Uncle's nephew, to be known as Melusi.

Does that make sense?" The two doctors laughed at his easy manner.

Bernard approved. "As far as it went, it made sense, but you missed out on two things. Firstly, you are an almost qualified doctor yourself and Tara is an expert in genealogy. Why do you think I employed her?" Melusi could think of many better reasons but stayed silent.

As they were speaking, Simon Lancing drove up in a shower of gravel.

Bernard couldn't resist taking over. "That must be Simon, late as usual. Thank you for coming Simon. May I introduce Arthur, general practitioner; Uncle, dermatologist; Melusi, almost doctor; and Tara, genealogist; Professor Simon Lancing, retired Professor of History at the School of African and Oriental Studies in London, to be known as Simon. He is currently living with Jane Harvey's mother Rebecca on the Costa del Sol."

Melusi raised his eyes.

How does Bernard get away with it? It must be something to do with highly intelligent great age. Simon doesn't appear to be the least put out by the introduction; he must have known Bernard for a very long time.

"Greetings to you all." Simon's white hair bobbed up and down. "And thank you, Bernard, for asking me. I am intrigued."

"There now; Melusi will take orders for drinks and Hobson will deliver them." Hobson was attending to a panic in the kitchen, so Melusi did both. Four gin and tonics, a beer and a glass of white wine swiftly appeared, and the conversation went into second gear.

Bernard started the ball rolling. "Lady and gentlemen, we have all had a somewhat busy day. Please relax, drink up and chat. Perhaps I will take you round the garden and show you some of the unusual plants that Great Uncle Ted brought back at the end of the last century from Zimbabwe."

They strolled across the lawns as the heat started to go out of the evening sun. Ted had brought back some very curious looking trees, some of which were approaching their adolescence after a hundred years. They admired Bernard's trickle watering system that he had installed ten years before it was hailed as a brilliant discovery in Israel. They relaxed and Melusi fetched a further round of drinks. When these had been consumed Hobson came out ringing a hand bell to summon them to dine. They walked slowly up to the house and Melusi noted with pleasure that Uncle was chatting up Tara. He had not seen Uncle so animated for a long time. Melusi had presumed that Uncle's normal aloofness in recent years was partly because of his natural shyness and perhaps because it might be thought that Bhekitembo Makuthwane, the consultant, might be accused of favouritism if he was seen to be too friendly with a medical student.

Uncle grabbed Melusi's arm. "What a lovely girl. She makes me want to lose forty years."

"You looked as if you were having a jolly good try at doing just that."

Bless you Uncle; I believe you might just have leapt to the right conclusion.

Chapter Fourteen

Dinner was served on the great refectory table. The dark African wood, polished to a pool of jet, slumbered under the fine linen and glowing silver. Regiments of cut glass sparkled in the light of the three trefoil candlesticks. Pure white linen napkins rested in neat little parcels on the crested white and gold side plates. Surrounding the table, fourteen magnificent matching carved and padded mahogany chairs, made by Messrs W and C Wilkinson in 1834, originally supplied to Goldsmiths' Hall under the supervision of the architect Philip Hardwick, completed the picture. The result was pure magic. The serene ambience was a tribute to the two days of spit and polish by the Hobsons. Three of the guests were seated on either side of the table with Tara in the middle of two men; the heads of the table were used for serving. Tongues loosened as they went through the leisurely meal that started with salmon mousse, followed by a lemon sorbet to aid the digestion. The main course was roast duck with a delicious crispy skin followed by a selection of cheeses. The final course was a magnificent Pavlova. The wines changed with each course, port with the cheese and a sweet white wine with the Pavlova.

Bernard stood up to indicate the end of the meal.

"I would like to give you all a plan of campaign for the evening. I suggest we have coffee with brandy or liqueurs in the drawing room. Each of us in turn will then attempt to detail everything we know. As host's prerogative I will start the ball rolling so that you have time to adjust your thoughts. I suggest that Arthur follows me, as he was the first observer of the rashes, then Uncle since he is the clinician looking after the cases. Melusi, would you talk after Uncle and then Tara? I hope you don't mind speaking last, Simon? I know you to be something of a philosopher; I also know perfectly well that when the spirit moves you, you are quite capable of interrupting. If necessary, I will sum up, but I suspect that we'll all be so tired that we'll want to go to bed and meet in a few days' time. Does that sound satisfactory?" The guests nodded their heads.

They rose from the table and drifted slowly across to the drawing room where there were six comfortable chairs with little tables next to them. The chairs were facing the north end of the room that had two large boards on easels, each covered with a cloth. A slide projector on a stand at the other end of the room pointed its lens towards a white screen. The guests were served coffee, brandy, and liqueurs by the Hobsons and when they were settled Bernard stood up to talk.

"By now most of you will know that my life's work has been dominated by an attempt to neutralise an ancient Curse on our family. It has worried a great many of our line over the last few hundred years to my certain knowledge and I suspect for many more years before that, although there is little documentation to support that statement. To tell you the whole extent of my research would take many weeks and most of it would be merely of casual interest and therefore not immediately relevant. Also, we do not have the luxury of time, so I shall, therefore, only tell you the bare bones of my story. I was born in 1907 in a house that no longer exists in a little village called Cothele which is a few miles up the Tamar River. At the age of ten, in 1917, my mother, Sarah, who had been born in 1877..."

Melusi started, wide awake, his heart pounding. Tara put her hand on his arm and whispered. "Not yet, love." Melusi's heart stilled a little, but Bernard's glance ensured his silence.

"My mother told me that there had been a curse on the family and that one day the revenge would occur, and we would all have a horrible death; this was all very exciting for a ten-year-old. She did not know exactly the threat implicit in the curse, nor why it had been placed on our family in the first place. She said she had no knowledge of misdeeds committed by our forebears, or even the country of origin of the curse. Sarah had promised her father, Jack Abercrombie, as he was dying, that she would pass on such information of the curse as she knew to continue the message as it had been passed on for many generations before her. She gave me to understand that she didn't place much credence on the curse but as she was honour bound to tell me all she knew, and so she was simply doing her duty. If she had been alive today and seen the rashes, perhaps she would have been more convinced of the power of the curse.

As a family we were all financially very well off. We had little in the way of illnesses and other traumas, and no one had been killed or even injured in the Great War. In fact, some members of the family made a lot of money out of the two world wars, making uniforms, constructing weapons and so on; you can imagine life was relatively easy for most of us. Although my mother had been dismissive about the curse, at the time I was so impressed by the fact that she had told me about it that I vowed to identify its origin and, if possible, neutralise it. I have now been working for seventy-eight years on the subject and I believe I am almost there..." He looked at Melusi and Tara, "*we* are almost there. I am now too old to have any chance of solving this puzzle alone.

"I would like you to have a look at this." Bernard removed the cloth from one of the boards, revealing an ancient document, mottled beige and creased with age. "When you come closer, you will see in minute writing a series of names linked by black lines. I have a lens to help you see them."

Those who did not know of the existence of the document craned their necks to see more clearly.

"I will start with the origin of this document which as you have probably guessed is a genealogical tree. My story starts with my Great Uncle Ted, a missionary, who doesn't appear since he was not in the direct blood line of descent. Ted's involvement is through his sister Olive's marriage to Jack Abercrombie. Here she is." Bernard pulled a tiny cylinder from his pocket and identified the position with the bright light of a laser pointer. The tremor of the bright red arrow was the only sign of Bernard's nervousness.

"Imagine Ted's thoughts when he marries into a family that has had a curse hanging over it for hundreds of years. Imagine also, that there had been no evidence of any sort of harm ever having occurred to that family. Out of the blue, you are informed that the curse exists, and your dearly loved sister is terrified. Naturally you would like to have known more, especially if you are a man of the Church and uniquely inquisitive at the same time. Ted asked many questions and was told a little more, but since he was not directly in the blood line the information given to Ted was slightly different and did not contain any sort of threat to himself. He was told merely that a curse existed and would take its toll of his sister's offspring at some time in the future.

"Now Ted had the call to become a missionary and was determined to root out what he considered to be evil; in effect, to expunge the curse. He eventually became the Dean of Salisbury

Anglican Church in Rhodesia, but in his early missionary days, before Salisbury was even thought of, he must have been given a clue about the origin of the curse and in typical fashion he and his wife beavered away to amass a considerable amount of data concerning African curses. Later, after his wife died, he went off into the mountains with a servant, more of a friend really. He disappeared for three months and returned rather the worse for wear in possession of this document that eventually passed to me.

"The document is made of vellum – animal skin, but from which animal I don't know, probably antelope. It was prepared as a writing material over three hundred years ago. This date has been verified by modern dating techniques which also verify that some of the original writing at the top is of the same age with a potential variation of only five per cent. When you get a chance for a closer look, you will notice it starts with a date of birth, 1528, adjacent to a name. The forename begins with a J and the surname starts with the letters Haw; the rest of the surname is illegible. There are other data, since lost unfortunately in the bombing of Plymouth during the Second World War, which reinforced my original guess that this person was a well-known English sea captain. I think you had better have a close look at it now. Time to stretch our legs, anyway."

Bernard's audience came forward to inspect the document. Melusi wanted to refresh his memory and as he leant forward to look more closely his face brushed against Tara's hair. She smelt so good, he at once lost concentration.

"John Hawkins," Bernard announced when they had returned to the comfort of their armchairs. "A famous man, for one reason or another… unfortunately, here in this room we must accept that one of those reasons was his involvement in the slave trade. It was a ghastly, ruthless trade which only stopped when it became uneconomic. It is my opinion that during one of his voyages to obtain slaves, John Hawkins captured the person to the right of his name on this document and made her pregnant. He wouldn't have thought anymore of her than of a mere animal, so this was likely by force – horrible, awful to even think about. However, I would also surmise from the gold flecks we can see remaining on the capital T, that she would have been a significant person in her own colony. Perhaps even royalty, so perhaps we will call her Royal T, for the purpose of our discussion? I think she delivered a son; the only legible letter is a J. The vellum continues down to the present day."

Bernard paused to see if his last sentence had sunk in. "You can digest that statement while we have a short break and some more coffee. You may smoke by the way as this room has enough air changes to allow a little smoke in the air."

Melusi had wondered why he felt so wide awake after such a splendid meal and now understood the function of the grills in the middle of the bookcases. Bernard handed round cigars and Arthur and Simon lit up.

"Why can I never find ashtrays? I don't think Mrs Hobson likes me smoking." Bernard was still complaining as he lit a strong-smelling cigarette. Melusi found a pile of ashtrays at the back of the room. "All is forgiven. Thank you, Melusi."

"What on earth persuaded you to have air-conditioning in a drawing room in this country?" asked Uncle.

"You might remember the heat in 1976. It was a very long, hot summer. My wife was not well, and the heat was making her feel much worse, so I had this room, the dining room and our bedroom air-conditioned. There is a central plant on the roof which is why you can't hear any noise. It makes life a lot more pleasant and certainly her last few months were much more bearable." There were tears in Bernard's eyes. He sighed sadly at the memory, took a deep breath, and shook his head to concentrate on the work in hand. Uncle felt dreadful and he put a hand on Bernard's arm to help him recover.

Bernard heaved a great sigh. "Let us return to our document. The last date that is clearly written is 1850. You will note that there are no names attached to the dates after 1700. However, I can ascribe names to all the visible dates, and they are accurate with respect to births and deaths. What I can tell you additionally is that there are indentations on the vellum dated up to this year, 1998. From where you are sitting you will only be able to see them if you have extraordinarily good eyesight. Melusi has seen them and will vouch for the accuracy of my statement. These indentations have been verified by the document section of the British Museum. It was suggested to me by the Keeper of Records that one scribe made the indentations in the material, and another then inked them in later; it looks as if his pen ran out and the writer never came back to finish the job. Nevertheless, the maker of the vellum and certainly the scribe who did the initial writing three hundred years ago could not possibly have known the names of people who were born and died after 1700, let alone to the present day. I would remind you that Great Uncle Ted would also not have known of the births and deaths that occurred after the early 1900s. We will study the rest of the document later. I suggest a stretch of the legs and come up to have another look."

Bernard was running out of steam. His audience stood up, went over to the old document, and studied the indentations.

"I shall stop at this juncture and ask Arthur to talk about the first two patients."

Bernard sat down, lit another cigarette, and inhaled deeply. His shoulders were hunched, and he had tears in his eyes. Tara felt like putting her arms round the old man, but she felt it was too private a grief.

Chapter Fifteen

Arthur finished his brandy, walked to the front of the little group, and took a deep breath.

"First of all, I would like to give you a little introduction. I have spent a great deal of my life in Africa and the Caribbean and until a week ago I have only been involved in this sort of complex problem on two occasions. The first time was about thirty years ago when I was in what was then known as the Belgian Congo. I was running a government immunisation clinic, miles from anywhere, when a young man of Aherero-Ambo origin came in, obviously terrified. His story was that when he reached the age of fifteen, he had been told that a curse had been put on his tribe over two hundred generations ago. Apparently, someone from his tribe had been so offensive to another tribe they had released a sort of long-term attack on my patient's tribe. According to my simple calculation the giver of the curse must have lived over five thousand years ago.

After telling me his story, the healthy young man simply dropped dead in front of me. I reckoned he must have been tough to have walked ten miles in a morning over difficult terrain to come and see me, yet I had failed him. Unfortunately, it was not appropriate to ask for a post-mortem, nor do I think it would have been allowed by his family. Fortuitously, I was taking his pulse at the time of his death. It had been firm and steady, a good solid beat of around sixty a minute. Suddenly, it went haywire and stopped. My guess was that he went into ventricular fibrillation because his pulse suddenly rose, became variable and then chaotic. I could hear a few sounds when I listened to his chest but then nothing. He died calmly, totally accepting his fate. It was absolutely staggering and there is no medical explanation. I have heard of similar occurrences from colleagues working in the same area.

My second experience of the African curse was one associated with rashes. Some unfortunates acquired the most hideous deformities, others had rashes that suppurated until they died, and they died quietly with an unnerving calmness. When I first saw Jane and Elizabeth and heard the history of their rashes, I had a terrible feeling of déjà vu. I couldn't at first remember the time and place where I had seen these rashes, but it came to me in the evening of the day that Elizabeth first called me. The rashes, the speed of onset and the resistance to reasonable modern medication were like those I had seen in Africa.

"I do not, however, believe that they are inevitably fatal, as a witch-doctor friend cured one of my patients by rather unorthodox means. He first ground the very plant that was the reputed cause of the rashes in a mortar together with a rather spotty-looking tomato-like fruit, thought to be inedible. It was then left to ferment for a week and smeared over the lesions. The smell was disgusting but amazingly they started to heal from that day. I have very little else to say but I'll do anything in my power to help." Arthur sat down, took a large sip of his brandy, and lit another cigar.

The wind was getting up outside and the branches of the bushes lashed against the windows. This eerie sound made them all jump except Bernard whom, it appeared, had almost been expecting it.

"Perhaps the heat is breaking at last," said Arthur. "All we need is the monsoon and we could well be in the tropics. Now it's your turn, Uncle."

Uncle asked for another brandy and Hobson was summoned.

While they were waiting for Uncle's brandy, Melusi suddenly spoke. "Arthur, are you convinced that the answer lies in Africa? Perhaps it is hiding in the medicine chest of the witch doctors?"

"I am not suggesting anything in particular, but it's worth a try." Arthur simply shrugged his shoulders.

Uncle's brandy arrived and he stood up to speak.

"Do you mind if I interrupt again?" asked Melusi, Uncle nodded. "You were saying, Arthur, that you had seen a case that recovered. Tara and I went to see the four cases in Plymouth. Nigel, who incidentally is a cousin of Laurie, another affected person in Plymouth, has very mild lesions. It may be of some relevance that he has a significant amount of African blood. In fact, it was Nigel's own suggestion that his African blood had protected him against the worst effects of the rash. Obviously, he should be observed for some time, but Tara and I noted that he was not particularly tired, he did not look half as ill as his cousin and made very little complaint about the rash, merely finding it tiresome and embarrassing."

"This is very exciting," said Bernard. "We need to know a lot more about Nigel; would you mind paying him another visit before I go off to Africa?"

"Not at all," said Melusi, thinking of Auntie's secret cove.

"Perhaps Tara would go with you?"

"I'd love to," Tara said enthusiastically.

Turning to Uncle, Bernard said, "Uncle, the stage is yours."

Uncle took a little while to collect his thoughts. He was particularly cheered by Melusi's interruption since there was just a hint that a genetic element might protect people from the devastating effects of the rash.

"As you know I admitted the first patient, Jane Harvey, to my ward on Tuesday 18th of July. She was suffering from oddly demarcated linear rashes on both arms and the small of her back. The areas were a purplish-red colour, but not raised or blistering and they did not blanch when viewed through the bottom of a glass that had been pressed against the skin, thus indicating a severe inflammatory process.

"Jane was tired and suffering with a severe headache and a slight temperature. Otherwise, there was nothing else of note. Three days before presenting she had been to the university midsummer ball wearing a dress made of the cotton material that does not need the thirty or so chemical processes that have been used in the production of woven cotton for many hundreds of years. One-week later Elizabeth Clarke came to visit Jane in hospital after hearing about her terrible rash, as she too had bought the same dress and. had also developed multiple areas of inflammation. Both patients were referred by Arthur. When I examined Elizabeth, it was clear that the distribution and colour of the lesions were remarkably like Jane's. Notably the areas of skin covered, or protected, by underclothes were initially unaffected, but the rash seemed to be more violent in those parts of the skin that had the most constant contact with the cotton dress. In the small of the back where the hot, sweaty hand of the dancing partner had pressed the dress against the skin there was a substantial rash which, with a little imagination, one could perhaps see the outline of a hand. Now the lesions are gradually becoming worse in both patients and although we seem to be able to slow down their progress with steroids and drugs that suppress the immune system, we don't appear to be making much headway to cure them.

"The third patient under my care is Samuel. Samuel had bought a shirt made of this 'new' cotton, as I will call it, and had worn it sitting in the sun in his garden on a hot day in June. The distribution was different; the inflamed areas were again mainly on the arms but there was a line across the back of the neck corresponding with the bar at the top of the garden chair. Melusi has pointed out on a previous occasion that Samuel's rash appeared a good three weeks before Jane's. Presumably because of this, his rash is significantly more advanced than the other patients; indeed, the centres of some areas show some evidence of hardening which I find ominous, perhaps indicating severe damage to the small blood vessels.

"Incidentally, I have checked with the manufacturers of the material, and they have reassured me that the three garments must have come from three different rolls of material and, moreover, from three different production runs. They are naturally very concerned about the rashes and have been most cooperative.

"When he came to my out-patients Samuel told us of the death of his cousin Ellie Mackenzie in Zimbabwe. Her illness, which was ultimately to prove fatal, started with a series of linear rashes that looked much the same as those affecting Jane and Elizabeth and Samuel himself. I have spoken at length to the pathologist Valentine Johnson at Harare General Hospital where Ellie died and another common feature of the cases that came to light was that all the patients suffered from the most frightening dreams. Originally, I thought that this was merely evidence of encephalitis or inflammation of the brain, but the specific nature of the dreams and the remarkable similarity of the images, for want of a better word, would lead me to conclude that there is something more sinister afoot."

Uncle paused on this strange note and took a sip of his brandy. Bernard waved the bottle. "Anyone for a refill?"

Melusi left the room with the tray of glasses and returned with two glasses of beer for himself and Tara and a strategic reserve of brandy.

"Where was I? Ah yes, Ellie's rashes. Simeon did the post-mortem on Ellie Mackenzie. Ellie's rashes progressed to the stage of blackening and necrosis and as you can imagine this inevitably led to progressive system failure and death. None of their treatments had more than a moderating effect on the progression of the disease, and I have to say that medical and nursing staff are heartbroken. The first thing that Simeon noticed was that despite a massive power failure which included the body refrigerator, Ellie's body had not deteriorated perceptibly in the two days that it took to restore the electricity supply. This startled him as normally bodies decay very rapidly in the heat of the tropics. Secondly, the day she died he had noticed that there was a strange white film on the surface of the lesions, and it was still there on the post-mortem table. His comment to me was that since her lesions had been slightly sticky, they could have picked up cotton dust from the bedclothes. I took this as rather odd. However, if that was the simple explanation, why did he bother to mention it?

"The post-mortem was not helpful. All the organs looked relatively normal apart from terminal effects. Sections of the blocks taken for histology, however, showed something rather startling. Without exception, every organ had evidence of invasion by some fibrous material. There was some minimal reaction to this material, in other words, the body had made some attempt to limit the damage but had failed. Simeon had no idea as to the nature of the material and very kindly sent me some sections that my histopathologist has examined."

Uncle went to the back of the room and picked up his brief-case from the table, opened it and took out a large envelope and a box of slides.

"I shall need the projector." Tara helped him load the machine, hoping that the slides would not be too gruesome. She was already feeling slightly ill at the thought of poor Ellie's illness and death and was glad that the air-conditioning was so efficient.

"I am expecting a phone call this evening on the electron microscopy of the fibres. I hope you don't mind, Bernard, I gave the technical expert this phone number as he was unable to look at the section until this evening."

"That's not a problem, we all want to hear about the fibres. Already I think some of us have our suspicions."

Uncle sipped his brandy and continued. "I have here sections of some of the tissues obtained from Ellie's post-mortem. You will see the fibres as I point to them." Uncle drew from his pocket his own laser pointer and again, a bright red arrow appeared on the screen. "This is a section of the skin from one of the worst lesions. You will note the wide spaces in between the few living cells. That is fluid leaking out of the blood vessels. Clinically the skin would be tense and, in some places, quite hard. Those long things," Uncle pointed to them, "are the mysterious fibres that I was talking about. Neither of the histopathologists have ever seen anything like them before. They bear no resemblance to any of the abnormal storage diseases that have a hereditary basis or indeed to anything animal at all. Nor do the microbiologists think they resemble any fungal material. For one thing they are far too big, several hundred times larger than any fungus element, so they must be vegetable or mineral.

"I am afraid that they are indeed what we are all dreading: cotton fibres. It appears that Ellie died because she was infected, or invaded, or perhaps it would be better to say colonised, by the cotton from the material which we must presume she was wearing.

"I am also expecting a phone call from Valentine. You will remember his name; he is the pathologist in Harare. He has promised to ring after he has spoken to Ellie's friend, Alice. Alice is the friend who also went on the diving expedition during which Ellie's rash started. Alice should be able to tell us whether Ellie was wearing anything made of the new cotton within the last few days before the rash developed. Particularly if she had been wearing a shirt of that material when she was scuba diving. I mention the scuba diving, as one of the most severely affected areas was a mirror image of the metal structure that supported the compressed air tank on Ellie's back."

Hobson came into the room. "Excuse me, Bernard, there is a long-distance telephone call for Doctor Makuthwane: I understand he goes under the name of Uncle."

"Thank you, Hobson, will you bring the telephone in here, please? I hope the lead is long enough." Bernard looked at the speaker. "Would you mind, Valentine, if we all listened?"

"Please feel free."

"Ah, hello again Valentine. Thank you for ringing, do you have any news?"

"Indeed, I have. I found Ellie's friend Alice and she confirmed that Ellie had been sent a new shirt made from a special form of cotton that was supposed to be environmentally friendly. She was into all that sort of thing and found the shirt very comfortable. The shirt is in Alice's flat now. Shall I send it to you?"

"Yes please, it may be helpful. It would be interesting to see if the sea had any effect on the material. Do you know who sent the shirt to Ellie?" asked Uncle almost as an afterthought.

"That's another mystery. The shirt came in a parcel which had been posted locally, Alice did notice at the time that there was a local stamp, but when Ellie opened it, she just accepted the shirt without comment. Apparently, Ellie never said where the contents of the parcel had come from, and Alice didn't remember seeing a letter. Bless her, she turned the flat over and emptied all the waste-paper baskets but there was no sign of a letter. The parcel wrappings went long ago, unfortunately. Have you discovered anything new at your end?"

"I do have some news for you. The fibrous material is not of human origin nor is it some unusually large fungus nor is it a mineral precipitate. It is, in fact, vegetable matter and, as I believe we were all dreading to hear, it is almost undoubtedly cotton. Light microscopy shows that the fibres are opaque, but the outline is characteristic of cotton fibre. I am waiting for a phone call from the electron microscopist in the botany department, but I am certain that he will confirm that the structures that we can easily see under the light microscope are indeed cotton fibres. So, we are now faced with the strange finding that would indicate that the cotton from the new material of the dresses and the shirts is capable of invading human skin, probably encouraged by sweat and pressure and undoubtedly enhanced by intimate contact under the sea."

"So, what on earth could we have done about it? And how many more cases are we, or you, going to have? I must go and study cotton and see what kills it. Please keep in touch; I'll ring you again if there anything more comes to light."

"Of course, I'll keep in touch, probably within the next few days. Thank you for ringing, Valentine, goodbye." Uncle pressed the button on the heavy old phone and the group sat digesting the latest piece of the jigsaw.

"I will now thoroughly depress you and show you sections of the skin biopsies from Jane, Elizabeth and Samuel."

Uncle went quickly through the slides demonstrating the damage. There was very little to choose between them. Ellie's slides were a lot more advanced in the destructive process, but they could clearly see the fibres within the tissues of Uncle's three patients. The fibres looked as if they were actively penetrating the deeper layers of the skin.

"There is one other item that I had hoped to have for you and that is the scanning electron micrograph of the sections. I understand that this shows not only the mature cotton fibres but also the typical picture of the structure of the live cotton plant tissues. The photographs of this will be available tomorrow, with any luck. What we need is a lesion that is healing. Melusi's statement earlier on this evening intrigues me. Do you think Nigel would mind if one of us took a small piece of his skin? Under local anaesthetic, of course. Would you mind asking while you're there, Melusi?"

"Certainly, I will. I am sure Tara could persuade him to agree – she had more success chatting up Nigel than I did."

"Now I have another matter for you to think about. This is science at its best, or in our case, worst." The listeners looked expectant and wondered what other rabbits Uncle was about to pull out of his hat. "We know about the three cases in Bristol, four cases in Plymouth, two of whom are known to be related. Then there is one fatal case in Zimbabwe who was related to one of the cases in Bristol. I also understand from colleagues that there is a case in Liverpool and one in Harwich.

I am not an expert in genealogical trees, but it struck me that if all the cases known to us can be linked into one continuous genealogical line, then we are perhaps looking for a mutational event at some unknown time in the past. Bernard has produced his vellum document and I gather that Melusi and Tara have a superb genealogical tree from Plymouth. It might be theoretically possible to identify the time within the last five hundred years when the mutation occurred.

"I have two warnings; the first one makes me feel most uncomfortable. I have the impression that our investigations seem to be too successful. It is all suspiciously fast work, as if we were meant to discover the data very quickly. Now, if that is the case, who or what is the higher authority that is handing it to us on a plate? Could it perhaps be bracketed with Bernard's curse into the realm of such mysteries as we dream about?

"Secondly, if one assumes that on average each marital relationship, or at the very least, coupling, from the mid 1500's to the present day produces three children, then the expected number of people this year, 1998, at risk of reacting to the new type of cotton should be well over a thousand. Even at a conservative estimate, I would wager that at least two hundred blood line descendants of J H and the Royal T could be traced today. If we had the time, it would be an interesting and probably salutary exercise to determine how many of these had worn clothing made of the new cotton and had or had not developed a rash."

Uncle, his eyes glimmering in the thrill of the science swirling around in his head, went on to discuss in detail the molecular biology behind a potential diagnosis, and the role that DNA – specifically the genetic make-up of each individual sufferer – could offer in tracking down the origins of the disease.

When he was sure he had thoroughly blown the minds of his audience, Uncle sat down quite exhausted. "Your turn Melusi, I think I've said enough."

Uncle had a large sip of the brandy and waited for Melusi to spring a few surprises.

Chapter Sixteen

Melusi picked up his briefcase and walked to the speaker's end of the room. The briefcase bulged with books and notes to which he referred frequently during his talk. He laid some of these, with markers projecting from their sides, on the table and spent some time shuffling them about. He knew what he had to say, and he had to get it right, as if he was even now in the throes of his final examinations. He needed the notes to be readily available more to reassure him than anything else. Unnervingly he felt that in a very short time he would become the mouthpiece for something, or someone else, probably from another age. Melusi was oddly at ease with the idea that he should be used in this way. The sweat trickling down his sides and the adrenaline racing heartbeat were indicators to the importance of his presentation; he was on stage, and he had to convince his audience of an idea that had not fully germinated in his own mind.

"Well now, for what it's worth, here is the gospel according to Melusi. As you all know by now, I have known both of Uncle's first two patients, Jane Harvey and Elizabeth Clarke, socially for something over a year. Elizabeth is in her first year studying the history of Africa and Jane is also in her first year, reading Zoology. I have done a small amount of tutoring to both courses and through that and because Jane lives in the same flat as two other friends, I have been introduced to most of the undergraduates in that year. Both women are naturally of above average intelligence, but I have to say that the illness that affects them and their reactions to the illness are so unusual and so out of character that it makes me wonder if there are forces at work that are currently outside our knowledge and certainly, outside our control.

"Samuel's illness, likewise, seems to be out of the ordinary. Uncle has dealt with the clinical state of the patients, but I would like to add something that has been of interest to me for the last four years. I have always had an interest in dreams and, without exception, all our patients and those under the care of others have suffered dreams of such a violent and unpleasant nature as to terrify them out of their wits. The subject matter of the dream's points to a time probably three or four hundred years ago and undoubtedly relates to the beginning of the slave trade. There is a very strong thread that follows through the dreams. The result is that the patients wake up feeling that what has apparently happened in the dreams has been their fault. They feel they stand accused of having participated in the subject matter of the dreams. Not to put too fine a point on it, they feel as guilty as hell. I believe this, too, has a purpose.

"To continue with my story, the Plymouth cases are interesting. Tara and I went down to Plymouth to try and glean any relevant crumb of information from the four cases who lived in that area who were reported to have similar rashes. We had some interesting experiences."

Tara threw him a horrified glance and then relaxed when she realised, with a smile, that he had cheekily said it that way for her benefit.

"Uncle asked us to go and interview the four cases and instantly determine their family trees back to the early fifteen hundred." His audience laughed. "The first patient we visited was a twenty-year-old female called Laurie Prendergast. She had the now-characteristic lesions following a hot, sweaty evening wearing a dress made from the new type of cotton. Happily, Laurie's father, Francis, came over from the Yacht Club where he worked and was enormously helpful. We were amazed to find that he had an almost complete family tree as far back as the early 1500s; it had been his hobby for many years and was too good to be true. Far too good to be true! I believe Uncle has hit on something unnerving. Bits of this puzzle are being solved much too easily."

Melusi turned to the second board and rolled back the drape that had been covering the second chart. He walked to the back of the room and switched on the projector to reveal a photocopy of the chart on the screen. "On this board is a copy of Francis Prendergast's family tree that he very kindly gave us. If you look closely, you will notice that it is remarkably like great-uncle Ted's document. You will also notice that just below the top of the tree are the same initials JH. This JH in both documents had consorted with a female with the sole identifying letter, a capital T. The JH, according to Francis, was indeed John Hawkins and he appeared surprised when I suggested the name. But while he had no idea as to the identity of T, he believes that T may have been mentioned in the Hawkins papers. I believe you have had sight of these, Bernard?"

"She is mentioned in those papers which, incidentally, are in the British Museum, but in the most curious fashion that perhaps I will tell you about later, probably at another get-together. It is all in the last filing cabinet." He waved his hand towards the corner of the north wall of the room. "Please continue, Melusi."

Melusi cast a strange look at Bernard. Why was Bernard keeping this a secret? It was the first hint that Bernard had ever studied the old papers in such detail.

"Tara questioned Francis about his methods in a roundabout way, but Francis Prendergast was only too happy to volunteer the information that he had a nephew who had similar skin lesions to Laurie's. We went to see the nephew who is the Nigel Mason that I told you about earlier. He had, strangely, much milder lesions following the wearing of a shirt made with the same new material. The lesions did not appear to worry him unduly and with a little imagination, they did look as if they were healing from the centres of the inflamed areas. It was Nigel who volunteered the thought that the mildness of his lesions might be attributed to the fact that his grandfather had been an African seaman who had been left in the lurch on Plymouth Barbican. Nigel's grandfather happened to see a lady in difficulties stuck up a tree and went to her rescue. To cut a long story short, they married, and Nigel was a grandchild of the union. It was Tara who wormed that information out of him."

Bernard felt a wave of optimism.

He's going to do it, bless him; Melusi is going to break the Curse and cure the patients! What power does he have that I have been trying to obtain for so many years? Never mind, he's a clever man with tremendous insight despite his impetuous nature. Perhaps he is the right person to be holding the flag in this project simply because he is an African.

Bernard came out of his daydream as Melusi started again.

"I do believe that we should take more account of the dreadful dreams suffered by our patients. Simeon told Uncle that Ellie also had horrendous dreams before she died. There is a clear thread throughout the dreams that relates to the slave trade at some time in the three or four centuries that followed the first shipment of slaves by the Arabs from East Africa. No nation can be said to have behaved any better than any other, Portuguese, Spanish, British and even the Germans; everyone jumped on the bandwagon. Initially the French wouldn't have anything to do with slavery but eventually they joined in..." Melusi could feel an age-old rage building inside him, one which was familiar but nonetheless a surprise to him every time it overwhelmed him, which it often did. He found himself delivering to his spellbound audience the most wonderful but heart-breaking speech – he delved into the horrendous history of the slave trade and all its intricacies. People, Melusi had realised, had often only scraped the surface in their knowledge of what the trade was and what it had meant to generations of enslaved families; he felt like he was imparting years – centuries, even – of history that would educate his friends and his beautiful love, and the emotion he felt as he spoke each word eventually bought tears to his eyes, and yet he couldn't stop – it was as though a force greater than he was using him as a mouthpiece.

Eventually, through deep, quavering breaths, Melusi bought his rousing speech to a close.

The room was pensive for a short moment before Simon leant forward in his chair.

"Melusi, your speech was the most wonderful exposition of justified racial anger that I have ever heard. I would like to congratulate you and say that the concept of retrospective anger is certainly not foreign to me. I could quote many instances not written about in books that would make a normal man's blood boil, but nothing is done, nothing is said, and the issues are pushed so far to the backs of people's minds that it is as if they had never occurred. Thank you Melusi, do not be upset with the tears that came to your eyes. I would have wept in similar circumstances. I deeply admire you for it."

"You're very kind. I think I've said enough." Melusi was feeling oddly elated, even more convinced that those suffering from the rashes had become caught in a web because they were the lineal descendants from one slaver. Their illnesses and in Ellie's case, her death, could be interpreted as revenge for a trade that turned barbarism into wealth and social prestige. Melusi felt again that he had been driven to speak; never in his life had he waxed so eloquently. There was someone or something with immense power driving them all.

Where will it take us next? I don't really care if Tara comes as well.

Chapter Seventeen

"Tara," said Bernard, "would you like to add anything to Melusi's information about the genealogical trees?"

"Yes Bernard, there are a few bits and pieces. The family tree that had been the long-term project of Francis Prendergast ties in very closely with yours, Bernard. Many of the light indentations at the end of the vellum discovered by Ted are easily filled by comparing the two documents. They are the verifiable births, deaths, and marriages of persons, some of whom are alive today. I must confess, as Melusi suggests, that I did pose some leading questions, but Francis gave all the right answers and I believe his chart is genuine and not merely pinched from other sources. I have highlighted our patients into a combined genealogical tree."

Tara went to the back of the room and fetched a roll of paper. She pinned one end to the top of one of the boards and attached a weight on the bottom end. She turned around to the audience with a smile.

"You may think that I have been up all night, but the truth is that it was surprisingly easy to combine the two documents and insert additional information later. There has been no time to do any verification through standard channels, but I have asked some of my friends from college days to check out some of the older names from Bernard's and Francis' charts. I, too, am worried that in the absence of further cases we have a hereditary story that is suspiciously neat and tidy. I find this unnerving, just as the other speakers have found other aspects of our discussions unnerving. To help us feel better about it, I have also asked these same friends to see if they can trace the whereabouts of half a dozen people who should still be alive. They will check to see if these individuals have rashes and will ask them if they have been in contact with the new cotton material.

"Let us now follow my combined document and where our cases slot in and how clearly, they can be traced back to John Hawkins and the Royal T. Uncle, may I borrow your magic pointer? We start with John Hawkins, the well-known slaver, born in 1528 or 1532 according to two authorities and the so far unknown Royal T at the top of the chart. They had a son, Jason, born in 1548 who married Ndola, an African. I use the term married as it makes it easier. Some of the inseminations may have been blessed by the Church and some not, but for the purposes of this discussion, couplings will be read as 'married'. I would also ask you to remember that this chart is a very bare outline with solely the blood line traced to the present day. There were undoubtedly other children but for our purpose, which is simply to link all our cases, the document is adequate. Additionally, in most cases, I have only inserted the forenames of the females since otherwise it would have made everything much too unwieldly.

"Jason and Ndola had a daughter called Katherine, born in 1569. She married Edmund Brereton and they had a daughter, Cecilia, in 1588. Cecilia married Samuel Strong, and their daughter was the lovely Ellie, born in 1613. I have given Ellie her married name of Lancaster since that is how we have heard of her. The loveliness of Ellie Lancaster can reasonably be attributed to the theoretical approximately eighteen per cent of African blood that was in her make-up. I must assume that our

Royal T was pure African, but there is always the possibility that being part of the ruling class she may have had a percentage of some invading race, perhaps what we arbitrarily call Caucasoid, or Hamitic, depending on the book you read, in her genetic make-up. This would perhaps have made Ellie a shade lighter than expected.

"I won't detail all the names for the next hundred and fifty years, but I would ask you to note James Newton, born in 1769, who married Bridget. Two of their children are relevant to our investigation. Richard Newton, born in 1792, married Sarah and they had a daughter Agatha born in 1817. I would remind you that Uncle discovered that both Jane Harvey and Elizabeth Clarke claim that an Agatha born in 1817 was a common ancestor. Both trees support that statement. The other child of James Newton and Bridget was Lydia, born in 1794. I will come back to her later.

"Agatha married John Masters and they had three children of interest to us. The first was Alice, born in 1838. She married Frederick Abercrombie whose son Jack, born in 1857, was the husband of Olive, Great Uncle Ted's sister. Ted's surname, by the way, was Longstaff. I don't think that has been mentioned before. Jack Abercrombie and Olive had a daughter, Sarah, in 1877 and she married Paul Charlton. They were Bernard's parents. Am I allowed to say that you really were born in 1907, Bernard?"

Bernard laughed. "Of course, you are. I am prepared to be called anything over sixty." He had been listening avidly to Tara and was spellbound by her clear exposition of the data that had taken him years to collect. He loved her as he would have loved a daughter, had he been blessed with children.

"Sarah and Paul Charlton had two other children. Michael, Bernard's older brother who was born in 1905, and Richard,

Bernard's younger brother. Richard was born in 1915. More of Richard later. Michael married Rosie and their daughter Sophia was born in 1925. Sophia married Thomas Mackenzie and their child Frederick, born in 1945, married Ruth, and it was their daughter Ellie born in 1976 who so sadly has died in Africa.

"If we can go back to Bernard's younger brother Richard, he married Margaret and their daughter Jemma, born in 1945, married Walter Blake. Their child born in 1977 is our friend Samuel Blake. So, you can see that Bernard really is the great-uncle of Samuel but the relationship between Samuel and Ellie Mackenzie is less direct. I hope you are following me?"

Tara's audience was attending. They were riveted both with Tara's clear lecture and her lovely voice. Melusi found it difficult to concentrate on anything other than her lips and the way her body moved as she talked.

"Now let us concentrate on the two cases in Plymouth from whom we were able to obtain sensible data. This line starts back with Lydia, sister of Richard Newton. She was born in 1794, married Stephen Wingfield and their son William, born in 1829, married Laetitia. Their boy David was born in 1860 and married Ann, to have a daughter Margaret in 1882. Margaret married Samuel Prendergast and their son Jack, born in 1910, married Sally, to have a son, Francis, born in 1935. Francis, you will remember, constructed our second tree that has been so invaluable. He married Leslie and it is their daughter Laurie, born in 1978, who also has a rash.

"To go back two generations, Jack and Sally Prendergast had a second child, Lucinda, in 1940. Lucinda married Joshua Mason who had been the offspring of Elias Mason an African seaman, and Amy, whom he found up a tree. Finally, in this branch of the family tree, no pun intended, Lucinda and Joshua had a son in 1973 who is Nigel Mason. You now understand the relationship between Laurie and Nigel in Plymouth.

"Uncle's finding out about the common ancestor of Jane Harvey and Elizabeth Clarke is quite extraordinary. They are descended respectively from the other two daughters of Agatha Masters; Georgina born in 1840 is the stem for Jane; and Olivia born in 1843 is the stem for Elizabeth."

The room was warming up and Uncle's eyelids were becoming heavier. He was not looking forward to tomorrow's clinic, which would be crammed full of unfortunate people for whom, sadly, he could do very little. He wondered why they were putting in all this energy and time for a relatively small number of patients. The family trees were interesting but could surely be studied some other time.

"Thus, the relationship between Jane and Elizabeth is tenuous in the extreme. But, as we now suspect, the devastating effect of a presumed genetic abnormality, the connection is still useful to us. I will not go through all Elizabeth's forebears as they are clear from the chart. You can follow the blood lines which I have highlighted in orange.

"We still have a great unknown and that is the identity of the person whom we have called the Royal T. I have a strong suspicion and I would almost be willing to put money on it that the only way we will find out the identity of the Royal T is to find an old person who has still retained the tribal memory. Such tribal memories used to be staggering in their completeness and were commonly rehearsed until word perfect by the heads of the ruling families until very recently; to within the last fifty years, in fact. I recently read of a Belgian explorer called Emil Torday who around 1900 sat and listened to the King of the Bushongo recalling the legends and traditions of the past. Torday noted down the unrolling list of kings, a list of some one hundred and twenty names, right back to the god-king who had founded their nation. The explorer was impressed but was also suspicious. Was this just a story, had the king invented the names? Torday nevertheless continued to make his notes until suddenly the king gave him a date. At the ninety-eighth chief, Bo Kama Bomanchala, the king said that nothing remarkable happened during his reign, except that one day at noon the sun went out and there was absolute darkness for a short time. On his return to Belgium, Torday visited an astronomer and learned, to his delight, that over the area of land occupied by the tribe the only possible date for a total eclipse of the sun during the seventeenth and eighteenth centuries was 30th March 1680.

"So, you see, your Royal T is most likely to be found in peoples' memories. Since Great Uncle Ted had acquired the vellum chart while he was in Zimbabwe, I suggest that is the place to look. I understand from those who should know that Zimbabwe is a big and startlingly attractive country." She looked at Melusi who nodded happily.

"What do you think, Bernard?"

"If that is so, then the answer may also lie somewhere in the loft with Ted's papers. I shall be calling for volunteers tomorrow to shift all his boxes downstairs - unless we have a look at them tonight?"

"We'll help," said Melusi and Tara with one voice, "in the morning."

Chapter Eighteen

"Yes please, Melusi." Simon held up his glass. "Not too much; an indefinable term, I know. However, it is time for my penny-worth."

"I have listened to all that has been said and I am impressed with the reasoning so far. Naturally I have an interest in these peculiar rashes and of course in the cure since Jane Harvey is the daughter of the woman I love. That all sounds rather precious, but I say it to emphasise that I, too, have a personal interest in the outcome.

"I find that I agree with most of your conclusions. There is one facet of your discussions that particularly interests me and which I have been studying for many years. That is the nature of the African curse. These curses, for there are many of them, are probably the oldest on earth. If the anthropologists are correct in their presumption that most of the present inhabitants within the species *Homo sapiens* are descended from the hominids who from time to time inhabited the length of the Rift Valley in Africa, then this is not unduly surprising.

"Firstly, I have to say that it is most unusual for the accursed individual or collections of individuals not to know that a curse is hanging over them, otherwise, surely, it becomes rather pointless. After all, a curse must produce fear and if it doesn't, it's pretty much a waste of time. It therefore worries me that not one of the affected patients appeared to know of the existence of the curse. Admittedly, it is not usual among Western

European societies to discuss the options on Curses except in a jocular way; so perhaps that observation may not be helpful.

"Let us assume that such a curse exists, and its devastating effects only become apparent after a span of some three or four hundred years. This can be classified as one of the very rare great curses. These are curses that can only be made by those of royal blood, usually female, and seem to have an almost random culmination after relatively long periods of time. They invariably end in the death of individuals and sometimes of whole tribes, but they must be paid for. They are paid for either by the voluntary sacrifice of a significant number of people, or they are given to be used by another tribe as a sort of payment for a favour performed by that tribe. I suggest that the first type would be highly unlikely since the population of the whole African continent at the time of origin of our presumed curse was probably not more than a couple of million. There were vast tracts of land that had no human or humanoid inhabitants at all, and it would have been a pointless exercise to sacrifice significant numbers of people. We must seek a tribe that was persuaded to give a very great favour to another probably less powerful tribe; also, that the less powerful tribe must have held some lever over the more powerful one.

"Now to follow our deliberations held so far, one must presume that the curse that we are discussing was in some way linked with the beginnings of the slave trade. Well, the slave traders did indeed collect millions of souls over a period of around three centuries. Therefore, it is likely to be a curse given as an extreme measure by a royal African female who was captured. It is supposition, I know; but it is reasonable to suggest that whichever the tribe was, the curse had been kept strictly in reserve, perhaps assuming, even hoping, that it would never have to be used. But where did the curse come from? I am placing this rather elaborate story in front of you since the only way in which it will be possible to neutralise the effects of the curse will be to identify its origin and literally go and plead. But you must get the right individual and there must be a very good case to back up the plea. It is unlikely that the origin of the curse will have been completely forgotten, for if that were to be so, the effect would be nullified anyway. With luck, it may be that this curse will be reaching the end of its existence and we may not have any further deaths, but I wouldn't bank on it.

"The last comment I must make is that most curses are related to cave systems. Cave systems appear to have been the equivalent of our banks or storehouses, places where important objects or ideas are stored; even places to retreat to and study or worship the unknown. It is possible that Ted found the remnants of a dying tribe in a cave system and obtained the vellum document from one of the elders of that tribe. There are many, still unexplored, cave systems in Zimbabwe, some of them of great depth and often the ends of the chambers are sealed by water, so one should be careful. A trip to Africa is definitely on the cards as this is the most likely source of useful information." He drifted to a halt, scratched his mop of hair, and sat down.

Bernard stood up. "This has been the most amazing evening. Thank you all for coming. I am sure we have all learnt a tremendous amount and all we now need is to pull the strings together, at least I hope so. It is now two-thirty in the morning, and we are all very tired. Unless there is anything that anyone wants to say further, I suggest that we have a cup of tea, and I will ask Hobson to order a taxi. We must have another dinner when more information is to hand."

Bernard and the Hobsons were profusely thanked for the meal and for such a stimulating evening. Hobson called a taxi for the exhausted Uncle and Arthur and the others quietly sipped their tea trying to digest the evening's discussion.

Simon seemed to have a second wind. "One facet of this disturbs me. I may be the arch pessimist but remember you get what you pay for in this miserable world and I wonder what the price will be that has to be extracted if the plea is granted. What do you think, Bernard?"

"I think that will have to be one of those rivers to be crossed when the time comes. I don't see how we can make any prediction. The main goal is to find the cure and stop further cases."

Simon looked gloomy. "I agree wholeheartedly."

Bernard stood up. "I'm off to bed. Simon, your bedroom is at the end of the first landing and there is a bathroom attached to it. Good night, Melusi and Tara; don't dream too much and don't get up before eight in the morning. Meet you for breakfast at nine or later on the veranda."

Melusi and Tara were alone at last.

"What an evening; we all had quite an input. I am sorry I disgraced myself."

Tara put her arms round his shoulders. "You didn't disgrace yourself at all, my love. If a man can't give way to emotion it would be a pretty poor do. You had every right to say what you did and what's more you said it perfectly."

"Do you really mean that?"

"Of course, I do, and incidentally I love you. Come up to bed."

"Those are the best words I have heard all evening."

They went upstairs to Tara's room where they kissed briefly. They stripped, stepped into the shower together and soaped each other until they could not bear the strain any longer. They quickly dried and found that it was true that Tara's bed was big enough for two. They explored each other's bodies until Melusi finally entered her and they quickly exploded. They talked for a little while until eventually a calm, deep sleep overcame them both.

The moon peeped through the window and Tara heard an owl hooting. Naked, she slipped out of the bed, stood by the window, and looked out at the black and white garden. A small rodent, a bank vole, came out of a crack in the garden wall and scurried to the compost heap where the remains of the peanuts had been thrown. She was nibbling hard to feed the little bodies inside her and failed to hear the owl as it swooped down.

Oh, no! But what does one small rodent matter when there are millions more? Was this tiny tragedy to be compared with those of humans? How could the Royal T be concerned about a few humans with rashes? The pleading would have to be paid for, but how?

Tara went back to bed. She felt Bernard was too confident and it worried her.

Chapter Nineteen

It was Monday 31st July. Tara awoke to the sun rising over the Levels behind the Mendip hills. She drew back the curtains and stretched out her arms. She was about to touch Melusi but withdrew her hand at the last moment and decided to let the rays of the sun wake him. He was in her shadow, and she sat still watching him for a while. She marvelled at his smooth, shining body. There was a ghost of a smile on his lips, and it was as much as she could do not to kiss him there and then. She slowly drew back the bedclothes and marvelled at his manliness, his flat tummy, and the muscles of his thighs. His even breathing seemed to reassure her. She moved away a little and the sunlight lit up his face as he came to life. Melusi looked sleepily at the naked Tara and the smile on his face grew.

"Bonjour, Tara."

"Bonjour Melusi; why the French?"

"Because I have never woken up next to a French girl. So, the comparison is apt since I cannot get used, nor do I wish to get used, to seeing you in all your glory. Anyway, your surname sounds French."

"My darling lover, you are trying so hard to be gallant. Perhaps you are acquiring your uncle's pomposity."

He laughed and stretched out his hands to stroke her body. He kissed her mouth, her neck and her breasts until her nipples rose like ripening cherries.

Tara pushed the bedclothes onto the floor.

They made love as the sunbeams played on the bed with them.

"What a wonderful day!" Tara's breasts were still heaving. "I must remember to buy a bottle of Dubonnet for Mrs Hobson. I wonder what the percentage of Dubonnet bottles that is have been purchased to placate little old ladies who have secrets?"

"Pass, but you had better give her another from me. I think a shower is called for, perhaps separately. I expect we have a mountain of work to do today."

After the shower they dressed and went down to breakfast. They were the first down, greeted by yet another clear sky with blazing sunshine, already becoming warm after the dawn. While they waited for the others, they wondered what was to be done next.

"I know Bernard is an amazing man, but he is around ninety years old and I'm sure we have to go with him. It would be very unfair not to and we're much too inquisitive to let him go off on his own to find all the answers. How shall we tackle it? I've done a lot of camping and I can offer to carry the gin."

"Let's ask him at breakfast. If Bernard's willing to pay the air fares. I could be the bodyguard to protect against the wild beasts. I can always take my javelin, although I doubt if it would stop a lion. We must put it to him without hurting his feelings. You know him better than I do; he really has a shine for you."

"We'll play it by ear. Leave it to me." Tara laughed but was instantly serious. "I had another worry last night. What's going to happen about your final exams?"

"Don't worry, that's under control. There's a different system every year, but this year they've decided to award the qualification degree based on a written continuous assessment with only a piffling paper at the end. You can even obtain exemption from the paper if all your assessors say you're marvellous. Uncle has told me that, if necessary, I wouldn't have to take the final paper so there is no problem in that direction. It would be difficult to concentrate on the minutiae of the blood supply of the inner ear if I had to fly straight back from the darkest cave in Africa."

"That's a relief. Here comes Hobson. Good morning Hobson, another lovely day."

"Good morning, Tara, and good morning Melusi." Hobson's eyes twinkled. "May I lay breakfast? I hope you are hungry. I can cook you a proper English breakfast if you would prefer it to this continental style. You look hungry after the marathon last night and I am sure you need proper sustenance."

It would have taken a hide as thick as an ox to have ignored the hint in Hobson's voice that he would like to be asked to try his hand at a 'proper' cooked breakfast. Tara was unsure how much he could do in Mrs Hobson's kitchen; she could be a very fierce lady when roused but it was clear that breakfast was Hobson's province, and he was longing to show off. On the other hand, she was not wholly sure what Hobson had meant about the 'marathon'. Certainly, there had to be two bottles of Dubonnet.

"I would love to have the works. What are you offering today? Melusi is hungry."

Hobson's face was a picture; the biggest smile they had ever seen. "I can make you fried bread with bacon and egg and mushrooms and slices of tomato and there may be some sausages in Mrs Hobson's fridge. I am so pleased." He trotted away humming to himself.

"You really have made his day; I hope you don't get indigestion with your thousand calories; probably nearer two thousand."

Breakfast on the veranda was a quiet, restful affair. Hobson brought Melusi's enormous, cooked breakfast. When he started to tackle it, he realised how hungry he was. The evening had certainly used up more calories than there were in this little plate of energy.

Simon appeared and looked enviously at Melusi's plate. "It's many years since I was offered one of those. The smell's enough. Ah! Hobson is bringing more goodies. Hot toasted muffins with heaps of butter and, I hope, Mrs Hobson's home-made marmalade."

The coffee was hot and strong, just like the dawn. Bernard appeared at a quarter past nine looking tired but happy.

"Good morning, Simon. Hobson can make you a plateful of calories like Melusi's. It depends how hungry you are after last night."

"It does look good, and it smells very tempting. Perhaps I shall weaken and accept the offer, Hobson. That was an amazing evening. What a strange coincidence, everyone's hobbies suddenly becoming useful at just the right moment. Who do you think is pulling the strings? Is it you Bernard, or some wizened old African guru? Are we just puppets that jump and mime to order; or is there such as thing as free will?"

"That's sounded rather a jarring note. Carry on, old son. I suppose if we knew the answers to all those questions, we would be the deity and that would be very boring as we would be able to predict everything. I think I'll settle for the status quo."

Simon was winding himself up for one of his monologues when he was interrupted by the telephone ringing. Hobson brought the ponderous machine onto the veranda. "There's a call from Uncle for you, Bernard. You know, it sounds like that television serial many years ago with the two not very tough detectives. Was it called The Man from Uncle?"

Hobson did not often make observations of this kind, but his comment made Simon smile. Hobson shrugged his shoulders at the lack of a response from the others and remarked, "It was quite a number of years ago." He gave them a bleak smile and went back to the kitchen.

"Hello Uncle, I trust you slept well?"

"Yes, thank you. I hope I'm not ringing too early but in my internal mail this morning was the scanning electron micrograph of the tissue section material. The picture looks surely like live cotton. It is bound to look different from the prepared fibres. It looks like any cotton plant, even the cotton grass which is distantly related to the cotton plant from which we make clothing; they all look the same."

"Thank you for ringing. No, you're not too early. This is exciting. We were having breakfast on the veranda and philosophising about Fate while Melusi and Simon plough through Hobson's enormous, cooked breakfast. Simon was wondering if we were all just puppets on strings. But then who is pulling the strings? He makes it all sound so high-powered."

Uncle was not used to Simon's philosophical mind and continued with his report. "I have asked the immunology laboratory to see if antibody to cotton is present in the sera of the patients, and at the same time asked the molecular biology laboratory to see if there is a common stretch of DNA amongst our three cases and Ellie's material that will anneal with cotton. There are several different bits of the cotton plant which may react so they will have to do multiple tests on samples from each person. We can extract enough DNA from the cells in their saliva so that's no problem."

"Thank you, Uncle. Ring us after lunch with the answers. No, that was a joke!" he added hastily.

"I'll ring you as soon as there are any useful results." Uncle sounded rather put out.

"He must be tired this morning, in the middle of a busy clinic and not having had the luxury of breakfast on the veranda."

Bernard rose from the table. "I have been thinking, Tara. Not a great change from normal you might say. I'm not sure I'm well prepared enough to go to Zimbabwe this week; I might have to postpone it for a few days. There's too much to investigate at this end. We've not yet started Ted's boxes and I think it'll take a few days to digest the contents. Half the loft is full of his things. We must find the boxes to begin with; there should be eight of them and they're heavy. I hope you're feeling strong Melusi?"

"Don't worry, Bernard, we'll get them down for you."

Bernard sounded tired, but when Tara remembered his age, she was amazed that he was still in the land of the living after the strain of last night.

"How do you feel this morning, Bernard?"

"Not too bad, considering the late night. I have had many later ones studying old documents, but those were many years ago." Suddenly his mood changed. "Do I look as if I was about to collapse?"

Tara was thrown by this question and Bernard's flash of fire.

"Bernard, Melusi and I have discussed the African trip and if you think it would be helpful, we would love to come with you. I'm afraid we'll have to ask you for the air fares, but we want to help. Don't we Melusi?" She finished weakly with the feeling that she could have put the question better and looked to Melusi for support.

"Yes, we would really love to come with you."

There was a long silence eventually broken by Bernard. "Thank you both, I had hoped you would say that. In fact, I must confess that I was rather banking on you both coming with me. So now I hope you will both forgive me for ordering four tickets; I will not tell you who the fourth is for." He rose from his chair and walked towards the house. "Perhaps you'd better change them to next Monday, that's seven days from now and it should just give us time." His voice grew fainter as he reached the hall.

"Well done, Tara, brilliant timing."

Tara exploded. "The cheeky monkey! He knew all along we would come with him. He's led us by the nose. I wonder what he means by that last statement, 'give us time'. Time for what, Melusi?"

"He meant, I am afraid, that it will only just give us time to find the wizened old guru who is the repository of the curse, time to find the cure for the rashes and time to administer the cure to the patients, before they all die. I do realise that the old blighter knew we were coming with him all along, but I wonder who is the fourth person? Now who is pulling the strings. Perhaps Simon is right. Being practical, don't forget malaria prophylaxis. We ought to start it now and remember to go on taking it for six weeks after we return. I must think of work sometime and tropical prophylaxis might come up as a question. There are not many other things that can't be avoided by sensible eating and drinking. No, malaria is the danger, although not such an acute one on the high plateau. Perhaps we should take a course of antibiotics with us in case of injury. Sepsis can be very quick, even a prick with a thorn can cause a horrendous infection in a very short time. Uncle can write us a prescription; we'll probably have to pay for it."

Simon bid them goodbye after breakfast, wishing them well with Ted's boxes.

"Ted's boxes, of course."

"Nothing like the present," said Melusi. "Before the day hots up too much. I expect the loft will be like an oven. Bedson and I will find ladders and clear spaces for the boxes which will give Tara time to buy all the pills we need."

"I mustn't forget to rebook the flight tickets for Monday the seventh of August. Bernard insists we all go first class."

Chapter Twenty

"God, it's hot in here; we ought to try and open some of those top windows." Melusi wiped the sweat from his eyes, took off his shirt and handed it to Tara who threw it down the ladder.

"Catch, Hobson. A bit smelly, I'm afraid."

"One hell of a lot of very old junk up here; must be over a hundred years of the stuff. That must be a sight longer than Bernard's time in the house. There are some boxes right at the back; they have to be Ted's as there aren't any others."

"There's E L burnt onto their lids so they must be his. Bernard said there should be eight in all. If we stacked them by the trapdoor and tied a rope to the handles, Hobson could guide them down the ladder. Bernard is clearing the drawing room so we can examine them in a cool room. I must say, I'm looking forward to the air-conditioning."

A beaming Bernard greeted them. "Thank you all for doing such a splendid job. Now forget the dust. Don't tell Mrs Hobson I said that. We'll need to study the entire contents of each box; it'll probably take us a few days. You may have noticed that there is a small number, a Roman numeral, at the base of each E L; that indicates the order in which Ted stored his papers. He was a meticulous man, and he was convinced one day someone would have the energy to study the contents, but I suspect he thought there would be all the time in the world to do it. Never mind, don't lose heart; I'm certain we'll strike gold. Even the golden T! Let's open them all and stack the contents round the room. By the way, Hobson has found you a clean shirt, Melusi."

Tara fingered the boxes, eyes wide. "These are beautifully made, and the scent of the wood is still there after all these years. I can't see any splits despite them being in that baking atmosphere. Ted must have found an amazing carpenter when he was in Africa. What do you think, Bernard?"

"He did say they should be almost airtight. This overlapping lid is mighty heavy and the ebony, or some other black wood, fillet tight through the bronze rings should be enough to stop insects crawling in. Come on, line them up like soldiers and start on Box I. You open the first one, Melusi."

"It seems a shame to disturb these documents. They're all so neatly stacked." Melusi picked up a packet of papers and started to examine them. "These appear to have details of Ted's journey out to South Africa in the autumn of 1884. Here's a letter from the missionary society suggesting that Ted should make his own way to Southern Africa, as they called it, to spread the gospel. He was not to be out of pocket and a substantial sum would be made available to cover his expenses. Ted should therefore have felt free to travel in the vessel of his own choice."

"This must be where Ted found the travel company, Melusi?" Tara held up a torn newspaper page. "This is from The Times of September 15th, 1884, carrying an advertisement for the British India Steam Navigation Company, Mail and Passenger steamers to Zanzibar, Natal, Calcutta, Java and Queensland ports with liberty to call at any other ports en route.

'Interested persons are requested to write to Gellatly, Hankey, Sewell & Co offices in 103 Leadenhall Street, London SW.' By return, he received this mass of papers indicating firstly that the Company would oblige, for a small additional fee, since his destination was outwith the normal voyage, to take Ted and his wife to Cape Town."

"I wonder how much extra that was; sounds like our so-called cheap air flights! Sorry Melusi, over to you."

"'Ted was informed that the steamer, Kerbella, would be sailing on October 13th from their berth at the Royal Albert Docks, London E at 9.30. Boarding must be no later than 7 o'clock in the morning of the same day since the mail was to be loaded from 8 o'clock. Here we are Tara, your extras! The price, first class, for the outward journey only was £23 for one person, £42 for two. That sounds like the total price in those days.

"'The Company sincerely hopes that there would be no delays to accommodate quarantine.' All the rest in this bundle indicates that negotiations went smoothly. Your turn, Tara."

"There is a receipt for an overnight stay in a hotel in London. I must say he enjoyed his food. Look at this dinner menu! It makes me feel quite hungry. But naturally, the Missionary Society were paying, and they had loads of money then. Here's the remains of the Times newspaper with Ted's scribbled comments in the margins. 872 new cases of cholera in Naples. One shipping company had to advertise that their regular sailing to Marseilles had been cancelled due to an outbreak of cholera in that city. No wonder his shipping line was concerned about quarantine.

"Here's an interesting article entitled, 'The Scramble for Africa', which details the speed with which the European nations had annexed various 'protectorates' on the west coast. Ted seems to have distrusted the Germans in the rush to steal chunks of the newly opening continent. He then goes on to write several pithy comments about the inevitable political problems that will result in that part of the world. Ted noted his concern, posing a few stark questions about the political problems in the southern part of the east coast of the mysterious part of the world to which he was going. Bernard, there are two sealed letters to Mr and Mrs Frederick Abercrombie while Ted was on board the boat. Presumably, they must be Ted's sister's parents-in-law. They have been franked with the purser's official stamp and back stamped both at the port in Natal and Cape Town, where Ted disembarked. The vessel continued its journey to India and Ted's sea journey went without mishap. I think you had better open them."

Bernard took the letters and put them to one side. "Carry on, Tara."

"It doesn't sound as if Ted's journey to the missionary society headquarters in Cape Town was much fun. He writes that he is staggered at the casual demeaning attitude of the settlers to the Africans. He liked people, which is why he had joined the church to bring his view of The Almighty to grace the lives of many. That reads rather pompously.

"Anyway, Ted sounds determined to throw in his social lot with those who treat the inhabitants with civility and allow them to have some dignity. He is sad that generally his attitude is mocked. He writes as if he was the outsider and quotes the many times when remarks that he found offensive were flung at him because of his empathy with the Africans. Have you opened the letters yet, Bernard?"

Bernard looked around and picked up the forgotten letters.

"Oh, sorry. Yes, I have, here we are. The first letter describes much that you have read but the second one is more cheerful. They were allotted a pleasant single storey dwelling with a splendid view of the flat-topped mountain and the coast. Instructions from the church appear to have been confused. There was an initial contract signed in 1885 that didn't specify any work, but eventually the powers-that-be decided that Ted should break completely new ground. He was to join a group of people to move into uncharted country that had only previously been visited by a handful of traders and the original explorers, some of whom had also been in the guise of missionaries. Oh dear! There is a confession. Devious is not the word.

"They travelled in oxcarts for more than a thousand miles and finally took a small part in the hoisting of the Union Jack over a bare piece of ground that was eventually to become Salisbury. The trek was led by a fiery but generous little man with the name of Frederick Selous. In fact, the trek had been organised by Cecil Rhodes as a massive migration. Ted was given a contract signed by the British South Africa Company which had been granted a royal charter in 1889. His contract was to start the building of a church in the new township in 1890."

Bernard wandered over to see what Melusi was doing.

"What are all these, Melusi?"

"These are the rather stark negotiations, if you can call them that from behind pointed guns, with the kingdom of Ndebele in the former empire of Great Zimbabwe. There is a contract of 1888 which follows the 'official' treaty of friendship between Cecil Rhodes and the Ndebele King Lobengula in February of that year. Some of Ted's comments on these negotiations verged on the libellous."

"I hope his superiors didn't see these," remarked Bernard.

Tara grunted, "I suspect that the transfer of information was so unreliable in those days that it wouldn't have made a lot of difference. This is nice; he meets a man with the name of Saul and strikes up a friendship. He goes on about Saul and they are able to read each other's thoughts. Speech is often reserved for the cool of the evening round the fireside when they could put the world to rights. Ted thanks his god for Saul's friendship. That is just charming!

"The next bit is rather depressing. Ted writes that he is gloomy about his prospects of being able to perform good missionary work when he is so obviously associated with the ruling white army. The perceived need to accompany the pioneers with two hundred heavily armed troops has not gone down well, but Saul persuades him that at least he has a jumping off point for his missionary activities. Later, in the same year, he switches his efforts to the capital of Matabeleland, Bulawayo, when the company, using the excuse of a minor border dispute, invades that country. Unfortunately, the defeated Lobengula leaves his capital a burning ruin. It isn't too difficult to read Ted's diary and detect a great deal of sympathy for the Africans in their defeat.

"Now we seem to be rather out of character. His reward for not being openly in opposition to the company and through them the British government, was to be given a stake in the new companies that were set up to re-open the ancient mine workings. He does not comment on why he accepted these gifts, but I suppose we must presume he must have thought that he could benefit the Africans by participating in a wealth-creating enterprise. What do you think, Bernard?"

"Those mining contracts, essentially in the form of part ownership, were not the start of the wealth of our family but certainly contributed to the increase in that wealth at the time. They were usually mining shares, with the hope that they would find gold. Well, they found little gold, but other minerals were mined for years. Unfortunately, they also discovered substances like asbestos which turned out to be the magic fireproof insulation material that the building industry had been looking for. There was a tremendous demand for the stuff until the last forty years. Asbestos was thought to be innocuous when first discovered and it is only relatively recently that most of the mines closed after they detected an enormous increase in lung cancer in those who worked with it. That was a sad outcome that left a stain on the family."

Tara noticed that Melusi was looking upset and when he spoke, she realised why.

"So now we have two good reasons why the African has a bone to pick with the tree of John Hawkins. Firstly, the slave trade; and now the seemingly innocent trade in asbestos."

"But Ted could not possibly have known at the time that it would have been so damaging. The family can't be blamed for that."

Melusi stuck to his guns. "I'm sure that Ted was not the first missionary to accept gifts in the mistaken impression that they would somehow benefit the Africans and he won't be the last, but the principle is wrong."

Tara was becoming angry and upset with Melusi's belligerence. He was showing a side of him that she did not much like. She picked up a sheaf of documents and took them over to the table by the window to sort them out.

"These papers are much nicer. They are the final contracts that happily showed Ted in a much better light. He has started schools in every place that he has been posted and even some in towns over which he had no official religious authority. The money needed to start the schools must have come from his own pocket as the stake that Ted had in the mining ventures would not have produced any ready cash. That better, Melusi?"

"I certainly agree that's a plus. And these notes from fighting the Boers are good as well. He gave solace to the injured from both sides and gives a hint that it was the catalyst that started him on his surgical career. We even have some names of the combatants whom he helped during the conflict. This box is now empty, on to Box II, Bernard; your turn."

They opened the second box and the sweet smell of the ancient wood cheered them all.

"These would make a terrific book of short stories. They are Ted's comments, sometimes not too flattering, about his friends, both African and expatriate, over the earlier part of his life in Africa. Let me read some of them to you."

"We don't have time, Bernard. Listen to your secretary. Probably next year you will have time and the energy to go through those stories again. Then you can write your book of short stories. Let's go to Box III.

"This is more your line, Melusi. Here's an ancient copy of Gray's Anatomy. And what do you think of these?"

"Well, I never; this is a complete kit of surgical tools. They are not too different from the ones we use today. And this folder has his operating notes. My goodness, he was amazing. He did major surgery, removed huge tumours, performed hysterectomies and other operations within the abdomen which must have been recognised at that time as being hazardous in Europe. He's treated major cases of trauma, frequently the result of attacks by animals or the result of inter-tribal warfare. Ted's even amputated limbs in the most dreadful conditions and got away with it. Anaesthetics seem to have been provided by hypnosis induced by the local witch doctors. I guess he had to presume his patients were not feeling pain or perhaps they were able to block out the perception of pain. There was no alternative."

"Coffee time for the workers!" Hobson entered the room carrying a tray with strong coffee and enticing biscuits. "Unless you would like something stronger, Bernard?"

"Very tempting, Hobson, but we need clear heads."

The three read the stories of the operations as they drank the welcome refreshment. "Ted very quickly got on the same wavelength as the local witch doctors. Do you think, Bernard, he would have made a good psychiatrist in today's world?"

"He certainly needed their help, and he writes that they were very efficient assistants. They are, or were, a vital part of African culture and Ted was massively impressed with the faith people had in their power. That faith was absolute and unquestioning as the witch doctors used language which was understandable to the people and had immediate effect or solace. Ted must have found himself comparing the flaccid observance and droning, mindless, repetitiveness of his colleagues' parishioners, many of whom would quickly revert to their bitchy mentality as soon as they reached the exit of the local place of worship.

"The end result, I presume, was that Ted and the witch doctors recognised their particular expertise; so, between them they made a good team. There are loads of affectionate references to several named people and the startling results from their working together. What's next?"

Bernard ferreted down in the box.

"This might be interesting. A rather tatty, small, black leather-bound notebook." He opened it and started to read.

"Not so good, I am afraid. This is a very personal collection of Ted's private doubts, as he put it. He must have scribbled these while trekking and they encompass the fundamental wisdom of his calling. Here's a quote: 'Am I just an agent of destruction of a culture far older than Christianity by imposing the mores of the European nations on people who simply do not need them?'"

"There are dozens of pages of notes detailing Ted's soul-searching. And there is no mention of reassurance by his African colleagues who were probably too tactful to say so directly, but Ted felt that his Church was essentially destructive."

Melusi interrupted. "I don't think Ted's soul-searching can have been helped by his dislike of the bishop. He writes vivid details of the monumental rows between the two and he concludes that it was best they were kept apart. That must have had the effect of making him introspective, which was possibly the catalyst that made him throw himself more deeply into the medical and especially surgical activities he knew he was good at and loved to do for much of his life."

"That's enough, my darling." Tara gently extracted the little book from Melusi's hand. "There's just a few spearheads and gallstones in the bottom of the box. Let's go on to the next one, Box IV. More diaries, Bernard; this is exciting!"

"You're right, Tara. Box IV contains diaries. They describe the journeys Ted made with his wife, Priscilla, throughout their stay in Africa. Well, I never! One of their hobbies that must have taken on the quality of an obsession was to visit remote caves and make drawings of the ancient paintings. There is a large folder of these drawings in the box related to each journey. For an amateur archaeologist this would be an amazing find. We ought to study them."

"They are mostly of animals or, rarely, human stick people fighting with animals or with each other. Ted has copied the finest detail and sometimes inserted his own interpretation. He's compared them with the Upper Palaeolithic cave paintings that had recently been discovered in Western Europe; but I reckon they are tens of thousands of years apart."

Tara was rummaging in the bottom of the box. "Hang on a minute. There is a different sort of pictures in the folder underneath; I think we need Simon to give us a clue about these. At first sight they are yet more drawings of cave paintings, but there is something unusual about them. There are no animals, and the drawings look much more recent as if a story is being told. Now there are masses of stick people, many of them flat on the ground with flowering plants protruding from various bits of them."

Tara and Melusi placed the drawings on the carpet to see the whole story.

"There appears to have been an extremely high mortality of the stick people from some mysterious cause. Of course! They are dying, the stick people are dying. What do you think is happening to them? How about some sort of catastrophe affecting the whole tribe? Perhaps they're dying of some epidemic, and those who remain alive don't know what to do about it? What is unusual is that in the next picture, the bodies are piled one on top of the other. In all the other pictures we have seen from this box, when there is a death, the bodies are either eaten by the wild animals that have killed them or they are left out for the hyenas and vultures to consume. This folder is different. The death rate is enormous and has something to do with flowers and the bodies."

Tara jumped up and shouted, "I've got it. The bodies are in the same state as Valentine described Ellie's body. Her body was still fresh after three days in the tropics. You remember, Valentine said that the electricity had failed, and the refrigerator was warm. The bodies should have been absolutely disgusting with decay. Valentine was surprised that Ellie's body had not undergone the process of disintegration. The bodies of these people thousands of years ago were preserved even in the African heat. We've got it, it is all here! We have to find these paintings." Tara was so excited Melusi and Bernard had to both hold her steady and sit her down gently.

"Relax, my dear, we will study them later," said Bernard.

The precious drawings were gathered up and returned to their folder. Below the folder there were a few notes that did not relate to the journeys. Ted's system stopped abruptly with confusion in the dates.

"Perhaps this relates to the time spent in other countries?" Melusi suggested.

"But Ted would still have been taking notes of his travels," said Tara. "Surely it would have been just as interesting to travel round and explore in other countries as it had been in Matabeleland. It seems to be out of character, don't you think, Bernard?"

"I have the feeling that something awful happened. The answer may lie in the fifth box. Let us have a break and stop for something stronger than coffee. We must not have Tara getting over-excited again! Hobson has left some food for us on the veranda since the weather is cooler today. We have done well, four boxes in as many hours, with some tantalising clues. A few beers or gin and tonics should calm the minds."

After food and drink, Bernard volunteered to start on the next box.

"It is as I feared. Box V sadly reveals the answer to the sudden end to the travels. Priscilla becomes ill soon after they returned from exploring the caves at Sinoia followed by an exhausting trek up to the Mavuradonha range above the Zambezi escarpment. On their return to Salisbury, Priscilla spikes a high fever and a rash. She developed a severe headache and is unable to eat. She finally becomes jaundiced, gradually fades, and dies. Poor old Ted!

"Letters of condolence; plenty of them, some of them sensitive and helpful, most of them statutory and a stark obituary in a newspaper. Ted says he is overwhelmed. I am not surprised. He is certainly overwhelmed by the loss and sends a general letter of thanks to the local newspaper.

"I don't think much of the one from the church authorities. There is no element of the human touch and those from fellow missionaries are in the stilted language of the time. But the bishop's one is beautifully sympathetic and letters from African friends show exceptional loyalty and sympathy both with Ted's personal loss but also with his religious problems and they wrote with a mixture of grief, tenderness and joy for the life she led."

"What a meticulous man Ted was." Said Tara. "He's kept everything, and all so neatly done. Was the whole of his life run with such precision, Bernard?"

"I understand it was. That is why I am certain that we will find what we are looking for in one of these boxes. Perhaps that unusual folder will reveal all. I wonder what Priscilla died of. What do you think Melusi, what is your diagnosis from a distance?"

"The most likely cause of her death would have been malaria. The rash is unusual but does occur in a small percentage of cases and late in the disease there may be jaundice. Alternatively, typhus is a candidate or one of the haemorrhagic fever viruses; on the other hand, they are usually acute diseases. Even yellow fever is just on the cards, but I would be surprised if it had spread that far south."

Chapter Twenty-One

"Time for lunch, chaps, and it's Hobson's day off so you will have to make do with a dose of pseudo-continental for us all. Hot sliced French bread with cold meats, cheese, and salad, followed by damson ice cream to cool you down and energise the brain for another hard day; well, until the evening. Melusi, a beer for you. Bernard and I will have a mixture of rough cider and lemonade with plenty of ice. Then a dose of hard black coffee to get us going. Box VI we are up to."

Bernard took a deep breath. "I guess it's my turn for a bit. This one appears to be mainly religious texts and a mass of what look like very boring sermons. When Ted retired and returned to England, he took a few services at our local church. I remember he had a good voice, firm and resonant; he didn't speak too fast, not like some of the new ones nowadays, they always seem to be in such a hurry as if they're trying to finish before everyone becomes bored and their stomachs start rumbling. Ted usually sounded convincing, but I felt his heart had gone out of it. It was as if he had done his bit for the church and just wanted to be himself with his own thoughts and enjoy life with his second wife. She was a homely, charming woman who had been his housekeeper for his last years in Africa. He married her before he came back to England. They managed to have a few very happy years together.

"This is nice, the old family bible at the bottom of the box with a lot of prayer books. Again, all these were well-used with quite a few pencilled annotations in the margins. Now to Box VII. First is a large envelope addressed to Ted. I don't recognise the writing, let's see. Ah, from Ted's sister, Olive.

'The Long House
Little Ashby
Templecombe
Somerset
January 12th, 1901

My Dearest Brother,

I hope that I am not becoming the tiresome relative that only writes when she needs something. Life normally goes on here in such an easy fashion. We read and hear about all the battles and the deaths in Matabeleland and the countries round and about you and I feel reticent about writing. But I must write for reasons that will become apparent as you read. I am certain the rest of the family would support the plea in this letter. I am writing to enlist your help in a matter that at times I find hard to believe; it is so strange. Jack has helped me to write the letter, as by the very nature of the problem of which you will hear, he is more directly involved than me. He has always been encouraging to everything I have done. He is a wonderful husband, and I must try and do everything in my power to help him and the rest of the family.

You will remember about thirty-three years ago, Jack's mother Alice told me about the Curse on the family into which I had married. I married Jack when I was only sixteen and I had to be told all the family stories. Since I had married into the family, I was only given the bare outline of the Curse, but Jack had been given the whole story or at least as much as anyone knows. Alice believed that the Curse had originally been intended to affect the blood line. I had some difficulty understanding this. It was all very well talking about a blood line, but whose blood and which line? If we all came from Adam and Eve, then everyone on Earth is in the blood line. There must have been a point at some time in the past when this Curse was attached to us. I told Alice my thoughts on the subject, but she did not know anything more and did not appear to be particularly able to talk at length on the subject.

Even though I only seemed to have a part of the story you will understand my grief when I realised that potentially it could affect my children, their children in turn and so on for ever. You were also told the story at the same time; I can't remember by whom. But you are my brother and so you can't be affected by it. It is because you will not come into harm's way that I write to you for help. I also know that you are an honest man of God and can perhaps persuade the givers of the Curse of the error of their ways. I can't say that the Curse is evil or not evil since I do not know for what reason it was laid. What terrible deed was done to so impel a person or persons to impose such a burden on an entire blood line, and for so many generations?

One starry evening more years ago than I care to remember, when I had been married to Jack for three years, you made me a promise. It was on the night of your twenty-first birthday, and we were becoming very serious about something or other; I can't remember what. Anyhow, you solemnly promised me that if ever I was caught up by the powers of evil you would rescue me; you would be my knight in shining armour! You were intending to join the Church Missionary Society and would be spending many years abroad, probably in Africa, working as a missionary. To give me peace of mind, for we have always been close, you gave me this promise. It was not the sort of promise that you would have made without realising its full implications. I was very grateful for your statement and accepted your pledge, naturally assuming, that I would never have to call on your help except in extreme circumstances.

I have faith in you just as you have faith in your work. When you were twenty-one and I was only nineteen. I could not believe that this day would come. As I sit here by the window of the bedroom looking over the innocence of the sunshine on the rolling hills of Somerset, I am horrified by the burden that I know this letter will bring you. But I must force myself to believe that it is true. I need your help and your Faith as I feel all our family are in desperate danger.

My story is rather long. You will remember my stories usually are! I have just more or less recovered from what is normally described as a very mild illness. I was drenched by the rain one day when out walking the dogs and when I came home, I did not change my clothes at once. I now realise that it was entirely my own fault, but the result was that I developed a very nasty cold which a week later went down into my chest. It is now a month later and I am still coughing rather a lot. The inhalations of the balsam help somewhat, and the doctor believes that I am on the mend. At least you will be relieved to hear that I am not suffering from the tuberculosis that is so common nowadays, so I do not have to go to a sanatorium, they are mostly such dreary places although the ones in Switzerland do sound rather nice. I am wandering off the subject as usual.

When I was ill, I had a series of terrifying dreams. The dreams made me think I was in Africa. I can say that with some certainty because the countryside was just like the surroundings of the place you live in. I have very fond memories of our visit to you two years ago. I remember the huge expanse of the plains with all those animals that we only see in pictures in this country. I remember the quiet restfulness of the church and the township that is developing round it. I particularly remember the noisy cheerful greetings that so many people gave you as we walked along the dusty roads. The lovely brown faces, always smiling, which are so different from our pallid gloomy English ones are still fresh in my mind; so too is the memory of the dust and the flies, but as you rightly pointed out that is all part of the pattern of life in your part of the world.

I remember the open savannah country and the forests where you tried to take us on those long-suffering horses, or were they bullocks? I can't remember now. Anyway, they never seemed to tire of pulling the carts on the treks we made up into the mountains and, above all, to the caves with the prehistoric paintings. The paintings were almost as if they had been painted yesterday, they were so alive. And yet there was something ominous about them, as if they were trying to tell us something. You were a superb guide and Priscilla a wonderful hostess. How she managed to cook a tasty hotpot out of one of those little animals with the twisted horns I shall never know. You must miss her terribly, brother, and I weep for you. She is now in a Better Place and awaits us all.

To return to my dreams; they were dreams in vivid detail of evil deeds done by conquerors. The evil was unnecessary, callous, and performed on human beings. The humans were not perfect, but then there is no-one on Earth that is perfect. They were dreams that described the demeaning of the very basis of the human nature of those black faces that you live and work with every day. I find it difficult to put it into words but the most terrifying moment in my dreams was when I realised that whatever was controlling the dream clearly meant me to understand that it was partly my fault. I was one of the people who had been directly responsible for all this horror. At that moment I awoke and at once recalled the evening when Alice, so many years ago, had told me about the Curse on our family.

I suppose I have to believe that the Curse is a form of revenge. It is to atone for the destruction of many people, for the humiliation and death of countless numbers of human beings snatched from the coast, the plains, the forests, and the mountains. I believe she - for I am convinced that it was a woman - cursed the blood of the captors with the only Curse left to her, the most ancient Curse held by the tribe. Tandeka Thembani is her name; she was the daughter of the warrior king of the ancient tribe of the plains at the opening of the caves at the base of the mountains of the Matopos. She laid the Great Curse, and she gave her own life as the final sacrifice.

Brother, as I read what I have just written I am wondering if you think that my brain has turned? Please believe me. I am certain the name is correct although I do not know why I am so certain. Perhaps the name and the places came to me in the dreams. Brother, I am greatly disturbed by the dreams, and I believe that if we do nothing our family will suffer a terrible fate. I have convinced myself that there is something in the caves that can neutralise the curse and set us free. I remember from one of the dreams something about a great noise that will summon the Keeper of the Curse. I am sure he will speak with you for you are a man of God and will have his trust.

Perhaps the answer is in the caves with the paintings. I remember that you and Priscilla have made hundreds of drawings of the cave paintings. It might be possible to find a reference to the Curse in one of the caves. I have given you what from this comfortable little room would seem to be an impossible task, but you are the only person who can help us.

Please write soon. I can think of no one whom I trust more.

Jack is keeping well and sends his regards as do the children.

With kindest Love, your little sister, Olive."

There was silence for a few moments as they digested the message conveyed by the letter and the agonised plea for help.

Melusi broke the silence. "That seems pretty clear."

"A little too clear, if you ask me," said Tara. "It's all so neat and fits into place too tidily. Perhaps it is my suspicious nature, but I have the awful feeling that we are all being set up for something. How about that idea, Bernard? Do you fancy being led by the nose?"

"I agree. It does seem that whenever we ask a question, an answer pops up from somewhere like a Jack-in-the-Box. Then we go on to the next move, like playing chess with a computer."

"Do we have any choice in the matter?" asked Melusi.

"We have to play the game as the rules appear."

Instead of feeling elated with the new discovery, they felt wary.

Bernard tried to sound cheerful. "Tea-time, folks."

The heat continued and seemed to be at its height at around four o'clock. They went outside under the great twelve-foot umbrella, but it was oppressive and humid. The gloom was beginning to affect Bernard. "Strange weather; I wonder when it'll break? You know, we haven't had a proper winter for three years with snowballs and frozen ponds and the dressing up in furs and sitting in front of roaring log fires. Do you think we're all going to dry up and become like the surface of Venus? What do you think, Tara? What's is your knowledge of climatology?"

"I suspect a lot more than yours by the sound of it. I hate to be a spoil sport, but I do think it would be much more comfortable and conducive to thought if we had our second cup of tea in the air-conditioning of the drawing room."

"Out comes the whip then, back to work. But at least we can take a cup of tea with us." They breathed a sigh of relief as they went back to the cool room to see if there were more surprises in Ted's boxes.

"There's a great wedge of carbons. I suppose they are Ted's attempts to reply to Olive. He must have found it difficult to compose a rational letter to her. There is no date, but it must have been written in early March 1901. Letters took about ten days from posting in Somerset to reach the outposts of the British South Africa Company via South Africa. So, if we double this time and add on a few days for the inevitable delays we should be about right. Here goes.

The Canon's Office
Salisbury Church
Salisbury
British South Africa Company
Africa

My Dear Little Sister,

I am humbled by your letter. I remember the occasion quite clearly, how could I possibly ever forget the night I gave you my promise that I would do everything in my power to help you if you were involved in the powers of evil? I can understand your hesitancy in writing such a letter. What are dreams for? We do not know, possibly they are a means of analysing our activities and motives without the so-called civilised overlay which encompasses our prejudices. I put great weight on the actual information in the dreams to which you were subjected. I write in this fashion because I believe that you were merely a convenient vehicle to convey the information to me.

Do not be too upset, Little Sister. The dreams were meant for all of us, but you were the unfortunate recipient. I accept everything that you have written as I know you to be honest and you would not lightly enter the mischievous field of falsehood, especially to your brother. I can reassure you about one thing, my thoughts on the matter have no relevance to my so-called vocation. My religious beliefs have no relationship to the problem of the Curse that has threatened your, and therefore my, family for some hundreds of years. Although, as you correctly write, I am not in the direct blood line, I was given more information than most of the others. I have an irritating habit, as you have been known to remark on before, of questioning everything. When Jack's mother was telling me about the Curse, I asked so many questions that she told me the whole story.

I am good at reading between the lines and behind the covers of stories. As a result, I am reasonably convinced that the Curse will never be applied, at least not in our generation or in the next. The Curse was passed on in the middle of the sixteenth century. It seems to have been a tribal Curse, presumably from one of the primeval African tribes, more of that later. The recipients of the Curse are in the main one of the white races. I fear this is not very specific as it covers the whole of Europe and half of Asia. I must assume it had something to do with the slave trade, being the major horror at that time, and I have some sympathy with the giver of the Curse. The slave trade was a dreadful operation, one that is not easily forgiven even after the passage of hundreds of years. Sympathy, however, is cheap and easy. Advocacy to relinquish a Curse or annul a debt requires more than the easy virtue of sympathy. You have made the first plea, now it is up to me to make the second. I will do all in my power to justify your faith in me and I trust that in the fullness of time our hopes that your blood line will be relieved of this Sword of Damocles that hangs over it will be fulfilled.

We are so similar; I have just re-read my last paragraph and it does sound just like a sermon. I apologise; but this is the medium that I have been trained to use. Little Sister, I will do everything in my power to help us, not just you, but all of us in this great family which I have had the pleasure to join. There, does that sound better?

I shall be taking a few weeks leave, maybe longer, but you will not be able to contact me. Don't worry, I shall succeed, in what I do not yet know; I must be given adequate time. I know that, fortunately, I can obtain unlimited leave of absence from my duties. There is, by chance, a young eager clergyman who has just appeared on the scene and the bishop has made it known that he thinks it to be the Will of God that this young man should be given a clear field. I think it is not particularly a good idea, it resembles the standard attitude of the Empire to 'chuck him in at the deep end.' I am sure my African friends will be polite and tolerant, but I am hopeful they will ignore the excesses of the young man's zeal and go their own way. One should not condemn the enthusiasm of the young, but at the same time one should not be persuaded to accept actions which reflect a superficial thoughtlessness.

Thank you again for your condolences. I may have some good news for you, if I can pluck up the courage in a few months' time; now there is a puzzle for you."

My love and regards to Jack,

Your big brother, Ted."

Bernard put the letter carefully on the table. "What a wonderful letter. Just the right emphasis to say, I am jolly well going to find the answer. Calms her down but not too earnest. Well, how did he get that vellum genealogical tree? I can't find anything useful to us in the rest of these letters. Why did she think it necessary to go out and see him? It was probably just a holiday for Jack and Olive, more likely an adventure."

"Probably," said Tara, "but we still do not have an explanation for the discovery of the vellum."

"Thank goodness for that. We should have a few remaining mysteries. I am increasingly worried about having all the answers handed to us on a plate."

"Perhaps they heard us," said Melusi.

To their surprise Bernard rounded on him. "Do not joke; I am becoming very worried about that aspect. Perhaps, as you glibly say, they can hear us, whoever they are. I have had this hanging over me like Ted's proverbial Sword of Damocles for seventy years. It's no bloody joke!" he repeated, tears in his eyes. "Under no circumstances can it be called a joke. It is playing with fire and fire kills."

Bernard was so rarely upset, the effect was devastating and made him suddenly look his great age. After a shocked silence Bernard shook his head and seemed to recover saying in a matter-of-fact way, as he went into the garden, "Ah well. I'm sure you didn't mean it."

Chapter Twenty-Two

Hobson, poking his nose through the door of the drawing room, detected the tension. He quickly produced three tumblers as Bernard came through the French windows. "I'm back in charge, all. I hope Tara fed you well for lunch. It is a beautiful evening at the front of the house, Bernard. I have placed three chairs for you and a table with bits to nibble."

They settled and Melusi tried to make up for his outburst. "Bernard, I must apologise for my rather slick statement. The last thing I want to do is cause you to feel offended. I would go to the ends of the earth with you to find the source of the curse and stop it in its tracks." Bernard rose from his chair and gave them both the tired smile of an old man. They, too, stood up and he put his arms round them.

"All I can promise you is gratitude and my everlasting love and that of my family. Please help me to find, and plead to annul, the curse?"

"Of course, we will."

Bernard relaxed his grip. "Thank you both; and I, too, am sorry I lost control. I feel we are almost there. After all these years, there must be no mistakes. At the same time, we need all the breaks we can get. Now, as Winnie-the-Pooh says, and courtesy of Hobson, it's time for a little something. A cool gin and tonic cures most things. Let's take them and go watch the sunset."

The heat was less intense and the cool gin and tonics even more refreshing. For a moment, as the sun reached the horizon, there was a golden staircase across the water, beckoning them to come for a ride down to the other side of the world. Then it quickly vanished, and the undersides of the wispy clouds lit up red, purple, violet and finally a deep indigo into the dark blue of the night.

"Beautiful," said Tara. They talked of Africa, what they knew and what they might expect to find in that magical continent so full of inconsistencies; the corruption of the rich politicians contrasting with the dedication of the poor teachers; the economies that collapse as the populations rise. The devastation wrought by the ghastly letters HIV, contrasting with the infectious cheerfulness of the orphans of that epidemic, four in every ten of whom are HIV-positive.

The twilight had almost gone by the time they had talked themselves out. Hobson appeared and turned on the spotlights that made Ted's trees stand like guardians of the night. "Bernard, Simon telephoned and asked if you would ring him back?"

"I wonder what he wants. I thought that we had agreed to leave it a few days before we met again to review how far we had progressed."

"I suspect he wants to come to Africa," said Melusi. "After all, the woman that he lives with in Spain has a daughter who is ill and needs all our combined efforts to find a cure. He wants to be in on the act. When you think of it, he gave us a very clear exposition as to the whys and wherefores of the phenomenon of the tribal curse. He's a philosopher and has a wonderful way with words. Could be useful if we get into a tense argument or discussion with a high-powered African sage. I bet Simon could talk the hind legs off them."

"I wonder, perhaps you're right. I'll give him a ring before we eat." Bernard turned to his secretary. "How about room for Simon on the aeroplane, Tara?"

"For you, Bernard, there would be room anywhere, especially first class. I would remind you that there are four booked seats."

"Oh, dear me, yes." Neither of them believed Bernard's feigned surprise.

"For your information," she added, "I have hired a big Chevrolet four-wheel drive with a winch to pull us out of trouble, armoured glass, air-conditioning, long range tanks, additional water containers and enough toys to keep even you happy. The driver I have managed to hire is an Olympic runner. He sounds quite dishy."

"Ah, but can he throw a javelin?" asked Melusi, refusing to be wound up.

"Pass!"

"I'll ring Simon now. Hobson, we are still thirsty; it is very tiring putting the world to rights. I shall need his number and some sort of telephone."

Instantly Hobson appeared with another round of drinks. "Bernard thinks I'm deaf," Hobson said quietly to Melusi. ", he is a predictable soul, and the drinks were ready five minutes ago; you all drink so slowly. His old phone is on the side, the cable is just long enough."

Melusi adored the Hobsons. They looked after Bernard tirelessly, were the soul of discretion and, he hoped, had a taste for Dubonnet.

"Simon!" Bernard shouted to the old telephone as if Simon himself was about to appear through the earpiece. "You rang and asked me to ring you. We think we have worked out why you phoned. To be more accurate, Melusi thought that perhaps you would like to come with us. He said you had the gift of the gab, in the nicest possible way."

"Yes, I am asking to come with you, and this is a perfectly serious request. And I am also grateful to Melusi for analysing my motives so clearly. I believe that there may well arise awkward moments and confrontations when my 'gift of the gab', as he kindly puts it, might be useful, but that aside, the lady I love has a daughter who is not at all well. Currently we have no way of even having a clue as to her prognosis. I love her and I desperately want her cured and brought back to full health. I'm willing to stand as a final advocate, if necessary. I may explain that later."

"Simon, I can understand your reasons for wanting to come. Believe me, old friend, we look forward to your company. Tara will book the extra seat. Changing the subject, we are just about to have dinner and continue to examine Ted's boxes. We can give you twenty minutes to get here if you would like to come for the meal? We would love to have your company, if only to tell us we were all thinking along the wrong lines."

"Splendid, I'm on my way. Have a large gin and tonic waiting for me and, if I may, I would like to stay the night. I'll be with you in fifteen minutes."

Bernard put down the telephone. "That's the fastest reaction I have ever had from Simon." Sinking into his chair with a somewhat contented sigh, Bernard tilted his head up to watch the stars. The full moon hurrying after the sun was reflected on the water, just about to dip below the horizon.

"I expect you are used to this view, Bernard. What is your interpretation?"

"Melusi, I see the moonlit ladder as an ethereal climb towards our success. What do you see, Tara?"

"I see a long slog and a lot of hard work. But if we are honest in our dealings with whatever stands in our way, we will win out."

"Well, that's good!"

As promised, Simon arrived in exactly fifteen minutes and gratefully accepted the large gin and tonic. They sat for a while longer in the welcome cool of the evening watching the shooting stars.

"Thank you for coming Simon. You can have the same room as last time; Mrs Hobson will have left your sheets. Now, let us answer Hobson's call to dine."

Mrs Hobson's meal was excellent. Most of the discussion revolved around their various interpretations of the moonlit ladder on the rippling sea. At the end of the meal, they were feeling mellow and repaired to the comfort of the drawing room with generous glasses of brandy. Hobson served the coffee and left them to it.

Bernard started the ball rolling. "Well, Simon, to business. We started to open the first of Ted's boxes at about ten o'clock this morning. Tell Simon about the contents."

Taking it in turns, Melusi and Tara described in as much detail as they could remember all that they had found. Simon listened without interrupting, and when they had finished, he was silent for a full five minutes. They could see that he was churning round in his mind, analysing, comparing with previous observations, applying all his vast store of knowledge to the information that had just been fed to him. At the end of the five minutes when they were seriously thinking of asking him to speak, they noticed that he was frowning and pursing his lips. Simon stood up to speak. This was the last thing they expected.

"Puppets, that's what they think we are! Do we really appear to be so gullible? Eh! Are we the original simpleton that is supposed to have one brain cell that has lost track of the other? Right, my friends, this is a battle, and I shall enjoy winning it. We are being 'set up' to be the last fling of a dying curse. We will enter their little chamber of horrors and we will break, annul, neutralise, or straight up kill their curse. If we need to use other methods, it may take a little longer, or alternatively we may be able to short-circuit the whole damn thing. The curse has obviously passed its peak and is on the downward path to oblivion, which is the way of all curses, however powerful. Like the dying scorpion, it hopes to take one more life with it. It has killed poor Ellie and it is hoping to take more. However, we do have the ability to prevent it taking any more lives and of healing the half-dead. This is all very cheering." He finished on such a surprising note that Melusi and Bernard clapped.

Tara frowned. "What on earth makes you say all that? I suppose we did feel on several occasions that whenever we found a puzzling aspect of this affair that the answer appeared too quickly for comfort. For instance, we now have the full name of the Royal T without having to look too far, likewise we only had to ask Francis for his family tree and there it was. In comparison, Bernard's tree took seventy years to complete and during the last couple of years he has worked day and night on it. Would it be a reasonable interpretation that the extraordinary amount of work done by Bernard has been partially instrumental in the neutralisation of the curse?"

"You will make a good philosopher in thirty years, dear Tara. I suspect you may well be right."

"Do I now understand you correctly Simon; that we are on the right track? That we should gamble by going to Africa and having found a place and a person and an unknown list of other things, that with reasonable discussion and perhaps a few tricks all will be well?"

"My guess is yes."

They agreed afterwards it was the shortest speech he had ever made.

"I also predict that in the eighth box will be explicit instructions as to how to find the place where the confrontation is to be made, how to call up the appropriate people who understand the curse and how to neutralise the effects of the curse. Over to you, Bernard."

"Let us see then, I hope this will tell us where and how Ted found the vellum family tree."

He went over to the last box. It was not in such a neat order as the other boxes, the papers had been forced into it and the lid slammed shut. It was as if Ted didn't want anything more to do with it. Box VIII contained a thick folder that seemed at first glance to be a diary of events. There was very little room in the rest of the box for anything else. The folder contained details of the journey made by Ted to honour the pledge he had made to Olive so many years ago.

"What a mess! It's unlike Ted not to have packed all these documents neatly away; they're all jumbled together. This one folder starts with a rather cringing application for extended leave of absence. His excuse to the bishop was to enter a retreat for three months, but since there was no such place in the country suitable for his purpose, he proposed to emulate Christ in the wilderness. The bishop obviously thought this was an extraordinary idea and plainly said so. Ted set off on horseback with his friend Saul in the direction of the hills to the south-west."

"Do we have a name for these hills, Bernard?"

"We do, Simon. They're now called the Matobo National Park."

Tara took a long slug of brandy and started to read.

Chapter Twenty-Three

"The day after my fiftieth birthday, August 24th, 1902, I started the trip to the caves under the mountains. Happily, Saul kindly agreed to accompany me. He has been the most wonderful servant and friend for all my years in this beautiful country, so I am very pleased that he is coming. He is also a giant of a man and makes up for my skinniness with his muscles. We have bought two horses, a few stores and water containers since we intend to travel light. We are not armed to resist aggressors, merely to shoot for food, and will only take enough silver and cloth to be able to purchase the simplest needs. For the rest we put our trust in The Almighty."

Tara paused to take a short sip of brandy, which she followed with a crinkle of her nose. The men smiled at her, and she continued to read.

"September 15th. We have made good progress towards Bulawayo and have arrived at the northern end of the completed section of the new railway line that I understand will eventually link South Africa with the Victoria Falls and the copper mines to the north. We will try to use the railway extension from Que Que to Bulawayo if the engineers let us, but I am worried about being able to take the horses on the train. Saul has never been on a train, and I had to confess that I had only been on one or two. It is debatable which of us is the more excited at the prospect."

"September 18th. The engineers are very friendly, possibly I put on a little too much of the Irish blarney, but they eventually recognised my origin and they allowed both of us and the horses on the train to Bulawayo. I felt just like a small boy as they allowed me to stand on the footplate. I assume they were pretending when they assured me that I was driving the engine for

a few miles. At least they didn't ask me to shovel the fuel. Saul is very tolerant and allows me my eccentricities: the horses don't mind either way as they're safely locked in the truck at the end of the train."

"September 20th. Arrived in Bulawayo; we were sad to lose the jollity of the train crew, but we didn't want to delay and struck off into the Matopos hills. We have filled the water containers and have enough dried meat and biscuit to feed us both for ten days. Our two horses are in fine fettle, and I am sure will welcome the exercise."

"September 21st. A wonderful day, the air was fresh with an early morning dew which reminded me that the nights at this height above sea level can be quite cold. Saul shot an antelope which we had for supper. It seemed such a shame to take a very small portion of the whole animal with just a little we can carry with us and leave the rest to the hyenas and the vultures. We have seen none of the lions or the rhinos that are supposed to inhabit these hills.

There is still evidence of fighting here on the way to the Matopos. Piles of spent rifle shells and some simple graves litter the hillsides as mute tribute to the continuing folly of the white man to try to rule a country through the gun. Saul had a long talk with a passing herdsman who told him that they were preparing for the burial of Cecil Rhodes on the Malindidzimu, which is the Ndebele name for the place called the View of the World. I hope he, Cecil Rhodes, feels better about his plundering when his spirit looks out to a ravaged land. I continue to be hopeful that the land will recover, the bickering between the tribes will come to an end and the black races will eventually rule with pride and wisdom. I know this is heresy and it will probably take at least a hundred years to come to pass, but I am certain it will."

"September 22nd. It is overcast today, unusual for this time of the year. We are nearly at the ruins of Khami. The ruins, I hope, will give me a clue as to the direction of the caves that Priscilla and I found twelve years ago. The caves I seek contain wonderful pictures of a tribe far older than the

present inhabitants of the country. The tribe was in existence possibly several thousand years ago. The pictures tell the story of the dying of that tribe. Priscilla and I spent many hours recording the pictures by the light of a paraffin lamp. Unfortunately, those pictures are in one of the boxes that have gone back to England. I have been thinking about all the possible caves and must conclude that it is in this cave that I shall find the origin of the curse on our family. We must find that cave and all we have to go on is my visual memory of the area. When we find it, I have a peculiar feeling that we will be safely guided to the right place. I know from previous experience, some of these caves go on for miles into the mountains and are frequently blocked by water or rock falls."

"September 23rd. We have reached Khami. What a dismal place; it is as if the fire that engulfed it nearly ten years ago has only just died. The silence is very strange; where are the animal noises that have accompanied the rest of our travels? We climbed onto the upper platform of the central complex and looked around. I do hope my memory is correct, but I believe we must strike in a north-easterly direction; it is too late to start now so we must make an early start tomorrow."

"September 24th. It is one calendar month since we set out from Salisbury. I have a foreboding that things are going wrong. Saul awoke in the middle of the night having had a frightening dream. He tells me that over two hundred years ago a great many of his family were taken by Arabs to the coast and sold as slaves. He has had these dreams before, he tells me, in which it seems he is being forced to relive the experience of the lost generations. It is a strange experience for me to console an African for his dreams when the very reason that I am here is because of the dreams of my family. Saul was very grateful, and I feel this has cemented our friendship even more. I do not view Saul any more as an employee, more as a companion; he speaks excellent English and has a poetical way with words. When we return to Salisbury, I shall buy him a house so that he can settle down with his wife Miriam and have children. That will go down badly with the bishop."

September 25th. Sadly, we lost a horse in the night. She was suddenly taken by a lion and there was nothing we could do.

September 26th. Found two caves with paintings at the entrances. I have seen these ones before, but they are relatively simple paintings of a successful hunt and are not the ones that I am looking for. It is cheering to see that the paintings were still as bright as the last time I saw them. There is a superb one of a cheetah with striped legs and some of a group of people clearly herding what are probably early cattle. I suspect they are stealing them from another tribe! The people have a splendid array of weapons but strangely no protective armour or shields, perhaps shields are too heavy and unwieldy, and they relied on agility and speed of manoeuvre? Off again, although we are much slower with the one horse. We have abandoned the tent as it is too heavy. Saul and I walk and the horse carries our provisions, bed rolls, paraffin lamps and the cooking pots. Nevertheless, we still travelled about twelve miles.

September 28th. Nothing of note yesterday so no point in putting pen to paper. Today we had a startling rainstorm which literally drove us into a cave. We were pushed up a gully and found a small opening which turned out to be the mouth of a giant cave. It seemed to go on forever. We lit a fire and with the paraffin lamps walked what must have been a mile underground. The paintings were startling in their freshness, and I suspect that no-one has visited this cave for thousands of years. It had stopped raining when we returned to the mouth of the cave, and we camped there for the night. At dawn a very tall, gaunt, old man came near us, studied us for a while in complete silence and then walked away. He had only just gone out of sight when Saul ran after him, but he was nowhere to be seen. Saul accepted this as normal behaviour, but I find it distinctly odd. One meets so few people on these trips that it is usually difficult to get away from their friendliness. We set off again in what, we hope, is the right direction.

September 30th. Yesterday was a disaster. Our remaining horse slipped, and its foot went into a small hole in the rock. There was an awful crack and we discovered that the unfortunate beast had broken its leg. We had to put it out of its misery and then set about discarding everything that was not vitally necessary. We had to keep the lamp with plenty of paraffin and this diary and the ink. The gun is needed for food and matches to light a fire to heat up our one pot. Knives, spoons, and forks for feeding and spare footwear and two water containers complete our kit. We have two compasses and a very simple map, the only one available for the area. We found a comfortable spot for our bedrolls under a great overhang in a strangely curving hillside. Unfortunately, it became windy in the night and the structure of the rock, and the overhang produced a roaring sound which was most eerie. Could this have been the origin of Olive's 'great noise'? It was quite fearsome at times.

We trudged further over a series of identical ridges, maybe ten or twenty of them. It was extremely monotonous. Eventually we found ourselves scrambling through a magnificent rocky pass between hundred-foot vertical walls of smooth rock. Suddenly the view changed and there was a green valley with a sparkling stream winding out of sight, looking strikingly beautiful and strangely out of place. Alarmingly the view was slightly blocked by the most enormous black rhinoceros that was directly in our path. Our pace altered to a determined run in the opposite direction.

Saul stopped, looking puzzled. "This is very strange. They always charge, you can't trust them an inch. We'd be safe with a white rhino. But this one is quite out of character; very strange." However, to be quite safe we gave this magnificent beast a very wide birth and walked partly in the stream to the head of the valley. We saw no crocodiles, but Saul was always on the lookout for them and said he couldn't promise they were not waiting for us. We climbed to the top of the cliff, only a couple of hundred feet, and as the sun went down, we looked around us at the magnificent views. Saul shinned up a huge smooth boulder of the most peculiar greenish violet that changed colour with the dying sun; I presume this was a product of its metallic content. We decided this was the perfect site to bed down for the night.

Tara was tiring and she handed the diary to Melusi.

"October 3rd. I missed the diary yesterday as I was nursing a sore ankle. At the foot of the bluff is a series of cracks in the rock. The stream comes out of one of these and bubbles down the valley to where I hope the black rhino is having a good roll in the mud. We entered one of the cracks and were able to penetrate several hundred yards when we were stopped by a rock fall. There were several animal bones and a few paintings but nothing of note. As we started to explore one of the other cracks, I slipped and twisted my ankle, so Saul made a camp at the base of the bluff, and we had an early night with my foot suspended by a makeshift sling from the branch of a tree. I must have looked very silly and Saul had great difficulty in preventing himself laughing. Today, the ankle is much better; the leaves that Saul bound onto my ankle must have some healing property as there is no swelling at all. I must remember to find out more about them. I feel convinced we will soon find what we are looking for. There are three holes about a third of the way up the cliff face and if my memory serves me right, it was at Priscilla's insistence that we explored these many years ago. We will start with the left hand one.

October 13th. Note the date. What a time we have had. We entered the left-hand hole and when we had crawled along a narrow passage there was a shaft of light coming down from the roof. There must be a split in the mountain or perhaps it was produced by a volcanic blow out. We could see that the light came from a slit about a hundred feet above us. It was a most unnerving experience walking along a dusty track in very dim light. Our footsteps were muffled by all the material that had fallen down the slit over the centuries. There were paintings on the walls of this rock canyon which stretched up thirty or forty feet. We wondered how the artists could have painted them. I can't imagine prehistoric scaffolding. It would have been impossible to manoeuvre pieces of wood longer than ten feet to this point.

We walked more than half a mile along the canyon when we heard the sound of water. Ahead of us was a stream flowing from one side of the canyon to the other. Both the entrance and exit of the stream were tunnels some thirty feet across and twenty feet high, all below the level of our path. We thought there must have been a substantial river at some time in the past as the flow only filled about one per cent of the tunnel. We climbed down, took off our shoes and socks, paddled through the stream and climbed up the other side. At the level of the stream the tunnels on either side reverberated to the sound of our voices in a curious fashion, as if there was a distorted echo from somewhere in the distance. I had to confess that I had no memory of these tunnels.

We walked a further half a mile in the dim light which was making it increasingly difficult to see and we were considering whether to light our precious paraffin lamp when we heard a tremendous rushing noise which became louder and louder. It was coming from behind us, so we retraced out steps back to the stream which we were horrified to see was now a raging torrent, quite impossible to cross. So, either we waited until the water fell or we tried to find another exit. We did not fancy the idea of simply waiting. As Saul put it, "If someone has pulled out the plug, we don't know how much water there was in the bath." So, we followed our original route and went further into the mountain. After another two hours of struggling along the narrowing canyon, daylight was fading outside, and we decided to wait for the dawn. We had enough food and water for a few days so there was no cause for alarm.

We awoke early just as the first dim light appeared above us, ate some dried meat and a biscuit, drank some of our water and set off again. For six days we walked, sometimes falling over piles of sticks, or clambering over rock falls. Always there was the dim light from the top of the canyon which just revealed countless thousands of the paintings. This gave us hope that the end was in sight. At last, there was a light at about our level. We stumbled towards it and looked out of a hole about three feet across.

Imagine our surprise when the first thing we saw was our last campsite and the tree from which my foot had been suspended. Our laughter matched our relief and must have been heard for miles around. After eight days we had walked I don't know how many miles underground in a gigantic circular route to emerge precisely thirty feet from our starting point. One conclusion had to be that the mountain was peppered with such cracks and holes. There was just one more hole, the one on the extreme right that we had yet to explore, but not today. We decided to have a few days' rest and try the third hole when we felt refreshed.

Saul shot another antelope, and we had a splendid meal by our campfire. We talked far into the night. Neither of us had ever heard of such a canyon nor of the mysterious river. Strangely, there was no evidence of such a huge volume of water on the surface so it must be underground, but where? The entrance to the cave that became the cavern was at least fifty feet above the valley floor and we did not think that our path had pointed downwards to any appreciable extent; therefore, the mighty river should be just below the surface of the plain. This was another puzzle to add to the others.

October 20th. A long rest in preparation for exploring what surely must be the cave that we are seeking. We awoke before dawn and had reached the level of the caves as the sun rose over the middle mountain in the distance. We climbed across and entered the right-hand hole in the cliff face. Imagine our relief when we found that not more than twenty feet into the cave it opened out into an enormous cavern which was brightly lit by the dawn sun. On the opposite wall from the entrance were paintings the likes of which Saul had not seen before. It was, indeed, the cave that Priscilla and I had started to explore for about four hundred yards into the mountain until our paraffin lamp started to sputter.

This time we had prepared ourselves in a much more thorough manner in case we were caught in another water trap. We had a good supply of food and water with plenty of paraffin and ropes. We reached the point where Priscilla and I had to give up and continued a relatively smooth floor for a further half a mile with the aid of the lamp. At that point the cave opened out into another cavern with yet more paintings. At this stage I began to appreciate that the paintings were telling a story. Starting at the entrance to the cave the paintings attempted to represent a tribe of paler colour typical of the hunter-gatherer type of people who inhabited this country many thousands of years. They were presumably of Hamitic or even pre-hamitic origin. After a beautiful introduction with paintings of stick people at play, the story changed to tell of a high mortality as a great number of the people were horizontal, piled high in great heaps. But in contrast to the pictorials in other caves in the area the bodies were not being devoured by wild beasts. Was this an early form of mummification or were the bodies objectionable to animals? A third alternative could be that the tribe had no idea why the bodies did not disintegrate. Subsequent pictures showed fewer and fewer people were still alive. There were, however, huge piles of the perhaps-mummified dead. There was eventually a tribal meeting to which several members of a darker tribe were invited, presumably as honoured guests.

Saul suggests that the next pictures represent a great sexual fling of the paler tribe with some of the girls of the darker tribe. He also interprets subsequent pictures to indicate that the paler tribe die out completely and the ochre dot on the now predominant darker tribe represents the fact that they have an element of the hereditary material of the paler tribe. I confess that it is all rather startling, but it sounds a reasonable explanation, and I can't think of a better one.

There is a sudden change of style after another fifty yards with paintings which are much more quickly drawn or painted. There are pictures of what one must assume represent the beginnings of the slave trade. The bad men are obviously the ones painted in pink with beards and guns. The captives are all very dark and unhappy as judged by their bent shoulders and gloomy faces. The forked sticks at their necks and their chained feet and hands emphasise the purgatory they went through. Saul was greatly affected by these paintings, and I have great sympathy for him. However, all the sympathy in the world does not make up for the horror.

We walked on a little further and Saul pointed out a startling picture in which a girl was being sexually attacked by one of the pink people. The next picture could only be compared with a painting of the apocalypse by

William Blake that I saw in the National Gallery in London when I was a boy. The girl from the last picture has gold on her head, golden bangles round her wrists and round her ankles. She was painted much larger than the pink man and she was pointing at him and hundreds of other pink people, both male and female, all naked and in torment. From the ends of her fingers were painted red lines which seemed to be eating them up. Was this Tandeka Thembani? Was this the girl who was raped by a slaver? If the rape was such an insult to her and to the tribe, who was the slaver and what dreadful fate would he and his offspring suffer?

This last painting seemed to be the climax to the story and there was little else to be found in the cave apart from the bats which are, unusually, far from the entrance. We went on for another half a mile as the temperature became warmer. It was also very dry and the odd rodent that had fallen in through the cracks in the roof had not disintegrated but shrivelled and was so well-preserved that it was impossible to tell how many years ago it had died. We had found what we came for but were not sure what to do with the information, so as we mulled over our thoughts, we made rather a silent pair as we returned to the mouth of the cave. That evening by the fire we talked late into the night. Saul was certain that the queen or princess, whichever she was, had laid a curse on the slavers. He also thought that it was possible that the curse had been given to her tribe from the paler tribe in the first series of pictures. Otherwise, what was the point of that first series of pictures?

I listened to everything Saul said with my mind in torment. Could it be that these cave paintings were the story of the origin of our family curse? It all seems to be so far-fetched. Saul was still talking when we both became aware of the same tall, gaunt man standing at the edge of the clearing. Saul stopped in mid-sentence and stood up. The old man, for he was old, very old, probably the oldest man I have ever seen, motioned Saul to sit down. The old man moved over to the fire and sat down with us. He spoke in a voice so soft I could only just detect he was speaking. Saul strained to listen and whispered to me, "I can understand him."

The old man looked straight at me. His eyes were so dark that it was like looking into the abyss. He said some words to me, stood up, and glided away. Many Africans walk with one foot in front of the other as if they are following a narrow trail. This makes for a beautiful, gliding motion. The old man's walk was indeed smooth, so smooth that his feet did not appear to touch the ground. I started to get up, but Saul stopped me.

He says he has left something for you at the end of the cave. It will be there for three days, and you must go alone. I asked Saul who he was, how the old man knew who we were and why I had to go alone. Apparently, the old man just said, "There is only one man who will go into the cave without fear." He would not say any more.

October 27th. I could not go the day after seeing the old man. I have no idea why. Something prevented me. I hope it was not laziness and I don't believe it was fear. I never like to admit that I am tired, but by golly I was. The next day I set off alone with enough paraffin and provisions for three days, in case of disaster. I told Saul to come after me if I had not appeared after five days, as by then I would be short of water and food.

Dawn broke with brilliant sunshine as I entered the cave beyond the entrance. It seemed even more brightly lit than two days ago. The first paintings glowed, and the little stick people seemed to be alive. Even the piles of the dead had a glow about them. My imagination was playing tricks and I had to be careful as I followed the gruesome story again until the princess was cursing the pink people. It was at this stage that I began to feel that something had altered. I could not put my finger on the feeling, but it had no menace and I walked on. Eventually I came to the point where Saul and I had given up. I had until then imagined his ever-cheerful presence was with me in spirit. As I stepped further on, I realised I was on my own, further into the depths of the mountain. The cave paintings became few and far between. Some of the paintings undoubtedly pre-dated all those towards the entrance; they were tens of thousands of years old. There were smoke marks on the roof of the cave and the animals were like nothing I have ever seen or even read about in books. They were very old indeed. They resembled the ones recently discovered in the south of France.

I entered another huge cavern, so high that the light from my feeble lamp did not reach the roof. The sides of the cavern were smooth and had a wonderful gentle curve to them as if a great river had swept out this hole millions of years ago. As I dislodged a stone a great echo rang down the cavern. I shall never know why, but I tried out the trick we used to do as children in the dome of Saint Paul's in London. I whispered. "Anyone there?" I heard a definite laugh, a smiling laugh, a friendly laugh, so I had no fear. I walked into the middle of the cavern, forgetting to use the rope to guide myself back. The cavern was far larger than the previous ones. Unfortunately, after a few hundred yards I lost my sense of direction. I whispered again but since I was not near the wall it did not carry, and I had no reply. I sat down to think. The compass, of course, I had a compass! I pointed myself to walk due north and set off again. After a while I came to the end of the cavern. The floor was now sand-covered, and I thought I could see footprints into one of the entrances, or exits, to the cavern. Still going north, I followed the footprints for what seemed like ages until I entered what must have been a man-made room cut out of the solid rock many thousands of years ago. They would have had to use wooden wedges which then expand with water to split the rock. The splinters of the rock could still be seen in the dry dust of the floor. The wooden wedges should have disintegrated long ago. There were objects in the dust, but they fell to dust in my fingers. Was it my imagination or were they the remnants of the wedges?

In the middle of the room was a stone table and on the table was a roll of what looked like parchment or vellum of a soft beige colour. So, the old man had kept his word. Could I have doubted that he would? I said out loud. "Thank you, old man". There was a movement of air behind me. I turned around and for a fraction of a second there was something or somebody that left behind a smile in very old lips which in turn vanished. I picked up the scroll and put it under my arm without examining it, picked up my lamp and started the long trail back. I reached the giant cavern and tried to retrace my route across it using the compass and heading due south. I came up to a blank wall. Which way should I go? I sat down and put out the light to think. At once I could hear breathing. My hair stood on end until I realised that I was playing just the same trick as I had done before. It was the sound of my own breathing that had travelled round the cavern back to me. I then made the great mistake of laughing. The noise was incredible and did not die away for a good three minutes.

The rational brain is a wonderful thing and after a while I thought along the following lines. I am right-handed; thus, my right side should be stronger and my right leg longer. Therefore, any journey in the dark would naturally tend to veer to the left. So, to compensate for the error I should be able to find the entrance to the tunnel by facing the wall of the cavern and edging to the right. So, I lit the lamp and, slowly keeping the wall of the cave in sight, I walked to the right. So clever of me, I thought, as I quickly came upon an exit, and I gratefully started down it. I had not walked for more than a few yards when I sensed someone behind me, and I turned around. There was no mistaking the old man with his staff and his black eyes. He smiled in a tolerant fashion as if to an erring child and pointed with his stick further along the wall of the cavern. Indeed, there were two openings quite close together. I had not noticed the second one. I turned to thank him, and he said quite clearly in English. "You will need me again; I shall be in the valley for one hundred years." Then he glided away into the darkness. When I say he spoke clearly, I would like to record that I use the word 'spoke' because I can think of no other. Although his mouth was slightly open his lips did not move. My interpretation is that he was using telepathy for which, perhaps, language is not necessary.

I walked until I could walk no more, so I lay down and slept. It took until today for me to reach the last sun-lit cavern close to the entrance to the cave. I entered it just as a petrified Saul was coming in from the mouth of the cave. We fell into each other's arms with relief. I had been in the cave for five days.

November 5th. For seven days we stayed and rested at that site at the top of the valley. Most of the time we just slept and ate and wandered over the hills, marvelling at such a little jewel existing in that part of the country. We examined the vellum scroll and there indeed was our princess, poor girl. She had been mated, for want of a better word, with a person whose initials were J H. With a little imagination the further two letters of the surname could have been 'aw'. The only slaver that we knew with the initials J H is John Hawkins, but how this relates to our family I do not know. Can it possibly be the case that the rape of a princess in the sixteenth century was enough of a tribal insult to set such a major curse on its dreadful journey? Can this curse hang over a blood line whose descendants must have had an ever-decreasing amount of the original hereditary material? These are all questions that come to mind and questions that I am increasingly minded to dismiss. I shall write to Olive and try to reassure her that whatever the rights or wrongs of the family curse I believe that it will not affect us in our lifetime, or in those of our children, nor our children's children. The best person to study the vellum scroll is probably Olive's daughter; she is practical and has lots of energy. If she can make neither head nor tail of it then she had better hand it on to the next generation so that before the hundred years is up, we may have an answer."

Simon interrupted Melusi. "We must therefore assume that Ted considered that despite the fear that the curse had produced over a great many generations, this fear had fed on itself, and the curse was extraordinarily unlikely to become active. I sincerely hope he thought so, otherwise his subsequent inactivity is peculiar. It is easy with hindsight, of course, but our problem about that conclusion is that we have one death under very mysterious circumstances. We also have some still very sick people with, as I understand it, no proper diagnosis and I would point out that the hundred years is almost up, and we are no further towards a cure. I can see no alternative but to seek out this cave and the old man to have any hope of finding a cure.

Interesting, the description of the lines of red coming from the fingers of Tandeka Thembani I wonder if that is relevant. Could those lines represent the rashes? Shall I read the rest?"

Melusi, exhausted, handed the diary to Simon.

"It must be November 5th still."

"We started to pack up our, by now, small bundle of belongings and, with a compass bearing north-east, we headed for Bulawayo. The engineers recognised us and allowed us to take the inspection train to the end of the construction at Gstooma. They asked after the horses and when we told them what had happened, they were very sad. We now had only about ninety miles to go.

"November 11th. We decided that we would walk back to Salisbury to give ourselves time to think over the adventures of the past few weeks. The journey took us six days, mainly walking at night by the stars, as it would have been much too hot during the day. At times we walked along the track prepared to take the railway, but it was often easier to walk along the old animal trails. Each morning, we found a friendly farmer, and Saul negotiated with them for somewhere to rest for most of the day. The farmers were most surprised that a tall white man wished to sleep in a barn. We fed well with dried meat, maize porridge and papaya or mangoes. We drank milk still warm from the cow and walked and talked the nights through. It was a wonderful spiritually satisfying experience.

Saul hesitates to agree with me about the curse. He is full of foreboding that one day before the hundred years is up it will begin to take effect. I suppose I shall have to tell Olive this but not just yet. Saul is convinced that the old man is friendly. If left to his own devices, he would abandon the curse. But Saul also thinks there may be other forces at work that are outside the control of the old man. However, I see little point in going back to the cave again. After all, what is there to do? The only possible next move would be for a member of the family in the blood line to go to the cave and tackle the old man to see how it is possible to lift the curse and stop the family worrying about it.

November 12th. We are on our way back to Salisbury. The bishop seems rather quiet about my journey. We were pleasantly greeted on our return; not asked too many questions. Rather a pity, as I am dying to tell our story to someone. We just seem to slot into the old routine without so much as a murmur. I must write to Olive and reassure her that there is no need to be concerned about the curse for the foreseeable future.

"November 20th. Saul now has a new house; Miriam and he are very happy and have invited me and my housekeeper, Hilary Beadle, to a party tomorrow. It should be fun. Hilary is making a present for them. The bishop collared me today and much to my surprise asked me all about our 'little trip'. He was equally surprised that we were going to a party in the house of a servant. I gave him merely the outline of the story including some of the details from my diary, omitting my comments about him. I was most pleased by his interest and, I am ashamed to say, flattered by his seriousness. He considers that I should take the matter much more seriously and has offered the full weight and majesty of the church to help me. He was therefore not particularly pleased when I declined his help and the help of the church. I do not think that he is personally offended but there was a certain tension in the air. However, it can't be that bad as he has asked Hilary and me to dine in a week's time. The bishop's wife is an excellent cook, and we are looking forward to the evening. We have decided that there will be no mention of my trip in the diocese."

"There the diary ends," said Simon. "It seems to end on such an ordinary note. I can now understand why it had been put about that Ted did not want to talk about his 'little trip' as he called it. I can imagine that it might have been an embarrassment to the bishop to have one of his colleagues rushing off into the bush to uncover a primeval curse. I am also a trifle suspicious about the binding of the diary, there is a loose feel to it at the end, as if a section has been carefully detached and either discarded or put elsewhere. It is as if this diary is the one for public consumption. That is yet another puzzle."

"Is there anything else of interest in the last box?" asked Bernard.

Tara rummaged amongst the pieces of paper at the bottom of the box. "Not a lot, just a few loose ends. I think I'd better try and put these in some sort of order tomorrow."

Chapter Twenty-Four

The morning of Wednesday 2nd of August dawned bright and clear. Yet another sunny day with not a hint of rain to break what was being predicted as the worst drought for many years. The four came downstairs rather sleepily to the breakfast which Hobson had laid on the veranda.

"Morning all, another warm one," said Bernard with a yawn.

Hobson appeared with the telephone.

"It's Uncle asking for Bernard. He sounds rather upset."

"Good morning, Uncle, what can I do for you?"

"Bernard, I am worried about my patients. There is no improvement in their rashes which are gradually spreading and becoming indurated. That means the centres of the rashes are becoming harder as if the skin is thickening. Also, the colour of their skin is changing to a darker hue. Both women are having awful dreams every night and even during the afternoons if they are lucky enough to drop off. The trouble is that they're both exhausted. I would like to give them something to help them sleep. So far, they have, not unreasonably I have to confess, refused to have any pills, since as soon as they are asleep, they dream. It's a Catch 22. Samuel's condition is worse. In fact, his systems are showing signs of collapse. His kidneys are gradually packing up and his blood urea is rising. We'll be able to keep him going on dialysis for a long time, but I'm not prepared to subject him to that if there is no hope of a cure soon. Sorry, Bernard, but the pressure is on us all.

"The dermatologist in Plymouth tells me that Laurie Prendergast is also getting worse but, as Melusi predicted, Nigel Mason's condition is static. The dermatologist even has a suspicion that Nigel is recovering. Incidentally he was certain that Nigel wouldn't mind if a small biopsy was taken from a part of the rash as long as it didn't interfere with his job. In fact, the dermatologist volunteered to take one for us, so Melusi need not drive down."

Bernard thought for a little while before he replied. "We are booking a flight to Africa for Monday 7 August." Tara looked up quickly, but Bernard put his finger to his lips, and she said nothing. "That is if we can't fly earlier. Simon is coming with us to give us moral support."

"I wish I could come as well, but all my clinics are full to bursting and I should stay here anyway to see if there is anything I can remotely do for our patients. Take my blessing with you and please telephone me if you find any hint of a clue to help me treat them."

"Certainly, we will. Thank you for the blessing." Bernard put the phone back on the receiver. "Well, Tara, did that sound confident?"

"To a limited extent, Bernard. Obviously, I have homework to do. It might even be easier to hire a plane and fly the thing myself. I had a pilot's licence a few years ago."

"Now don't be upset. We must hurry and the quicker we find this cave and the old man the better. Remember that our directions are sketchy to say the least."

"It is now my turn to surprise you all." Tara couldn't keep the excitement out of her voice.

"I can guess the nature of the surprise," said Simon.

"All right, you tell me."

"Might it have something to do with Saul, perhaps?"

"That's not fair, how on earth did you work that one out?"

"Male intuition; it does exist, you know."

"You're not supposed to have any. Yes, as a matter of fact, the driver's name is Elijah. He is Saul's grandson and he's all fired up to repay the generosity of Great Uncle Ted."

"Coincidence? If I were a betting man; but I'm not. How did you find out the relationship?"

"Simple. The name of the driver rang a bell, Simon, and I asked him direct. He didn't think it was at all peculiar."

"Hum, interesting! What do you think, Bernard? Are we being led by the nose into something awkward?"

"No idea, Simon. I rather like the idea. Not about being led by the nose. If it is a coincidence, I'm all for it. I still think you're wonderful, Tara."

"Say it again, Bernard."

"You're wonderful, Tara."

Tara tried to keep her telephone voice calm. "I am absolutely certain that is exactly what I want. It is vital that all four passengers have their flights changed to early Saturday morning the fifth of August. I realise that early means very early, seven o'clock and they have to check in an hour and a half before that."

She waited for the response and smiled.

"To hell with the extra costs; just do it, please. And send me the receipts and tickets and anything else you can think of, by courier."

She breathed a sigh of relief.

"Now for the hotel at Heathrow with an early dinner and decent, quiet rooms. At least we can get a few hours' sleep. Next step is Zimbabwe Airlines to book a connecting flight from Harare to Bulawayo. I hope they are on the ball for speed. Saul's grandson can meet us there."

Melusi came into Tara's office. "Have you ordered decent trekking kit for us all?"

"Of course, I have. Oh Lord, here comes Bernard fussing about something."

"Tara!"

"That's ominous; Bernard's tone of voice usually foreshadows a whole evening's work."

"We arrive in Harare at, say, seven o'clock in the evening. When is the connecting flight to Bulawayo?"

"I've booked seats both on the nine o'clock plane that evening and the seven o'clock plane the next morning. Elijah will meet both planes. It's only an hour or so to Bulawayo."

"Good work. So, we may be camped at the cave entrance before sundown on Monday 7th August. Has Elijah explored the area before?"

"Don't worry, Bernard, he knows it like the back of his hand. It's become part of the family tradition that they must be ready at any time to help Ted's family."

"Well done, Tara. Now as to the return journey, what arrangements have you made for that?"

"There are two flights a day from Bulawayo to Harare and a daily service from Harare to London. There are always plenty of seats at this time of year and there should be no need to book. Which day do you hope to fly back, Bernard?"

"I plan to fly back to England on Thursday the tenth if everything goes our way and back home that night."

"I will make sure the magic carpet is capable of flying us anywhere, any time. How does that sound?"

"Perfect!"

The taxi journey to Heathrow, the night or as much of it as they were able to sleep, and the flight to Harare, went like clockwork. Tara's organisation had been meticulous, and they arrived at Harare airport as the sun was sinking with tropical speed below the horizon.

As the four released their seatbelts, the air was pierced by a shriek. "Found them!" The two words had been uttered by a tall woman of about twenty-five. She wore a crimson bow in her hair and her smile reached from ear to ear to reveal the whitest teeth and a bubbling laugh.

"Don't be frightened, I'm Elijah's sister; he sent me to make quite certain the plane transfer was OK. My name is Dia, which Elijah says means daft. I will leave the interpretation to your better judgement! Welcome to Harare, to Zimbabwe, the most beautiful country in the world, a bit dry now but we'll survive. If you are happy with your stay you will have to come back. We would also like your foreign currency. By the way, my job here is immigration. Like the uniform?"

This last statement related to the bright suit Dia was wearing which they had presumed was that of a very important person. Dia took a casual look at their passports and took them in tow.

Melusi's pulse shot up the scale. "She's quite something!"

"Wow, so that's the opposition," whispered Tara.

Dia's hearing was sharp as a razor. She turned to Tara and said so softly that the others couldn't hear, "Don't worry, our family know everything, or almost everything, about the curse, the sick people, Ellie's death and why you four are here. We all want to do everything in our power to help you. The curse is on the way out. But that dishy young man, he is yours, if you love him."

"How can you be so sure and how can you sort us all out so quickly?"

"Sixth sense and a glance or two is all I need." Dia flashed another brilliant smile as she chivvied them onto the connecting plane. "I have to make the trip to Bulawayo today to do some business, so I'll be joining this plane in a few minutes."

The short flight between Harare and Bulawayo was over quickly. They had not talked much but Bernard noticed that Simon was looking morose. He had become gloomier as the travel arrangements had been successfully completed. During the flight he declared to Dia, "It's all too slick and quick; it has to go terribly wrong, and we have to be prepared for it."

Simon turned to the others. "I want to discuss my thoughts with you. I trust you accept that I have another sense, call it sixth or even seventh sense about the way to achieve what we have come here to do."

Heads nodded and they wondered what Simon was about to propose.

"We have travelled several thousand miles to attempt to remove a family curse which must have been in existence, as far as we can guess, for over four hundred and fifty years. And we are attempting to neutralise one of the oldest tribal curse memories still in existence. We are attempting to do this in just four days. You could well say that we might be accused of being impatient, at the very least. The urgency lies in the occupants of several hospital beds in England; we know nothing about other countries. I believe that when we are called upon to act there may be times when we must act very quickly indeed. Are you with me?"

Bernard, Tara and Melusi were puzzled by Simon's speech, but they all nodded. Dia was silent but was on the same wavelength.

"Now listen carefully. I hope what I have to say will not be interpreted as the vivid imagination of an old man, but it is very simple. Times of great stress logically need instant action, but we have a thin veneer of what we curiously call civilisation, and this tends to slow our innate protective responses. I rarely shout, but if I do so you will act as your honourable instincts tell you to do at that second. Instant action is what will be needed but wait for my command. Is that clearly understood?"

Bernard butted in. "Surely Elijah should be party to your last order. I have not met him, but I am sure he'll agree. Do you think he would, Dia?"

"Oh, yes, he has been looking forward to this trip for a very long time. He'll be on side, Simon."

"Thank you, Dia."

The plane landed at Bulawayo airport where a particularly belligerent official seemed to take great pleasure in holding them up with minor quibbles about their documentation. Dia was eyeing him with disgust. He was becoming intolerable when a huge beaming extrovert, very like his sister, charged into the room like a whirlwind. Elijah hugged Bernard, Simon, Melusi and Tara, spending slightly longer with her than with the others.

Elijah ignored the official. "Wonderful, after all these years, we can at last repay Ted. Did you have a good flight? How are you all?" The questions poured out of him like a flood, giving them no time to answer. He turned to the official. "Belt up, Mosa, why are you so bloody difficult. These are friends of mine."

"So, I see. I must do my job properly and check all unusual groups of people. Everyone knows why they're here. They are here to destroy something very precious to all of us; something that has been with us for thousands of years."

"You always did talk rubbish. Live in the present and don't be obsessed with the past. Anyway, I'm sure this is the first time you've heard of it. You knew nothing of Edward Longstaff until you read about him in the local paper. All he did for this country, so back off. Are their papers in order or not? If they're not, then blame me as I filled them in and verified them."

The travellers did not appreciate what had been going on as the two had been talking in hushed voices. But now the voices were being raised and they realised Elijah was as cross as hell. Eventually Mosa grudgingly agreed that their papers were in order and Elijah could take them off in his truck. They loaded the cases, said good-bye to an unusually pensive Dia, and like his biblical namesake, Elijah drove them away in a cloud of dust into the dark. Dia stood still and watched Mosa for a while. He whispered something to a colleague, packed up his books into a briefcase and went quietly off through a door marked 'Private: Staff Only'. Dia went to the airport exit road, took off her official hat and jacket, sat down and chatted with the usual crowd of people waiting for the next plane.

"OK, folks we're off to the hills." Elijah was enjoying himself.

"We're setting off tonight?" Melusi was surprised. "In the dark?"

"Don't worry, only some of the way. We are going to a sort of safari motel for the night at Matobo. Then tomorrow we find the cave which is not far from there. It will be a difficult drive and this tank may have to be winched occasionally up the odd riverbank. No-one has been to the caves for years and we may have a little trouble finding somewhere to camp. By the way, no open fresh fruit please, elephants can smell it a mile off and they are very nosy."

When they arrived at the motel Bernard introduced them all in a rather formal fashion. Tara's expectations of Elijah were confirmed as he courteously kissed her hand with one beady eye on Melusi, who was unsure whether to smile or scowl. Elijah was instantly serious when he welcomed Simon.

"We will certainly need your help."

It quickly became obvious that Elijah knew every detail about the travellers. Tara had spent many hours on the telephone telling Elijah about the cases in hospital and their rashes. Elijah was already fully aware of Ellie's death and the mystery surrounding it. He had already suspected that Ellie's death may have had something to do with Ted's family curse.

Chapter Twenty-Five

The night at the safari motel was such tremendous fun that they almost forgot why they were there. Elijah was the life and soul of the party and even Melusi fell for his cheerfulness. They ate and drank well and, in the moonlight, saw the white rhinos and other more delicate animals down by the water hole.

They were tired and ready for bed when Elijah dampened their spirits somewhat. "We get up at four o'clock sharp in the morning and we breakfast at a quarter past. I plan to be on the road at a quarter to five so you must have used the loo by that time, as we leave on the dot. I hope we'll reach the mouth of the cave by six o'clock in the evening. There we pitch tents and, in the morning, wait for our friend to arrive. By the way, there are no guns on board. I have a licence, but I've made sure there were no guns in the truck and no sign of them. It is wiser that way, there are far too many of them loose in this country. If we need armaments we have to rely on the countryside, the sticks and stones that we pick up as we move around."

The next morning, they had their marching orders, and the party was dutifully waiting at the front of the motel at exactly 4.45 in the morning on Monday 7 August. They were a day behind Bernard's schedule, but they thought that they had done well. Elijah drove up at his usual speed and they all piled in with their luggage and extra rations. Elijah had boxes up to, and on, the roof of the truck, filled with food, torches, tents and every conceivable item that might be needed. Five miles along the A7 he veered left onto a dust track.

Tara surveyed the scene with wonder.

"Where did those strange rocky outcrops come from, how did they get there?"

She pointed to unusual piles of smooth black rocks that looked as if they had been stacked by a giant hand.

"They're called kopjes and they are unique to this area of the dry bushveld," said Melusi.

"Oh look, Elijah, there's a pair of tiny animals, only about eighteen inches high. And what tiny little feet, they look as if they're dancing on tiptoe."

"They're tawny short-horned antelopes, very common around here. The unusual delicate gait helps them keep their balance on the slippery rocks as the dew comes down overnight. The local name is klipsingers. Now, if you look in the distance you can see a small herd of wildebeest. They're not interested in us, just wary of the lions following behind the truck." He laughed as Tara turned around in panic. "A joke!"

"You beast!"

After a while they came to a waterhole and a herd of elephants could be seen in the distance, followed by the excitement of two adult giraffes with a newly born baby.

"Isn't he beautiful, Melusi?"

So, this is the chosen country of the man I love. I like it, there's room for everyone and, apart from the airport bureaucrat, they've all been nice. It has a good feeling about it, and I don't feel threatened.

They passed another herd of wildebeest and saw three hyenas, chancing their luck. The hills were now capped by much larger groups of the smooth granite stones in strange piles, in contrast to those of the plain. These piles looked as if a breath of wind would blow them over, they were so precariously balanced. Rounding one pile of these stones, the travellers came face-to-face with an elegant group of grazing sable antelopes. They were almost black, less than three feet high; they looked such a complete scene that photographs had to be taken. The first few hills were crossed with relative ease but as they went further from the track beaten by the tourists, they found the going harder.

"Compass bearings are a bit more difficult off-piste; got to concentrate. Don't worry folks, I've done this journey a few times, just as my father and Grandfather Saul did. We have been waiting for you to come and I am the lucky one, so you are certainly going to get to the cave. Now I switch to a satellite compass bearing. Remember your Uncle Ted and my grandfather both talked about the three mountain tops, the mine that could be seen from the top of the cliff and the morning sun comes up over the middle mountain. Don't worry, I know the way."

Elijah was a happy man and entertained them all singing a haunting song that his family had known for many generations. They came to a dried-up riverbed and Elijah drove along it for a mile to find a place on the further bank that was easily driveable.

"Don't think much of this; it looks as if the last flood washed away my landing place." He turned the truck round and got out onto the riverbed. "Now you will witness one of the marvels of modern technology. Everybody out! See that tree, Melusi, about ten yards back from the top of the bank. Take this sacking and tie it to the base of the tree and I'll bring up the winch cable."

Melusi did as he was told and looked down as Elijah turned around the truck and backed it as near as possible to the bank by the base of the tree. Elijah struggled up with the cable and he and Melusi attached it to the tree.

"Don't anyone try to help push the truck," Elijah called as he scrambled down again. "Stay well clear. The truck weighs well over a ton and any effort you can produce is so piffling it's not worth the risk. If it falls on you, you've had it, but if the tree is pulled over, we just start again." He engaged the winch and gradually the truck pulled itself up the incline and onto the flat ground by the tree.

"Why did you use sacking on the tree?" asked Tara. "The cable would have bitten deeper into the tree if you had just tied it round."

"Practically, we may need that tree again. But apart from that, you should not needlessly harm even a tree." Elijah was so serious that Tara was at a loss for words. She wondered what Melusi thought about Elijah's statement, but he was too busy studying the winch to take much interest in anything else. "I've done this a few times before but not with such an efficient vehicle."

Bernard put an arm round Elijah. "It's yours if all goes well. It wouldn't be much use to us back home." It was the only time Elijah had been at a loss for words. His eyes filled with tears, and he hugged Bernard, unable to speak.

Elijah engaged the winch and slowly the heavy truck reached the top of the bank. They freed the tree of its burden and drove off. After a while he started to sing again. This time it was a fierce, joyful song, a song of a successful warrior. A mile further on they came to a narrow gorge between the smooth granite cliffs. "This journey is a damned sight easier on foot, but I have done it once before in a truck. Thank goodness for tough springs!" Elijah had to shout as they crashed from rock to rock.

At one stage they had to use the forward winch since the truck was stuck in a gully. Eventually they came to the top of the pass and the going was all downhill. It was here that they understood why Elijah had insisted on the steel bars on the sides of the truck. They lurched from side to side, the bars striking sparks from the rocks as they screeched and squirmed their way down to the valley where they stopped for a rest.

"It's quiet here, Elijah?" Tara sounded puzzled by the calm after all their horrendous noise. "What's happened to all the animal noises?"

"This valley is always quiet. Saul noticed it all those years ago. There's a wonderful peace here. It is a place not touched in any way by our modern civilisation; no tourists are allowed here. People only come here when they have some great problem to solve, or when they need to be alone. It is a strange place, a place with great power to heal the mind or the soul. If you are clever enough to define the difference between the two. It used to be called the Valley of the Gods a thousand years ago. But you must be warned, those who come here bent on mischief do not leave the valley.

"Officially the cave shrines are out of bounds to tourists. As it happens, I won't be taking you to any, so there's no worry about offending the locals." His gentle, deep eyes turned on the travellers, assessing the motives of each one in turn. Satisfied, he turned and walked away from them and sat down on a rock some fifty yards away.

"Do you think we have passed Elijah's test, Simon?" Melusi muttered.

"I believe we have." Simon seemed to understand Elijah. "Elijah has temporarily taken on the mantle of the Guardian of the Valley, and he is not prepared to tolerate sensation seekers. This valley is too precious to be messed about by those with sticky fingers; the pillage by the earlier white settlers is still a too-recent memory in places like the ruins of Great Zimbabwe. It is now extremely difficult for archaeologists to discover local history, which goes back for many more centuries than European cultures in these sites. The greedy gold hunters destroyed far too much. Primitive greed, I guess, but unlike the Spaniards in South America, those who stole from Africa came back with very little and usually accompanied their thievings in a coffin. Serve them right!" He was pleased with his little joke.

The valley they had entered was well-wooded with lush vegetation. A few overhanging branches had to be removed to allow the truck to make progress until eventually they found they were by a stream which flowed down the middle of the valley to the plain below. The stream flowed clear with a flat bottom and Elijah steered the truck upstream.

Bernard was feeling upbeat. "I now see why you wanted to take the exhaust pipe up to the roof. You think of everything, Elijah. Does this thing sprout wings?"

"I'm sure that could be arranged for you, Bernard. No-one I know has driven up this river before. On foot it's much easier to follow the line of the bottom of the cliff. But we must get to the top of the river at the point where it comes out of the cliff so we can camp. We could stop here and walk the rest, it's about a mile. But since we can, we'll do it in comfort. Now folks, if the truck comes to a grinding halt, don't get out and wade to the bank. Wait until I've checked the area for crocodiles first. That's not a joke, Tara." She smiled.

Elijah and his truck splashed their way with not too much difficulty through the water, until rounding a bend in the stream they came face-to-face with a very big black rhino.

"Good heavens!" Bernard said to nobody. "I wonder if he is the same one as frightened Ted and Saul?"

"They live a long time, but not that long. You're lucky to see this one; sadly, they're being poached out of existence. The poachers are even taking the ones in the Ngorongoro crater in Tanzania. Let's hope he's as placid as the one Saul met." Elijah calmly pressed the horn. The noise echoed round the valley, frightening the egrets that had been picking grubs off the back of the rhino. The rhino started to paw the ground in anger, but then its eyes looked upwards.

"Now that is very unusual," said Elijah. "This great big animal has notoriously bad eyesight. It's looking down again; very strange! Now we have a wonderful view of his huge back end just to show what he thinks of us!"

"I have a feeling," Simon remarked, "that this unusually well-behaved black rhino is a sign that the old man is somewhere near, and we should be seeing him within the next few days."

A few more bends in the stream and they came to the cliff face. Just as Ted had written in his diary, there was enough flat grass to camp at the base of the cliff. The stream bubbled out of a narrow hole in the rock into a deep pool from whence it flowed down the way they had come. The truck skirted the pool and there was enough room to leave it on dry land with plenty of flat grass to pitch their tents. The cliff was steep with a series of ledges that could be used as a way up to the three cave entrances that were visible fifty feet from the valley floor.

"One, two and three," Bernard counted, looking at the holes above him. "We're here at last. You are quite right Elijah. This place really is calm and beautiful. We have arrived in superb time, six o'clock on Monday seventh of August, spot on! Just look at the light from that tropical sun as it rushes down to the horizon. And there's another beautiful animal." He pointed to the sky above them as a black eagle disturbed by the noise of the strange machine flew off without a sound. It soared silently overhead, waiting for the disturbance to finish.

"Isn't he a beauty? What would you like us to do next, Elijah?"

"I have three tents," said Elijah. "You can sort yourselves out as you wish. I also have six large sleeping bags as the nights can be cold and there was always a chance that Dia would have been able to come along with us. If you hear anything moving outside the tent in the night, don't get up and investigate. Wild animals are still puzzled by tents and are not usually that inquisitive. They won't do any damage apart from, perhaps, peeing on the outside. And if you need a pee in the night find some receptacle."

They put up the tents; Bernard and Simon were to sleep in one, Tara and Melusi in another and Elijah in the third. They lit a fire and heated up some tinned corned beef in a saucepan. They ate this with a spoon and plenty of bread. It was disgusting but it was food, and it satisfied their hunger.

"I don't think Mrs Hobson would approve of this," said Bernard.

The fresh fruit made up for the spartan first course. They washed it down with cool beer from the truck's fridge.

"Breakfast at five o'clock," said Elijah.

"Good heavens, why so early? Simon, is that your idea?" Tara had been looking forward to a longer night.

"I am afraid it was. Because we have no idea when the old man will appear, and we must be wide awake and ready to follow him. He may appear with another as you will remember his time is almost finished. I fear we may be in the proverbial limbo; we have to be patient."

They talked for another hour or so, about their own views of the quest, of Ted and Saul and the events that had conspired to collect them at this remote and beautiful spot in Africa. At ten o'clock they began to prepare for the night. They washed in the stream, relieved themselves by torchlight in case of snakes and bedded down in the sleeping bags. Simon and Bernard talked far into the night. Bernard's voice was so soft that his words could not be clearly heard, but Simon was making up the volume and his worried voice was quite clear. Eventually, even he succumbed to sleep.

Tara and Melusi were side by side in each other's arms. "What a wonderful place." Melusi searched for her mouth to kiss. Tara arched her body towards his and felt down into their sleeping bag. When she had found what she wanted she whispered to Melusi.

"Make love to me."

"Quietly, love!"

"I have to make a little noise. I feel like shouting to the hills."

"Marry me?"

"Impetuous youth; we will have to wait until you have killed your lion."

"I'm sure it won't be long before I do just that."

Elijah pressed the horn of the truck at five o'clock sharp and a cloud of birds rose-up in panic at this intrusive noise. His infectious laughter cheered them up in the cold pre-dawn glow. They washed in the ice-cold stream and ate the fry-up that Elijah had prepared.

"Almost as good as Mrs Hobson's." Bernard remarked.

"What do we do now, Simon?" Tara was feeling wonderfully at ease with the world.

"We wait."

"Wait for what?"

"For the old man, of course," said Elijah. "Saul saw him first all those years ago, so I suppose I had better be on the lookout."

The morning sun became hotter and Tara and Melusi decided to have a swim in the pool.

"Are there any crocodiles here, Elijah?"

"Not yet! We could all have a swim. The water's as clean as a whistle and we are a long way from that rhino."

Bernard and Simon and Elijah stripped off and relaxed in the stream.

"This'll cool your worried brain, Simon."

"It helps!"

Elijah prepared the tinned baked beans for lunch, and they ate them cold on dry bread. During the afternoon they watched a variety of small mammals and insects around the site.

"Is this snake dangerous, Elijah?" called Tara from halfway up the cliff.

"Don't disturb it!" Elijah shouted the warning. "Puff adders are poisonous but very slow and if you don't mess with them by treading on them, they won't harm you."

Tara didn't think much of that advice and came down the cliff a good deal faster than she had intended. More of Elijah's cooking completed an otherwise uneventful day and by sunset they were becoming impatient.

"We have to wait, there's no alternative," Simon pleaded. "Be patient, Melusi."

"Why don't we have a preliminary exploration of the cave? At least we could have a look at the paintings that Ted saw and follow the history of the Royal Tandeka and the pictures of the subsequent revenge."

"No, we have no permission to enter the cave. We have to wait for the old man." Simon was adamant.

"How will he know we're here?"

Elijah laughed. "There are a number of people in Zimbabwe who know about you and your visit. They are in two minds about it. They're not sure we're doing the right thing; to try to alter such an ancient curse. I believe Melusi's presence may have changed that attitude somewhat. At least his family came from this country."

"I'm not particularly happy about that. But we must live in the present and my life is geared to healing people, not killing them."

"The fact that a lot of people know the reason for our visit may lead to problems. That's what worries me. It could lead to a lot of nastiness." Simon lapsed into gloomy silence and would not expand on his statement.

Chapter Twenty-Six

Another of Elijah's enormous breakfasts again on the third day, Wednesday 9th; the group were talking about the various merits of four-wheel-drive vehicles. Bernard, who did not have much interest in the subject, walked a little distance down the stream. The air felt strangely heavy, and an odd noise rattled round the ring of mountains; it could have been thunder, even the primeval remnant of an ancient sacrifice of some animal or even a human? Could it be Olive Abercrombie's great noise of her dreams?

Something in the distance attracted his attention; it was as if a blade of the tall grass had moved beyond the distance of his clear vision. Bernard shook his head to clear his old eyes. He climbed higher up the bank of the stream back to the campsite. He met Simon who had come to find him. They turned and had another look. There it was again; far away in the dawn light there was something moving, and it wasn't a wild animal. Slowly the will-o'-the-wisp was coming nearer. Bernard saw his shadow first, a long shadow of a tall man gliding towards him, in and out of the sunlight the tall man moved without a sound until he stood before the visitors. The two men smiled a greeting and walked back to join the others. They all stood up to greet the apparition.

"I'm pleased you saw him first, Bernard," said Simon softly. "Since you are in the blood line, and it is up to you to plead."

There stood the old man, tall, almost seven feet in height, so thin they were amazed he had the power to stand up. His claw-like hands grasped a beautiful throwing spear slightly taller than himself that he seemed to use as a support. The wood of the shaft was so old it had bleached to silver and the barbs were golden. Round the old man's neck was a beautiful golden medallion. From time to time, he touched the medallion, as if for reassurance. Everything about the old man revealed his great age. There were wisps of white hair surrounding a face so lined that it could have been carved in stone. He smiled as he motioned them to be seated and his eyes, dark as jet, travelled slowly from one person to another. After what felt like an age, they knew their souls had been turned inside out. He had waited a very long time for this meeting, and he had to be certain that those that were here were the ones Tandeka was expecting. When the Old Man had studied them all and was happy that they had the correct credentials he spoke.

"Welcome." The single word rang in their minds like a bell, so clear it took them all by surprise. "Follow me."

The old man moved between them and started to climb up the cliff face. Melusi went to help him, but the old man turned to him. He smiled as he raised one hand as one does in the giving of a blessing, to indicate that help was not needed. Melusi nodded.

"If he is the same old man, he must be at least a hundred and fifty years old, but he is going up that cliff face like a ten-year-old. Incredible!"

"But is he the same man who befriended Ted and Saul?" asked Tara, who was already breathing hard. They reached the mouth of the cave with no answer and entered where the passageway opened into the dawn-lit chamber. There they sat and waited for the old man to say something.

"I am, as you hoped, the same old man as you have read about in Ted's diaries. By your calendar I am a hundred and seventy years old. It is near the time when I should hand over to another. First I must take you on the journey."

Bernard looked at Simon to interpret the old man's cryptic statement, but Simon simply frowned and looked more worried.

Eventually he spoke, "I have to confess, I am rather at a loss to understand the meaning of the 'hand-over'. I had hoped he would have said that the life of the curse was coming to an end. Let's see where he leads us."

They followed the old man, who glided ahead of them into the darkness. His step was sure and steady, and they realised he knew every inch of the way and didn't need the torchlight Melusi tried to play on the tunnel ahead of him. When they reached a narrow part of the cave, the old man stopped and pointed upwards. Their torches revealed pictures of animals, some extinct, coloured with red and orange ochre and charcoal black.

"My goodness, these are wonderful pictures," said Simon. "Typical Upper Palaeolithic cave painting. Archaeologists would be able to date them from the carbon. I would guess anything from between twenty and thirty-five thousand years ago. That takes us to a time before the end of the ice age, which was around ten to fifteen thousand years ago. It's very curious, but the expertise, or perhaps the need to paint, seemed to evaporate after that time. Hunter-gatherer societies rarely draw to indicate a story. But since most of these drawings are at presumed sacred sites, they must have carried, what we would now call, a strong religious element. You will see predominantly large animals and several geometrical designs with only a marginal role for humans and often strange composite creatures.

The deepest caves often with very difficult narrow access tend to have more pictures of lions. They were probably visited by shamans. Some writers suspect the shamans were in self-induced exotic neurological states, maybe with the help of hallucinogens. They would be alone or bringing a sick person who they were attempting to cure with the help of the spirit world that they hoped to ally with behind the solid rock. Then you might have noticed little dots and lines; they just maybe the origin of writing. Oh dear, I'm so sorry, it's such a fascinating study, I do get carried away. Sorry, old man."

The old man had waited patiently for Simon to finish. His face was now glowing with pleasure and his smile seemed to light up the cave.

"We ought to press on," said Simon, pleased with the response.

A short while later, the old man stopped again and motioned Bernard to look at the walls.

"These drawings are quite different." Bernard remarked. "What say you, Simon, about these ones?"

"They're much younger; between four and five thousand years old. But still, much later than the Upper Palaeolithic ones. They must be what Ted described in his diaries. They do look like a depiction of the huge mortality suffered by the tribe with the pale skin, and, incidentally, the origin of the donated ability to use the dreadful curse. I suppose it ties up a few loose ends. On we go."

Eventually they came to the giant cavern with the smooth walls and experienced the strange way in which every noise they made echoed and re-echoed. The roof of the cavern was so high that their powerful torches could only just make out the structure of the roof several hundred feet above them. It was festooned with delicate stalactites many thousands of years old hanging down in drapes and fronds like an upside-down forest. The floor was not as even as they had assumed from Ted's diary and Melusi tripped on a rock as he was looking up at the roof. The noise was so tremendous that even the old man looked back and smiled.

"Careful," said Bernard. "For goodness sake don't break anything this far from the entrance, you're much too heavy to carry."

"Thanks a million."

"Thinking of your survival with a broken ankle, the air in here is curiously fresh and not as cold as I suspected it would be. There must be another entrance or a blow hole somewhere."

The old man looked back at Bernard but said nothing. He gestured towards the far end of the cavern where they came to the hewn-out circular chamber.

Simon studied the stone slab in the middle of the chamber. "I wonder if this was an altar. Or perhaps this was where the elders of the tribe met to discuss matters of state."

How could they know? There was no immediate comment from the old man who went to the opposite side of the altar and motioned them to sit on the floor. He started to talk to them in his soft calm voice that at times they had to strain to hear.

"Long ago, before the moon was hit by the gods, there was a tribe that lived in the plains to the North of the Great Mountain. The tribe that had been there since time began and had been created by one who had been sent by Olorun, God of the Sky."

"He is probably talking of a time between fifteen thousand years ago," Simon explained. "That was the beginning of the end of the last ice age, and twelve thousand years ago. There were great primeval gatherings of late Stone Age people that attained a very sophisticated civilisation. They're impossible to classify now but they were the origins of both the Caucasoid and Black races; probably not of the Mongoloid races who left the Rift Valley well before that. And for your interest, it is probable that the moon had been hit by a giant comet."

The old man had stopped while Simon had his say. Simon apologised and the old man merely smiled again, his dark eyes as enigmatic as ever. Melusi noticed that the old man's chest did not appear to move.

Surely, he must breathe, unless he is a figment of our imagination? Or perhaps he is using telepathy.

"You are correct," said the old man, who had clearly heard and understood every word that Simon had said. "The tribe started to die, but the bodies of the dead did not decay, and grasses grew from their bodies. The chief of the tribe at the time noticed that only those with fair skins were dying. The tribe had a mixture of skin and those with dark skin were only a little affected and could be made to recover. The chief knew that the gods wanted the tribe to survive to keep their knowledge. The only way he could think to do this was to pass their seed to the tribe by the sea, as they had a darker skin which he thought would protect them. They had a meeting with the elders of the tribe by the sea and the females of the tribe by the sea were pleased to receive the seed of the dying tribe. From that time on, the tribe by the sea had great strength and wisdom and they prospered. The curse was the gift of the Gods to the tribe by the sea in gratitude for the continuation of the race. It was only to be used by a woman of the royal family and could only be used once.

"Over four hundred years ago, pink-skinned sailors came in great ships to steal a great number of our people to make them slaves and destroy our tribes. There have been slaves for thousands of years; they were the defeated ones. But the sailors reduced their captives to worse than animals and the contempt was too great. In those days the headship of the tribe passed through the female line to help the tribe to grow in number. This was enough when there was an empty world, but with the multiplication of peoples, they were about to change to have the headship of the tribe pass through the male line to increase their fighting ability. The last princess, the Princess Tandeka Thembani, was about to be crowned when the men from the ships came and captured her. When they took her to the shore, they took off her clothes as they did to all the slaves, and they branded her below her breast. The Princess Tandeka endured all these insults, and no sound passed her lips. The captain of the ship took a liking to her body and used it for his pleasure, and it was at that time that Princess Tandeka laid the curse on your family." He looked straight at Bernard as he said his final sentence.

"You will now know that it is as you thought. It is true that Ellie Mackenzie died by the same cotton grass that killed the tribe beyond Great Mountain. The Wise One knows that the Curse has almost finished its time; it is almost spent. I am the Messenger to gather it in. That is what I have to tell you and you may now speak freely with me."

Bernard stood up and was trembling as he spoke. "I would like to be allowed to plead for those who are now ill. I am of the blood line of that very family and in my country, there are nine people, possibly more, who are ill with the most dreadful rashes. I recognise that terrible deeds were done by our ancestor, however I plead for no more cases and for the healing of those are now ill."

"I am nearly at the end of my time and on behalf of the Princess Tandeka Thembani I accept your plea," said the old man. He raised his hand as if in salute to the perseverance of the travellers. Simon sighed with relief.

"I don't!" The voice came from the entrance of the chamber behind them.

"I recognise that voice." Elijah sounded angry. "It has haunted me since school days. You remember the belligerent official at the airport? His name is Mosa. Never did like the bastard. What has this got to do with you, Mosa?" he shouted.

"I'll tell you. A couple of years ago I was travelling in these hills, and I found this valley. I was interested in the development of a string of tourist centres. The valley was ideal and as a bonus there was the advantage of the remains of the old religions. Tourists are easily hooked on defunct religions. I was wading up the stream the other side of the mountain when your old man over there walked up to me and we got talking. I told him my idea and suddenly he brightened up and offered me a job. For want of a better title, the Guardianship of this Curse."

"There was no money in it, and it seemed to be only for a short time, so I turned it down. I did nothing for a while and then, I am not sure why, decided to take it on. I came back and managed to get away from an angry black rhino, when there he was again, the old man. The old man then made me the same offer. He described the curse in greater detail and the idea of getting back at the white races for all they have done to the blacks appealed to me."

The old man walked slowly round the altar with his black eyes blazing and stood in front of Mosa, who would not look him in the eye. Simon sat quietly, watching the two.

The old man spoke, "I thought you were a man of peace, but you have destroyed my faith in you, and you are too late; I have accepted the plea. This family have suffered already one terrible death for what happened too long ago. There will be no further deaths and the sick ones will be cured."

"No, they won't!" Mosa pulled a gun from his pocket. He fired at the old man who dropped his spear and fell to the ground without a sound.

"Oh my god!" Tara screamed and started towards Mosa. She stopped when he pointed the gun at her.

"There are more bullets in this gun!" Mosa shouted. "And I have a packet of primed dynamite to seal you in. There's no hope for you or your precious family. I don't know who the rest of you are, but you are all here so you must all die, and the curse must continue."

Melusi was like a coiled spring, wondering how to disarm Mosa, but he was forced to relax when he saw Simon lower his wrist as if to tell them all to 'cool it'. Mosa turned on a torch and started to run to the other side of the giant cavern, making a great deal of noise. Melusi was poised to run after Mosa, but again was stayed by Simon's glance. The sound of Mosa's retreating footsteps echoed until there was such a roar, they had to hold their hands to their ears.

Simon suddenly shouted, "Melusi!" He pointed at the old man's spear. Immediately Melusi sprang up and with one continuous movement raised the throwing spear, balanced it as he was trained to do with his javelins, drew back his arm and hurled the spear as hard as he could toward the diminishing light held by Mosa. The spear shone silver and gold in a beautiful arc to the other side of the cavern. There was a hollow thud as it landed in the back of the running figure. A shrill cry was all they heard from Mosa as his body hit the ground just at the exit from the cavern. The cry was followed by a deafening roar as the dynamite exploded bringing down the roof of the tunnel on Mosa's body. The travellers shrank back into the chamber to avoid the falling tons of stalactites dislodged from the roof. The noise took some time to die down and when their ears had stopped ringing, they crouched down beside the old man.

The old man was obviously dying but he smiled at them. "I can go now. The curse is over. The cure, my friends, is the little white tufted grass at the base of the smooth purple stone at the top of the cliff; take the grass and wipe it on the skin of the sick people and you will save some, perhaps all of them. The stages will be stormy. Some will die if you are too late. Be careful, my friends, do not expect justice. Justice only exists in another life; it is not meant to be here." The old man paused as his life began to ebb away. "I can go to Tandeka at last. You, Bernard, and your family, are free. We will meet again." Bernard nodded his head with tears in his eyes.

The old man looked at Simon. "Thank you for your help, Wise Man." Simon, amazingly at a loss for a moment, smiled with silent understanding. The old man finally looked at Melusi and Tara and, fixing his stare on Melusi, said with a twinkle in his old eyes, "I was young a hundred and fifty years ago. I have given you the key to open the door; I hope you will be happy. Tread carefully, young man. That was well done." He glanced in the direction of Mosa's retreat. He laughed a great laugh; a young man's laugh which echoed round the great cavern as he died. And as he died, he flung out his arm and pointed in the opposite direction to the one from which they had come, into the darkness along the far tunnel.

"That must be our way out. Thank you, old man. Look, he's smiling. So, Bernard, there must be another exit to these caves. That's why the air is so fresh."

Elijah started to sing softly. He sang a lament, a lament for the loss of a wonderful friend. A friend who had stayed loyal for a hundred years.

Chapter Twenty-Seven

"Tara, tell me, what did he mean by giving Melusi the key to the door, and all that business about being careful?" asked Simon.

"You are very clever and wise about most things, Simon, but some secrets are hidden even from you." Tara's words made Simon realise that it was a very personal matter of great joy to them both.

Elijah stopped singing. "There's another question that doesn't seem to have an answer, Simon. How did that little shit Mosa get involved in this? He was always a nasty bit of work, even at school. I find it unbelievable that the old man asked him to take over the curse."

"Try and do a bit of lateral thinking, Elijah. Pretend that you have been the guardian of the curse for one hundred and fifty years. The old man, the guardian, called himself the Messenger. You know full well that if there's any time left for the curse to function it's very short indeed. You have come to like the family who are under threat. Ted sealed that little bit of the scene for us. How are you going to make certain that the curse will not continue? I told you about a month ago that a curse tended to finish if there was no living memory or at the very least no specific handover. Now then, what would be your next course of action?"

"Sorry, Simon, no idea. I need spoon-feeding."

"You choose a nasty bit of work who is going to be so obnoxious that he comes to grief. This is what I was dreading was going to happen. It could have gone so horribly wrong, but Messenger got us all off the hook. He gave his life for us. The fact that he wanted to go anyway is not relevant, he timed his going for us and in the most wonderfully human way." Simon paused to think. "Was he wholly human? Anybody got better ideas?"

They all looked at Messenger's ancient body, now at peace.

"My God," said Bernard.

"He comes very near that category," said Elijah. "I hope Tandeka will be pleased with him."

"Tandeka was also very pleased with you, Melusi," said Simon. "Do you realise, young man, that Messenger's throwing spear travelled a good twenty metres further than your record?"

"What are you trying to tell me?" Melusi thought he had done rather well. "The balance of that spear was brilliant, one of the best javelins I've ever held. I did feel on a real high. Are you suggesting anything else?"

"Oh no, of course not; just that to hit a moving target at that distance in the dark is absolutely impossible." As Simon said this there was a rumbling sound and more rock fell to the floor of the cavern.

"I think she is telling us to get out quick. Come on, folks. But first, goodbye, Messenger." Elijah knelt and kissed the dead forehead, followed by Bernard, Simon, Melusi and Tara. Then silently, with tears in their eyes, they made their way in the direction indicated by Messenger. About half a mile further into the mountain they felt safer as the noise of the falling rocks became more distant. They turned a corner and were aware of a soft but powerful sound in front of them.

Melusi studied the torrent. "Oh Lord, this must be the river that forced Ted to go so far on his circular journey. There is one hell of a lot of water flowing and fast too. What is it? Twenty feet wide, ten feet deep and flowing at ten knots at least, probably fifteen. Tara can swim that, but no one else has a hope. How did Mosa get across?"

"I suspect there was a bridge of sorts between those two outcrops of rock." Tara pointed to the other side of the river. "Mosa must have dislodged it thinking he would be able to get out on the other side of the mountain. Now come on you big strong men, how do we get across? This is the sort of problem that the Girl Guides solve every day. Come on lover!" She waited patiently while they all thought about the problem.

"Elijah and I could jump it and go and get help when we get out the other end."

Tara laughed. "Don't think much of that idea. How about this; I want everyone to take off their trousers. And before anyone gets any funny ideas, I do have a practical solution to our problem, and I also intend to take off my own."

Light was beginning to dawn in their mathematical minds. "Now tie them together to make a rope and Melusi attach a stone to the end. Then will you please throw it so it catches between the two rocks on the opposite side of the river where the bridge must have been. Then we keep it tight while each person struggles over; the last person is pulled over by the rest of us."

Melusi must have tried twenty times to make the stone catch in the V of the rocks, but each time it slipped back into the water. "What now? I can't get the confounded thing to stick; those rocks are too smooth."

Tara thought for a while. "OK, off with the shirts, we need a longer and stronger rope. I'm the best swimmer and I'll swim across. The rope is to pull me back if I am being swept into the tunnel. I don't fancy that at all."

Shirts came off and Melusi marvelled at this wonderful woman who now looked like a goddess in her bra and knickers clinging to her cold flesh. Melusi and Elijah looked at each other, blinked and shook their heads to concentrate on the problem of their escape.

"Obviously I can't swim straight across as the current is much too strong. With a bit of luck, I can swim the diagonal, so there must be enough rope to stretch that far. For goodness' sake don't let it go if you reach the end; I don't fancy being swept into that black tunnel. Now you men keep your thoughts on the immediate problem!" she said severely. "I'm sure you have all seen young ladies in their bra and knickers before; perhaps a long time ago!" The two old men laughed.

Tara entered the ice-cold water and started to swim, but very soon they realised that she had only reached the middle of the river and was being swept towards the tunnel. "Back!" Tara shouted and the line held. "Christ, it's cold. Think again, old girl. I should have dived in, that will get me halfway before I start swimming."

They clutched the loose line of clothing as Tara ran and launched as high a dive as she dared before swimming for all their lives. She was making good progress but there must have been a faster current near the other side, and she was losing the battle. They made ready to pull her back again before she was swept into the tunnel.

The cold was getting to her, and Tara looked up in desperation. Standing gloriously before her was the most beautiful princess, smiling and waving a hand. Tara cried out "Tandeka!" She held out her hand to her saviour and she was on the far bank. The watchers saw a flash of light and before anyone had realised it Tara was standing ready to take the strain of the line of clothing.

Tara turned to thank the beautiful princess only to catch a glimpse of a shadow and the memory of a smiling girl.

"What on earth was that, Tara?" Bernard shouted. "Did anyone else see a flash of light or was it a reflection of the torch-light on the river?"

"Tandeka, of course. She's on our side now, thank goodness. We can't fail. It's up to a bunch of live human beings from now on." Simon was becoming chirpier by the minute. "Keep the line taut round a rock and we're on our way."

Tara made sure the line was out of the river and with Elijah on the other end made a stiff enough cable to help Bernard, Simon and Melusi across. Finally, Elijah tied the clothing round his own waist and was pulled to the other side. They undid the line, put on their cold wet clothing, and continued their flight along the tunnel, shivering with cold.

"I can see daylight!" shouted Tara. "It's bound to be warmer outside. Come on, hurry or we'll all freeze to death." They came out of a tiny hole on the opposite side of the mountain into the blessed light and the warmth of the evening sun.

"Let's stay here for a bit while we warm up in the sun. Tara, tell us more about the lovely Tandeka."

"No time, Bernard, we have a visitor."

"Hello folks, welcome to the outside world." A familiar voice.

"Dia, darling sister; how on earth did you get here and why? And a whole lot of other questions."

"I followed Mosa; I didn't trust him. He's a nasty bit of work and I couldn't understand why he was being so obnoxious. As soon as you had left, he went off-duty, so I followed him to the gates of the airport. He cycled off and I followed him on foot to his new home which is not far from the airport. He collected his new mountain bike that he's so bloody fond of and batted off into the Matobo. Now we've all known for years where the cave is, but he wasn't going in that direction. I hurried off and found Rex. Rex, come and meet the team. Elijah my brother, Great Uncle Bernard, Professor Simon Lancing, Doctor Melusi Makuthwane and Doctor Tara Vaux, meet Rex. Rex is the chief warden and knows this park like the back of his hand. He always knew that there was another entrance to the cave system on this side of the hill, but he's never explored it. So, we followed Mosa who came straight here. We came in Rex's four-by-four which we left about half a mile over there." Dia gestured vaguely towards a dense outcrop of trees and rocks.

"We made the last bit on foot as quietly as we could and then sat down to watch him. He seemed to have some sort of sound detector as he was listening all the time to something, pointing down this entrance to the cave. It was just as well he was concentrating on the entrance as I'm sure he would have heard us as we approached. Anyway, we watched him and after a couple of days he popped down the hole just like a rabbit. After a few hours there was one hell of a bang. We weren't sure what to do so we waited. We heard you lot talking ages before you appeared but thank God you did."

"Oh, Elijah I'm so pleased you're all right and that explosion wasn't the end of everything." Dia was crying with relief.

Rex was puzzled by their story and by their wet clothes.

"Why are you so wet? There's no water on this side of the mountain."

"Oh yes, there is, young man." Bernard was resurrecting his old cheery self. "Just nip down that hole and you'll find plenty of it, a bloody great river in fact."

"Go on, I could make a fortune if it was true. We've had a drought for over a year and an underground river would bring new life to the whole area."

"Tandeka would be pleased as well."

"Who's she?"

"Someone we have all grown to admire in the last few weeks. Right now, take us back to the other side of the mountain and Elijah, in a week's time, will make you a rich man."

"OK, we're off and don't spare the horses."

They climbed down the hill, found Rex's four track, roared round the hill, up the stream and there was their truck and the tents just as they had left them. Rex and Dia dropped them after great hugs and kisses.

"See you in Harare," said Dia. "First one to the airport treats the others."

"I am glad she didn't say the last one's a sissy," said Melusi. "You just might be tempted, my darling."

"There might be two views of that. Down boy."

As the sound of the four-track died away, the silence returned. It seemed such a long time ago Messenger had led them into the cave system and so much had happened that they felt like strangers to the place.

"What do we do now, Bernard?" asked Tara.

"The grass, where is the grass? The purple boulder must be the one that Ted wrote about in his diary."

"At the top of the cliff, there is a coloured boulder. But not a lot else," said Elijah.

"Come on you lot," Bernard started to climb. "Last one up is a sissy."

Bernard never did work out why Melusi and Tara collapsed with hysterical laughter, leaving Elijah to win easily. The couple recovered and joined Elijah at the top. There was the purple boulder just as Ted had written.

"Where is this special grass? Is it this miserable stuff, Melusi?"

"Fantastic. This is wonderful. How about another piece of lateral thinking? Have you ever read a poem by Jonathan Swift?

'So, naturalists observe, a flea
Has smaller fleas that on him prey,
And these have smaller still to bite 'em,
And so, proceed ad infinitum.'

How wonderful, so simple; we should have thought of it ourselves. This is grass that is dying, and it is dying because it is heavily infected with a virus. Simon, this is the cure."

"It is a variety of grass closely related to the mallow-type of plant that produces the cotton that we use to clothe ourselves. How do we apply it, Melusi?"

"There are viruses that kill cotton grasses of any sort and if what Messenger says is true, it will also kill living cotton inside people. We need this virus or a closely related one in high concentration. Virology has progressed quite a lot since Messenger learnt his tricks and our scientists will have a range of viruses that attack cotton plants. We can certainly pick the grass and take it back to Jane, Elizabeth, Samuel, Laurie and the others. Better not to pick all of it as it may be needed by others. As soon as we return, we must contact Bernard's friend, Kit Pearson; I'm sure one of her scientist friends has preserved cultures of all sorts of plant viruses that we could try on the patients. Perhaps as Messenger suggested, the easiest way to get it into the patients will be to smear it on the skin, but we could also inject it into a vein. The patients could even breathe it in as an aerosol; there's nothing to lose. I can predict as Messenger hinted that there will be a big battle within the patients. They're going to have quite a problem getting rid of all the rubbish which will probably come out via the kidneys as a sort of dust. We should have listened to Valentine."

They climbed down and found Bernard sunning himself with half an eye on a kettle that was just about to boil. He had changed his clothes and warmed up after the drenching underground. They showed him the wizened, tatty-looking grass.

"That doesn't look very impressive as a miracle cure. Are they supposed to wave it about like a magic wand? What do you think, Melusi?" Melusi gave Bernard a long discourse on fleas and viruses and what they did to people and plants. Bernard listened and finally said, "I suppose I should be able to understand the thought processes behind the idea. If you say it'll work, then I believe you. To my mind it all appears a little far-fetched but all we can do is try."

He sounded tired now, as if the drive that had kept him going for the last fifty years was running out of steam. "Victoria, my dear wife, always said there was a lot more to botany than meets the eye. Perhaps that's why gardeners are usually such old men." He shook his head as if he was returning from a pleasant daydream. "Time for coffee; the water's boiled."

After a while Bernard's spirits, revived by the coffee, turned to Elijah. "Can't sit about all day, we have work to do. Elijah, can we leave as soon as possible. Can we use your satellite phone to ring the airport at Harare?"

"Sure, I'll do it."

"Good, thank you. Tara, can you please make sure that we have seats on the next flight from Harare back to London? I also want the plane to make available a radio-telephone link, or whatever you call it nowadays, for us to make a very long call to Uncle and perhaps others. Now Melusi, it was your idea and I think it would be most appropriate for you to organise the virus side of it via Kit Pearson. She knows all of us and she won't mind if we ring her in the early hours of the morning; she owes me a few favours. Tara, can you make the papers for the truck over to Elijah and everything else here? If we come again, we'll start with a clean sheet. I'm going for a pee." Bernard walked off into the bushes.

Tara turned to the others with a worried expression on her face. "What's the matter with Bernard? He suddenly seems strange, as if his thoughts are no longer with us. He is trying to distance himself onto another level. Come to think of it, I have never heard him talk of Victoria before. Hobson says he still desperately misses her. Perhaps Bernard's engine is winding down now that the cure is, hopefully, in sight. I hope he doesn't give up now, to my mind there's still a long way to go. He should be allowed to enjoy his success."

The others nodded, mournfully, not quite knowing what to say.

Tara walked a little way along the bank to be on her own. She felt at ease with nature and was thinking how wonderful it would be to come back to this country and make it her home, to bring up children with all this space and to mix in with such cheerful people. She realised that she had only experienced a very small and selected part of the country, but she still wanted to live here.

Bernard came back looking cross.

"What's the problem?" asked Simon.

"I slipped, put my hand out to save myself and skewered it onto one of those bloody thorn bushes. Come on doctor, do your best."

Melusi made sure all the thorns were extracted, put lots of antiseptic on Bernard's hand and bandaged him up with a sling.

"That's a bit over the top, old son."

"Not taking any chances. Now, I insist you have an antibiotic."

Chapter Twenty-Eight

They packed up the tents, loaded the truck and started to drive back. The black rhino was nowhere to be seen. Elijah drove the truck like Jehu, crashing and screeching its way over the pass and they seemed to reach the plain in no time.

"Do you think it would be wise to use Bulawayo airport?" said Tara, voicing all their thoughts. "We may be associated with the non-appearance of the dreaded Mosa. You never know, but that little bastard may have told one of his cronies where he was going and who he was following. Questions may be asked after the row we had with him at the airport. What do you think, Bernard?"

"Good point. Do you feel strong enough, Elijah, to drive overnight to Harare and catch the first plane in the morning? I believe it leaves at six and Tara has made sure there are seats for us?"

"No problem. Look at the full moon, we've got light all the way. I've phoned Dia and Rex, and they are going to meet us there." He changed gears, drove onto the tarmac road, and roared towards their goal. The four travellers slept fitfully most of the way and were wide awake as they entered the airport grounds. Dia and Rex had arrived first, and so strong reviving coffee was ready for them in an instant. There was also a ring on one of Dia's fingers that had not been there the day before. Tara noticed it, smiled, but said nothing; there's a time and a place, not now. Our time will come. The travellers were ushered safely onto the dawn plane of Thursday 10th of August with more fond farewells and were off. They sank back into their first-class seats and, for the first time for many days, relaxed. The plane rose to thirty-five thousand feet and the captain's voice came through on the tannoy. "Is there a Professor Bernard Charlton on board?"

Bernard shook off the fronds of sleep and sat up. "Yes, here I am, promotion at last." He raised an eyebrow at Tara. Thank goodness, she thought, the old Bernard's sense of humour is coming back. The stewardess handed a phone to Bernard.

"We have an open telephone link with a Doctor Bhekitembo Makuthwane in Bristol for as long as you wish, sir. The captain may interrupt you, but it won't be for more than a few minutes at a time."

"You start, Melusi. Give him the facts about the sick grass until he's got the idea. Make sure he has every single piece of information."

Melusi talked at length with his uncle. Bhekitembo was initially filled with disbelief, but the more he thought about the idea the more attractive it sounded. "Set a thief to catch a thief, eh? What a super idea!" Melusi breathed a sigh of relief; the message had got through.

"Now, uncle, do you think you could face waking up Kit Pearson and getting her interested enough to ring the research establishment run by the Ministry of Agriculture, Fisheries and Food? I think it's called the Central Science Laboratory in Harpenden. Would you ask Kit to ring them at once and persuade them to make an ultra-clean preparation of the cotton wilt virus, because that is the most likely candidate? If they started today filtering and spinning to clean up a stock culture, they could have it ready by tomorrow. I hope they have a good bulk of stock culture frozen down, as a fresh culture would take quite a while to produce. I think we may also need the services of a medical virologist. He'll be initially as horrified as you were but I'm sure you can persuade him to work quickly for us. All these clever people enjoy a panic. I suspect the medical virologist will insist that the purity must be so good that the virus can be crystallised. I don't think that's necessary. See how you get on, but the final preparation must be able to be injected into a vein at the right pH and be compatible with human plasma. We need about six hundred ml of the virus suspension at a concentration of about ten to the power of nine virus particles per ml."

"Hang on, dear boy; I will get all that technical stuff from the virologists. But that concentration of virus seems an awful lot and may destroy so much of the cotton at once that the kidneys will be blocked getting rid of all the rubbish. They may clog up; I suppose we can always dialyse it out. Anyway, you can rest assured that I have the story now. Fascinating. Can I talk to Bernard, please?"

Uncle and Bernard talked for half an hour; then it was Simon's turn asking after Jane. He was reassured by what he heard. Uncle then asked to speak with Tara. She blushed scarlet and said to Melusi, "Uncle wanted to know if you are behaving yourself; I told him that you were."

"That's a shame."

Simon laughed. "Tara don't forget to tell Uncle about Melusi's throw of the javelin. Well, we can't do any more, folks. Let's enjoy ourselves with food and wine at Bernard's expense. Then we can sleep the sleep of the winners."

Chapter Twenty-Nine

The Chief Scientist at the MAFF research establishment was not used to being telephoned at midday with an urgent summons, but when he discovered it was his old flame Kit Pearson he brightened up. He listened to the whole story for a full hour, asking her a series of sharp questions. Finally, he put down the phone carefully and breathed a great sigh. "Wonderful." The single word was enough. He picked up the intercom to his secretary.

"I want you to find the two scientists to whom I was talking yesterday and get them to ring me at once."

"It might be their lunch hour."

"At once, please."

She had only had this order twice before and each time there had been war on. She found the two scientists and they came on the line at the same time.

"Connect them both to my line."

"I'm not supposed to do that, sir. It's strictly against regulations."

"Bugger the regulations. This is an order; just do it."

She connected them both to the Chief Scientist's line. They talked for twenty minutes and there were a few words never overheard in the secretary's office. She took him in a cup of tea, and he was smiling to himself.

"I love a panic; it helps the adrenaline flow. Now get me first Professor Kit Pearson, you know her number. And then

Doctor Bhekitembo Makuthwane at the Bristol Royal Infirmary; now, please."

Ten minutes later Kit was on the line. "I can produce for you an almost crystalline suspension. How much do you need?"

The Chief Scientist was excited. "Probably about a litre of it at the concentration your colleague wants by tonight. There is a reliable motorcycle courier standing by to take it only to Doctor Bhekitembo Makuthwane in person at the Bristol Royal Infirmary. The driver is instructed to place it into the hands of Doctor Makuthwane himself and no-one else. There is another line flashing, and this is probably the good doctor. Thank you, my dear, for waking me up from the torpor induced by the mountains of administration. Do you realise that you can't even fart nowadays without filling in an application form in triplicate? Love to the children; goodbye.

"Other caller, please. Hello doctor, I have just been speaking with our mutual friend Kit Pearson. There will be with you at approximately two o'clock tomorrow morning a litre of fluid with the required clean virus in a suspension compatible with human plasma. It may be injected neat, but I would be marginally happier if it were to be diluted one in a hundred with dextrose saline. It is only to be delivered into your hands. You will be pleased to hear that this is classed as an emergency procedure and therefore there will be the absolute minimum of paperwork. My instructions, you understand. There will also be no charge."

"I really am most grateful, amazing speed and service. Thank you so much."

"Not at all, it is wonderful to be challenged for once by a real problem rather than mounds of useless paper. Best of luck with the treatment. Good-bye."

By the time the four travellers were back in Bristol, Melusi's uncle had Jane, Elizabeth and Samuel's rashes all covered with polyester mesh that had a few drops of the precious virus suspension diluted and spread over them. One of the scientists from MAFF, David Prouse, had come to see the patients and discuss their findings with the botany department at the university. A handsome thirty-year-old bachelor, David's hobbies were climbing mountains and potholing, which he liked to think were opposite ends of a spectrum. He also enjoyed travelling to tropical countries. It was not surprising that he took a great interest in Elizabeth's rashes and even less surprising that she responded to his interest. Simon had contacted Jane's mother and they went as quickly as possible to the ward to see Jane, only to find Bernard hovering over Samuel, not knowing what to say. The three patients were overjoyed with all this attention and for the subsequent few days they all waited for something to happen, for the waving of the magic wand.

Melusi and Tara decided to leave the tense atmosphere of the ward and flee with their ration of the virus in a cool box to Plymouth, to treat Laurie, Nigel and the other two patients. Their mission accomplished, the lovers spent a blissful night at Auntie's and then drove back to Bristol the next day, where they found a furious Uncle storming at the masses of visitors and giving them a dressing down in his office.

"You are disturbing my patients. They are stuffed full of rubbish and with even the most effective virus it will take an unknown time to clear it out of their systems. If you had a garden full of weeds how many weeks would it take you to clear it, even if you knew that the weeds would not come up again? My patients must get rid of the broken-down products of a couple of pounds of cotton. They have two kidneys, the active areas of which only weigh a few grams, and these organs can only eliminate about an ounce a day. The patients will have all sorts of side-effects from the treatment, their kidneys may well give up for a while. We can cope with that by dialysis but if other organs pack up, we'll be in deep trouble." Uncle paused for breath; he was short of sleep and the strain was beginning to show.

"We are using an ancient magic wand. I want you all to go away and let me and my team get on with our work. We'll keep you informed daily at a time of our choosing, and you may visit socially at the recognised times. Please leave us to get on with what we are generally recognised as being the experts." Glancing up he saw Melusi and Tara.

"Doctor Makuthwane, can you come here a minute please, and Doctor Vaux?"

The meeting ended and most of the visitors left. Uncle was very tired but at the same time happy with the travellers. "It looks as if you four will have saved the lives of our patients, but I must emphasise again that it will undoubtedly be a very stormy course. Particularly Samuel, his systems are showing signs of failure and I am very worried about him. He has such a charming, fatalistic attitude to life and death that I fear that he has accepted that he will follow the same route as his cousin Ellie. I wish I could put some fire into him. I suspect you, Bernard, are the only person able to do that. We have our hands full now but happily I have a splendid new junior doctor with excellent references joining me tomorrow. Can't remember her name."

Simon interrupted. "I can hazard a guess at her name. She will come with excellent references from Central Africa. I suggest you simply call her 'Princess'".

"You know, she is rather lovely, good idea. Well now, you don't think…?" He stopped in mid-sentence. Just what was Simon trying to convey to him? Concentrate, he told himself. Concentrate on healing the patients and leave the mysterious for another day. Uncle reckoned that he had enough problems for the moment.

"Samuel will recover with her help. Don't worry, she is very reliable." Simon laughed and raised an eyebrow at Tara, who said, "I can second that."

And they told Uncle about the magical rescue of Tara in the cave.

"Not sure I believe a word of that. But it makes a good story!"

The patients did recover after the stormy passage predicted by Uncle. Jane was sick so many times she lost count. She then found that she couldn't pee for a while and her kidneys had to be helped with dialysis. The damaged kidneys recovered, and she started to feel better from that time. Elizabeth felt bloody, that was the best word to describe her feelings. Uncle was suspicious that her skin would scar rather badly.

"Don't worry," said Princess. "I'll take care of Elizbeth's skin."

Uncle looked at his houseman and remarked. "You deserve a medal if you can."

Princess turned her beautiful dark eyes on Uncle, and he thought she said she had thousands of years of trial and error to fall back on. But he was so tired perhaps his imagination was running around in circles. He watched Princess make her way in the direction of the pharmacy.

Princess spoke to the pharmacist. "I have a shopping list of very old medicines that were in common use in the eighteenth and nineteenth centuries. Do you mind if we can look in the cupboards in the back room and see if you have any old stock?"

"Feel free; anything to help those awful skin cases."

Two hours later, Princess emerged with a bag full of ancient creams and potions. She also had a large kitchen mixing bowl and a wooden spoon with which she vigorously mixed all the ingredients into a sticky, smelly mush.

Back in the ward, Princess caked her mixture over Elizabeth's damaged skin. "There, Elizabeth. Sorry about the smell. But I promise you it will work. Firstly, the skin will blister. Later all the damaged areas will peel off and the underlying skin will be perfect."

Samuel was the most difficult case to turn the corner. Tandeka sat by his bed for many hours. His kidneys also failed for a while, so he, too, had to be dialysed. Then his heart started to have the most peculiar rhythm in the middle of the night. Tandeka took one look at the decrepit machine that was purported to correct heart rhythms. One wheel had fallen off and the dials didn't work properly. Instead of making a row about the machine she sat by his bed and placed her hands on his chest. She talked in a strange language for a long time and gradually Samuel felt that things were looking up and life was for living. The next day an electrocardiogram showed that Samuel's heart was ticking nicely in normal rhythm.

Later, talking to Bhekitembo, Samuel was heard to say, "She is a strange person, that Doctor. One moment she is next to you and in seconds she is at the other end of the ward. She is very nice, but her eyes go right through you. She really is lovely, and she let me kiss her hand. I felt so good I cried."

Laurie's skin recovered, albeit at a slower rate than Nigel's. The other two patients in Plymouth and the ones in Liverpool and Harwich also recovered with no residual damage. One curious feature of the patients' recovery was the huge thirst. They would drink up to twenty pints a day; squash, beer, water, anything. And yet, they were still thirsty. Naturally they peed huge quantities. The weirdest feature of all was that their urine was dusty. The urine in the bowl was sometimes milky white. If the boys peed on the ground after a night out, it would dry to a dense white powder, which if disturbed, looked like talcum powder, blowing about in the wind. Under the microscope the dust was made up almost entirely of very fine fibres. Usually, the fibres were broken and distorted as if they had been forced through a very fine sieve. Gradually the amount of dust became less until after a few weeks the patients had cleared their systems of all evidence of the invading cotton.

Chapter Thirty

Late in the autumn Bernard summoned Uncle and Mrs Makuthwane, Melusi and Tara, Arthur, Simon and Rebecca Harvey and others to his house to dine and stay the night for a final conference, as he put it, on Friday 8th of September. The long, hot summer was beginning to break. There had been a shower or two of rain and although the reservoirs were still very low the weathermen predicted more rain, a time of mellow fruitfulness.

The guests were collected by taxi, arrived in evening dress, and were met by Hobson.

"Please leave coats and other discarded bits and pieces on the chairs in the hall and then go into the drawing room. Melusi oversees drinks, but you can help yourselves if desperate. Bernard will be down in a minute."

Bernard, in his 1920s smoking jacket given to him by his grandfather, came slowly down the stairs, hesitated at the door of the drawing room until Hobson escorted him to meet his visitors. He looked tired, with one arm sling supporting a heavily bandaged hand.

"Welcome, friends, I am so glad to see you all. Congratulations, Melusi, on passing your finals, very well done. And with so much time to spare," he laughed. "I have five more guests who will be coming down soon. Three of them have only just arrived after a long flight from Africa, and Kit Pearson and her husband may be a little late. You may have heard of the international prize that has just been awarded to her."

"Indeed, I have," said Uncle. "It is wonderful news and after all these years she deserves it."

"What's the matter with the arm, Bernard?" asked Uncle.

"Nothing much, I pricked my finger on one of those thorn bushes the day we left. Everything was so exciting and frenetic when we returned that I tried to forget about it, but it swelled up yesterday and I went to a doctor for the first time in twenty years. So, I am on your magic antibiotics." He dismissed the minor inconvenience. Uncle looked troubled and felt a prickle of apprehension. Every time he had entered this house something out of the ordinary had happened, but this time nobody else appeared to be concerned so he put his worries to the back of his mind. He was not going to be the one to spoil a jolly evening.

Tara entered the room in a stunning, bright red silk, full length dress. The front was cut so low as to be severely dangerous. The sweep of the V projected up to the shoulders which were a mass of puffed out material. The sleeves were short to reveal her muscular bronzed arms. The white petticoat flared out the base of the dress to reveal gold shoes. She had brushed her hair up high and wore gold earrings which matched the bangles on her wrists.

"Tara, you look wonderful," said Uncle and Simon at the same time. "So, this is the shivering little creature that swam the river in her undies somewhere on the underside of the mountain. Who would have thought it?"

"I would," said Melusi, taking his courage in both hands. "And I am now brave enough to ask this beautiful goddess, whether she has made up her mind to marry me. What do you say, Tara?"

Tara swallowed and breathed very deeply. She had known this moment would come; she had been looking forward to it.

So, for the second time Tara jumped in at the deep end, but this time it was a metaphorical deep end and much easier to swim.

"Melusi, my love, you killed your lion at a lot more than fifty paces. That is what Messenger meant when he said he had given you the key to the door. Of course, the answer is yes."

Melusi, feeling like he might faint with joy, held Tara's hands and told her, "I will cherish you and be faithful to you for the rest of my life. Thank you witnesses, all of you."

Bernard hugged the happy couple. "That was well done. This calls for celebration. I have a suspicion…"

From the hall came the sound of the familiar 'pop' of champagne corks as Hobson and Mrs Hobson came, beaming, into the room with trays full of frothing glasses, quickly followed by Elijah, Dia and Rex Daniels with Kit Pearson and her husband. Hobson stepped forward. "I must apologise to you, Tara and Melusi. I thought – we all thought – that it might just be the right moment, the right occasion. Because, well… So, Mrs Hobson and I were all prepared and, well, I hope you will forgive us. We were listening behind the door." There were tears of pleasure in the Hobsons eyes.

Tara stepped into the breach. "You always do things for the best and at the right time, dear Hobsons, both of you. I hope you will join us all in a glass. Here's to us."

"Here's to you both."

They had succeeded in their quest for the cure of the invasive cotton disease, Bernard had successfully pleaded for the annulment of the family curse and now the two principal players were to marry? Only a few ends had to be tied together and a few remaining puzzles solved. The Hobsons served a magnificent meal and they talked until the early hours. Kit was congratulated on her thesis and the honours being showered on her. Elijah, Dia and Rex were thanked for their part in the adventure.

Bernard, who was sat quietly absorbing the happiness, joviality and love surrounding him, beamed at them all. "My dear friends if I may? There is still a skeleton in my cupboard that I am not particularly happy about. Some of you will know that Ted had been given part-ownership in various mining interests in Zimbabwe. It is certainly true that our family have benefited mightily from that gift. A great deal of the money has been ploughed back into the country in the form of funding for schools, but I think it is now time to relinquish our family interest totally. Would you please, Melusi, and therefore also Tara, take on the burden of distributing the remaining assets to the people of Zimbabwe? I think that is the least I can do."

"We would be delighted to accept, wouldn't we, Tara?"

"You bet."

"Thank you, my dears. You have taken a great weight off my mind. Bless you both. On a much more cheerful note," Bernard continued. "What gives me the most happiness now, is the outcome that you all heard earlier on this evening. There has not been a more welcome 'plighting of the troth', nor more heartfelt. I confess, I loved every second of it. I think you are both very brave to have done so in the presence of us all. I love weddings. It is one of the few times when I feel like crying; very strange, when you think of it. Tara, I must confess that I employed you simply because in your curriculum vitae there was a brilliant thesis in genealogy. I did not know such a gorgeous girl was going to appear. Then this splendid young man comes along and there just had to be a match."

"Yours will be the first invitation that we send, dear Bernard. We expect you to behave, but you may have the odd cry."

Bernard turned to Melusi and Tara and holding their hands found himself quite unable to speak. Dia helped him out by jumping up and dragging a sheepish Rex to his feet. She turned to face the others. "Tara and Melusi were not the only ones to take advantage of the adventure. Rex was brave enough to ask me to marry him. Some men are very slow, they say they must be sure, and this wonderful man has finally concluded that I am not as scatty as I seem, just wild, man, wild." She laughed her great open laugh and they all laughed with her.

Rex stood up. "Thank you for asking me to this special dinner, Bernard. Dia, my fiancée, told me of the invitation two days ago. You're all very kind and I thank you from the bottom of my heart, especially you, Bernard."

Later they were talking about the amazing, if stormy recovery of the patients, when Simon asked after Uncle's new junior doctor.

"I believe that you already have a very good idea of what happened to her, so I am going to throw the question right back at you."

"All right; I can guess that the lovely Princess Tandeka Thembani, for she is, or was, beautiful, has disappeared. I will also guess that despite all the hundreds of your administrators she will not be found on any register of doctors either in this country or Zimbabwe, for that is where she said she came from. Correct, so far, Uncle?"

"That's quite correct."

"I also suspect that if you go through her notes on the patients, she will have written in black ink using very old-fashioned script and when she signs her name there will be a pink dot next to her signature and the signature will be the same each time as if she had been using a rubber stamp. It will not, in fact, be a signature at all but the equivalent of a stamp as she is not allowed to sign anything, nor will she ever have been allowed to do so. Correct again?" The guests were silent.

"Correct again. I was puzzled over the signature, but now I sort of understand, go on."

"I will finish with a prediction that she will not have left a forwarding address. That she will have left little trinkets for the maids who tidied her room, and a host of other minor details. But what will have unnerved them will have been that she never appeared to use her bed. She did not sleep for the whole month and yet she did not complain of tiredness. She had no need of sleep. She will have had no pay as it is useless to her and there will be nowhere to send it. And now you all know who she is, another related thought. Tandeka's Messenger had given a pledge on her behalf, and she was jolly well going to make sure she didn't let him down. Don't waste your time trying to trace her as there will be no record of her having ever existed. She has returned to her God with pride, pride in the fact that she had done the honourable thing. She has forgiven without forgetting and she has minimised the devastating effect of the curse."

Chapter Thirty-One

Bernard and the Hobsons waved their guests good-bye on the Saturday morning. It had been a superb evening, and everyone had slept the sleep of the contented. They had enjoyed a wonderful adventure and solved the problems of the family related to John Hawkins.

Bernard felt empty, unwanted, and not needed any more. The ache in his heart following the loss of Victoria was becoming more acute. The pursuit of the curse had been his driving obsession after Victoria died and he now felt bereft, there seemed little point in going on. He shook his head and spoke his thoughts to the Hobsons.

"Hang on, old friend; I hope you don't mind me calling you that?"

"Of course not; you are making me feel better all ready. What is your remedy for my glooms?"

"Just think for a while. You have not one, but two weddings and you will be the honoured guest at both. You must think of presents and all the fripperies that go with weddings. Presumably Dia and Rex will be married in Zimbabwe, and perhaps it may not be too much to ask, but you might consider it to be fun if Tara was married from here. Mrs Hobson would be in seventh heaven if that were to be the case."

"Thank you, Hobson, you are both very kind. I must admit, I had not given much thought to the place of Tara and Melusi's wedding. Remember her parents live not too far away in Somerset. I seem to remember their local church is at Broomfield, on the Quantock hills, lovely church, carved bench-ends, and all that. Victoria was fascinated by bench-ends. We all have our funny hobbies.

"Now you have put the idea into my head, of course they could be married from here. Rather a good idea. We will have to see what she suggests. She is coming back next week from that wild aunt of hers in Cornwall. I have another little matter that I wish to tell you about. Most of my relatives are so rich that they are not in need of anything. To get to the point, would you like this house when I'm gone? Obviously, I shall have no further use for it and you two have done most of the work for the last, I daren't think, how many years?"

It was the first time that Hobson had seen Bernard at a loss for words with tears in his eyes.

"Come on Bernard, old friend, enough of that. Of course, we would love to have it, but you must stop thinking along those lines."

"It is done already, so there." To hide his embarrassment Bernard closed the conversation. He turned so that Hobson would not see that he also was near to tears and walked quickly down to the gates of his garden. He walked more slowly along the line of trees that had been brought back by Great Uncle Ted. His hand hurt and his chest didn't feel so good. He felt ill, very low, and made even lower by the dreams of the previous night. For one who very rarely dreamt it was even more surprising. Twice in the night Bernard had been woken by a glimmer of light piercing the curtain. Was there a voice or was it the wind blowing through the open window? Perhaps he had been listening too much to Melusi's account of the dreams of the distant members of his family? But at the same time there had been something familiar about them. They had not really been frightening, he was too old to be frightened, but he had the hint that there had been a call to participate in something. Bernard did not remember ever having been frightened in his life, and goodness knows he had been alive for a very long time, so why now? All very odd; was it the spirits of times past? Was Tandeka coming to commune with him in the winding up of the curse? Perhaps she considered that it was his fault that the curse had been such a failure? Perhaps he was becoming paranoid? Time for coffee, or better, a gin and tonic. Bernard increased his pace and went to sit on the veranda.

Hobson found him sitting quietly, "Bernard, the doctor is on the phone asking about your hand."

"Tell him that the bloody thing hurts, and I need some more of his unhurting medicine."

"I'll ask him to pay you a call."

"Thank you," said Bernard almost to himself. He sat and watched the bees find the remnants of the autumn honey in the end flowers of the year. Not many of you are going to survive until the spring, he thought. A bank vole poked his nose out of the wall and looked at the old man sitting quite still. Bernard moved and the vole jumped back to safety. By the pool a kingfisher flashed by and came to sit beside Bernard, unaware of his presence. It turned towards the pool, flew towards it and quick as a flash plucked a minnow from the water. Flying back the bird suddenly noticed that Bernard was sitting there and veered off towards the brightly leaved sumac tree where it ate the fish.

"Sorry, old son, I tried not to move."

Tara came back after lunch. She found Bernard hunched over a plate of half-eaten food on the veranda. Alarmed at the site, she quickened her step and put her arms round his suddenly very old shoulders.

"Bernard, you're looking tired. What you need is a complete break. I have wound up Auntie and she would love to have you to stay with her in her little cottage in Cornwall at least for a month. You can explore the range of my funny relatives for a change. I am afraid they are not as exciting as yours, but there are some fun ones."

Bernard looked at this bright woman and saw his youth. Her enthusiasm for life was so infectious that he had no option but to absorb some of her happiness.

Perhaps I'm not finished yet. I haven't been away from this house for a holiday for such a long time; ever since Victoria died. But why not? I love Cornwall and I can visit Victoria's grave in the churchyard at Callington.

"Yes, my dear, I would love to."

Bernard stood up a new man, clasped Tara to his chest and cried. She smoothed his hair, kissed him, and led him into the house.

"We'll go down tomorrow," Tara was determined to strike before Bernard changed his mind. "I'll ask Hobson to pack up some things for you. You must take walking boots, binoculars, and warm clothing. I know you used to play bridge, so we'll make sure there are two packs of cards. Auntie also has a very good music set-up and I'll add some records and discs. She also likes music and used to play the flute. She tells me there are some very good concerts in Plymouth this autumn. She often goes so she knows the ropes. She doesn't have a car, but taxis are so easy. The neighbours are always willing to help out with lifts and so on,"

Tara prattled on for a while as Bernard relaxed. Mrs Hobson came in at the right moment with tea and cakes and by the end of the afternoon Bernard was almost cheerful. Later, Tara went into the kitchen and found the Hobsons.

"I'm taking Bernard to Cornwall to stay with Auntie for a month. He needs to be taken out of his shell and a complete change of scene will help. Could you pack up what you think he will need. Don't bust yourselves, it's not as if Cornwall is a million miles away."

The Hobsons were delighted. They had noticed the change in Bernard and were very worried about him.

"What a wonderful idea. Mind she takes him for long, healthy walks, he needs the exercise. He's been moping around here for too long."

The next morning, Tara came down from her room for breakfast and found suitcases in the hall and a bright Bernard sitting in the sun, smoking his 'last cigarette'. The last fifty cigarettes to her certain knowledge had been the recurrent last one. Never mind, at his age, did it matter?

"Good morning, Bernard; packed already and raring to go?"

"Of course; I have been looking forward to meeting this aunt of yours for a long time. You have told me she's a good gardener."

"I can certainly reassure you on that front. She has won most of the prizes at the village competitions for years. She is also a good cook and can probably out-talk even you on a variety of subjects. She was an army nurse during the war, and she was also a crack shot, so be careful."

Bernard laughed; Tara had not heard that laugh for too long and it was good to hear.

Tara borrowed Melusi's car for the week. The Hobsons stowed the luggage in the boot, and they set off for Cornwall. The air had the beginnings of winter and a hint of frost clung to the grass. Bernard was silent for most of the journey and Tara was happy that he could mull over his thoughts in peace.

"How has Melusi liked his first six months as a junior doctor?" asked Bernard.

"As he predicted, at the time of qualification he knew everything there was to be known about medicine; he was going to be the best doctor ever. After a few days in the casualty department, the sister in charge had taught him more practical medicine than he had learnt in a year. She was very kind and filled with the wisdom of one who has had to think for herself in an emergency. She is also very pretty, which helps."

"I hope I do not detect the hint of jealousy?"

"Oh no; she's very happily married with three children."

"You may find you have a problem when you go to live in Africa. There will be no relatives living near you to give you moral support.

"We'll be all right, Bernard, don't you worry. Here we are at Auntie's."

They drove up to the little old cottage to be met by Auntie with her beaming smile. "Welcome, Bernard, I've heard so much about you from Tara. I have a spot of lunch ready, but first Tara will show you to your room overlooking the sea."

Bernard went up the stairs to his little room with the superb, almost fluorescent, view. He breathed deeply with the pleasure of it all. If only this confounded hand would stop hurting. He had a wash and came down to have lunch with Tara and Auntie.

Over the meal, Bernard reminisced about life as a child in Cornwall, "I was born in the doctor's house in Callington and spent most of my childhood on our estate, just to the north of the village. My older brother Michael and I used to walk over the hills to fish in the Tamar at Gunnislake. We caught the occasional salmon which we took back to our house to be cooked and served to our parents that evening. They always pretended to be surprised and gave us each three pence, a lot of money in those days. I can't remember what we spent it on, but we felt rich. I remember somewhere around this area there was a Lord Penrose who owned most of the local tin mines. He was always very kind to us. There were children who were a little younger than us; we sometimes went mackerel fishing with them. They kept a boat at Kingsand. None of the noisy engines in those days, we had to row out and back and be careful to keep the tides in mind. They even had some lobster pots which we had to pull at some ghastly hour in the morning."

Auntie was pensive. "One of those sons was my brother, Frank. He was torpedoed in the Second World War. George, another son, was my lovely husband who died ten years ago. And I fear the tin mines are no more, all that's left is this cottage with its view of the sea and a few acres rented to local farmers.

"Well, Auntie, what remains is absolutely beautiful."

That afternoon Bernard, Auntie and Tara went for a walk along the cliff path. They watched the yachts race out of Plymouth. The little sails danced and bowed to each other in the gusting wind, turned round a buoy and rushed back to the safety of their expensive moorings and the bar of the yacht club. There was nobody swimming down in the secret cove, and Tara ached for Melusi. The sea would be warm at this time of year. What a lot had happened in the last few months. During her life she had experienced the trauma of a few affairs, but nothing came within a million miles of her love for Melusi. When she had told her parents, they had at first been silent, then wary, saying it was her life and she must know best. She had taken Melusi to meet them at their farm on the Quantock hills and they had fallen over themselves with delight. What magic did he have that he could so charm people? Perhaps she was already far down the road of discovery.

Auntie suddenly asked, "When is the happy date, Tara? Your marriage to that nice young man; in case you think I was asking another question!" She added naughtily. "I shall wear a hat; must be the first time for many years."

"Melusi can get the weekend of tenth, eleventh November and there's a locum available for a week after that. We thought that it would best be on 10th November. Would that suit you, Auntie, and you, Bernard and, of course, the Hobsons?" They nodded with pleasure at the prospect.

They picked and ate blackberries on the way back to the cottage. Tara walked ahead and left Bernard chatting to Auntie. His height made him stoop slightly and when Tara chanced to look back, she could see Auntie's head bobbing up and down as she chatted away.

The evening meal was enlivened by quantities of Auntie's home-made elderflower wine. They slept well that night, with no dreams. The next morning Tara did some urgent shopping. She brought back a case of gin and a dozen large bottles of tonic for Bernard and an enormous bag of frozen pasties for Auntie.

Tara left a happy pair in great spirits and drove back to Bristol to the flat that Melusi had been allowed by the hospital.

Chapter Thirty-Two

Three weeks later Tara went to stay with her parents at their farm in Broomfield. The second day she got up with the dawn, fed the dogs and cats, mucked out the horses and was cooking breakfast when the telephone rang. It was Auntie, sounding quite unlike her normal self. Something was very wrong.

"Sorry, Tara, to ring so early. I'm afraid Bernard is not well. He was as happy as a sand boy for a couple of weeks and was great company; a good idea of yours. We had lots of trips round and about visiting the places from his youth. We went to a concert in Plymouth, and he even enjoyed a short sea trip to Polperro. Then one day he asked if I would mind coming with him to visit the grave of his wife Victoria in Callington churchyard. He was sure he knew where to find it, but when we got there, he seemed muddled and couldn't find the gravestone. We searched for some time and then suddenly he looked up and saw a very fine specimen of the tree mallow, in the corner of the cemetery. You know I'm supposed to be an expert in those plants; and it was a lovely specimen, in the wrong place, of course."

"'Must be over there', he said, and rushed over through the cotton grass, and there it was."

Tara breathed very deeply, and she felt cold fingers at the back of her neck, her heart was pounding. "What happened next?"

"Well, nothing particularly dramatic, except every bloody thing seemed to start to go wrong. As we left the cemetery, Bernard tripped on a piece of metal protruding from the ground, and I am afraid he hurt his hand again rather badly. You know, the one that he had pricked with a thorn in Africa."

"I remember that very well, sadly. It's never healed properly. How is he now?"

"Down in the dumps again, I'm afraid. I called the doctor last night and he prescribed some antibiotic for the hand which is all swollen and a horrible colour. That may have done some good, but I've put him to bed and called in a nurse to look after him. He refuses to go into hospital and, anyway, I would rather have him here, he is such a lovely man."

"I'll borrow dad's car and come down now. I may be able to get Melusi to come as well, or perhaps later. I'm sure he can change his rota and come down tomorrow. Bless you, Auntie, I hope you're all right."

"Oh yes, I'm all right, but it would be wonderful to have you here. Please come soon as you can."

Tara drove quickly down to Cornwall. When she arrived, she was surprised to find a battered Ford in front of the house. By the jumble in the back of the Ford it could well be the doctor's car. The front door was slightly open. Tara entered the cottage and listened; there was a hum of voices upstairs. She entered Bernard's room and immediately there was something odd.

Was it a smell from not so long ago in the ward of the hospital in Bristol, or in the flat looking over the harbour at the Barbican? Or was it my imagination playing tricks?

Bernard raised his head. "Ah, you've come, Tara. Your lovely aunt has been the most wonderful nurse and has looked after me like an angel. However, I fear it is an uphill struggle.

This confounded hand and now the arm is unfortunately my metaphorical Achilles' heel." He laughed a bubbly laugh, cut short by coughing. Bernard's eyes were glazed, and he looked flushed and uncomfortable.

Tara turned to the doctor. "Please tell me..." She started but he raised his hand to silence her.

"Let's go downstairs for a cup of tea. We'll leave Auntie in charge here."

The doctor knew where the tea things were kept. "Firstly, I have to say that Bernard will never agree to go into hospital. He has made it plain that he is very old and has outlived all his nearest relatives. He has had enough of life but at the same time has been very grateful for the life that he has lived. We do not therefore have the option for drastic treatment."

Auntie appeared. "Bernard is asleep; he's all right for a while. What's next, doctor?"

"I'm afraid Bernard's hand and arm are heavily infected with some pretty resistant germ which may or may not respond to the substantial dose of antibiotic that I am giving him. It is not the ideal treatment, but I suggest to you that he is doing the right thing and to subject him to anything more than tender loving care would be meddlesome medicine. Please feel free to disagree; you have every right to do so. I will get a hospital consultant to call in tonight to see if there is anything that I have missed, but I suspect he'll say the same. May I use your phone, please, Lady Penrose?" Auntie nodded her head miserably.

Tara and Auntie sat with tears in their eyes. Auntie rose to put on the kettle on again. As she did so the front door opened and Melusi rushed in. Tara leapt up and he opened his arms to her and to Auntie.

"Thank goodness you came."

"What's the news?"

Auntie made more tea while the doctor told Melusi the bad news. Melusi and the doctor went up to Bernard, who was awake and overjoyed to see him. Melusi had a look at Bernard's arm under the eagle eye of the doctor and they came downstairs again.

"I only qualified a couple of months ago, but I am certain you are right both in the diagnosis and the prognosis. Tender loving care is the best. Do you think Bernard is in much pain?"

"It is strange you ask that. By rights he should be in a lot of pain, but he denies having any pain at all. The odd thing is that he keeps on looking at the window, muttering 'Messenger' and smiling. When that happens, he's calmer. I presume it must be some old memory from many years ago."

Tara looked at Melusi, but they said nothing. The doctor wouldn't have believed it, anyway.

The hospital consultant called that evening and spent half an hour with them. He sorrowfully agreed that there was nothing more that could be usefully done to help Bernard. The infection was progressing up the arm, would soon invade the blood stream, and Bernard would be released. He, too, was amazed that there was no pain. He bid them goodbye and gave them his telephone number to ring.

"Do feel free to ring any time, Lady Penrose. I have known your family for many years, and anything I can do to help."

"Call me Auntie, everyone else does."

They sat by his bed for a while drinking Bernard's gin and tonic and worked out a rota to sit with him through the night. At one stage, Bernard awoke, opened an eye and asked them what they had in their glasses, "I'll have a large one."

"Why not? Cheers!" said Melusi.

Great Uncle Bernard died at four o'clock in the morning on Saturday 20th October, with a glass in his hand and a smile on his face, in the company of the two people that he loved most. As he died, a cloud moved over the moon and on the still silver sea there was a silhouette of a very thin, very tall old man leaning on a spear. The cloud moved slowly, and the old man seemed to glide away. As the silhouette faded and grew indistinct one arm appeared to be raised in salute. Tara and Melusi both shook their heads in wonder.

The funeral took place three days later at the little church in Callington. There were a great many wreaths and floral tributes. One of Bernard's very old friends, Geoffrey Allinson, came to the funeral. It was said that they had been at school together and had kept in touch ever since. Geoffrey noticed a particularly lovely arrangement of flowers of the various species of mallow surrounded by cotton grass. The card had a golden border, unusual at a funeral. Inscribed on the card were the following words:

From Tandeka With Love

Acknowledgements

I would like to thank Fiona Blackwood for her help, particularly with modern place names in Africa.

And my publisher for their assistance in bringing this book into the world.

About The Author

John Pether was born in London in 1934, and later moved to Buxton. His mother left when he was four and when his father went off to the war, John was raised by his grandparents in Bournemouth.

Haileybury, Oxford and Middlesex Hospital Medical School were next and then house jobs before moving into the field of pathology, where he subsequently chose to specialize in microbiology. Research in London was followed by 30-odd years running the microbiology service for Somerset.

An author of more than 60 papers, he spent a career discovering unusual germs and caught over 300 wild rodents for study at Porton Down.

Retiring in 1995, he took up silversmithing and started to write science fiction/fantasy.